TOPLOADER

Ed O'Loughlin was born in Toronto and raised in Ireland. He reported from Africa for the *Irish Times* and other newspapers, and was Middle East correspondent for the *Sydney Morning Herald* and the *Age* of Melbourne. His first novel, *Not Untrue and Not Unkind*, was longlisted for the Man Booker Prize 2009. *Toploader* is his second novel.

TOPLOADER

Ed O'Loughlin

Quercus

FT
Pbk

First published in Great Britain in 2011 by

Quercus
21 Bloomsbury Square
London
WC1A 2NS

A CIP catalogue record for this book is available
from the British Library

ISBN 978 0 85738 291 7

10 9 8 7 6 5 4 3 2 1

Typeset by Ellipsis Books Limited, Glasgow

Printed and bound in Great Britain by Clays Ltd, St Ives plc

To Gabrielle

ACKNOWLEDGEMENTS

Thanks to Nuala Haughey, Gabrielle Hetherington, Roisin O'Loughlin, both John O'Loughlins, Peter Straus, Jon Riley, John English, Richard Arcus, Jeroen Kramer, Conn Ó Midheach, Andrew Cuthbertson and Maeve McLoughlin for their support and/or suggestions, and to Sarah Bannan and all at the Arts Council of Ireland, which provided generous assistance.

Hong Kong is up for grabs
London is full of those Arabs
We could be in Palestine
Overrun by a Chinese line
With the boys from the Mersey and
   the Thames and the Tyne

from 'Oliver's Army', by Elvis Costello

AUTHOR'S NOTE

All this will really have happened, more or less, by the time
this account reaches you. For ease of comprehension, standard English orthography and translations are employed for
all proper names. The exact location of these events has
been redacted to protect the identities of the individuals
involved.

PROLOGUE

A very wise old lady – her name was Martha Gellhorn: look her up – once told me that you can only ever really love one war. Well, of all the conflict zones that I have covered, 'the Easy' holds a special place in my heart. I was there myself, all those years ago, when it came into being, the very first of the autonomous terrorist entities; I rode out on one of the last armoured vehicles to pass through the newly-built wall. And I have returned to the Easy many times since then, to stand on that wall, and to walk among the brave young soldiers, police and contractors who guard it; who protect all our freedoms; and who soberly deliver their commanders' responses, mindful of the purity of arms, to each new provocation. And I will keep going back to the Easy, year after year, as long as terror abides there, to remind all those who waver of the vigil that must be kept, by all good men and women, lest hatred and evil prevail.

Extract from the essay 'Why I still go to the Easy', by Flint Driscoll. Reproduced here by kind permission of Dr Flint Driscoll and blow-back.net

CHAPTER ONE

The contact was first picked up by the radar girls, shortly before dawn, when it was still too dark and foggy to see anything much from the wall. Alerted by the beeping in their earphones, they watched as the contact appeared on the fringe of the free-fire zone, a ghostly green blob on their ground radar, condensed from the shimmering haze of the trees.

It was mid-winter, and the night was beginning to fade into day. Yet the exact time at which the target was acquired is, curiously, not recorded. Afterwards, when technicians checked the logs for that watch, they found that key data streams were unaccountably missing. This caused quite a stir, in certain rarefied circles – the tactical computer is supposed to record everything, every contact, every fire order. The question was thus left forever unanswered: why was this contact allowed to get so far?

Deep in their bunker, the radar girls watched the blob move into the free-fire zone. It acquired confirmed mass there, tripping seismic sensors beneath the bulldozed ground, which in turn alerted the drone control room, just down the corridor from the radar girls. A small piston engine grumbled slowly up the sky, unseen, as the first armed drone moved into position overhead. A shepherd's dog barked somewhere off to the south, a kilometre or so into the misty Embargoed Zone.

The first visual sighting of the target was made at or around 06.25. Notified of the threat by the tactical computer network, the sentries in watchtower Lilac Three glimpsed movement out in the free-fire zone. Through their night-goggles they were able to make a visual identification, which they duly fed back to the computer: barnyard animal, medium-sized, probably a donkey.

The animal advanced a few paces more – head up, sniffing the air – towards the tower Lilac Three, observed by its sentries through blast-proof glass windows. The donkey was grey, as is usual, and two straw panniers were slung across its back. The panniers jogged heavily whenever it moved.

A proximity alarm jangled in the tower. The two young soldiers looked into each other's faces, then fumbled open their firing ports. They readied their weapons – the click of a rifle bolt, clack-clack of a machine gun's cocking handle – and waited for the order to fire: the contact was already well inside the minimum distance at which the tactical computer is automandated to initiate lethal force against all suspect individuals or objects. Hunched over their weapons, the sentries shook their heads and flexed their shoulders, working to steady their breathing, leaning into their aim. Yet still the fire order did not come.

The donkey moved forward again until it was only twenty

metres from the wall. It lowered its head, nosed the dirt, then raised its head again. A stubby butt of carrot protruded from its jaws. For the first time now it seemed to notice the wall, eight metres of concrete looming bleakly above it. Grass and weeds grew thick and long in a narrow strip along the wall's foot which the bulldozers could not plough, watered by the dew which trickled down the concrete. Still chewing, the donkey considered this unexpected feast, then moved towards it: it was now so close that the sentries could hear its teeth crunch on the carrot.

The donkey swallowed its treat, eyes half-closed in pleasure, then stooped to sniff at the fresh weeds along the base of the wall, its tail swishing at the first flies of day. Curling its lips to bare its teeth, it stripped the leaves from a stem of bindweed, chewed and swallowed. It swished its tail again and snorted contentedly, then made a half-turn to the east, spread its front hooves, extended its neck and brayed in thanks and praise to the rising sun.

And then it exploded, vanishing in a splash of violet light and a gut-heaving shock wave.

Sand and gravel lashed the watchtower, pitting the blast panes and jetting through the firing ports, scouring the night goggles of the two stunned sentries.

Sirens went off in guardrooms and watchtowers all along the wall. Boots thundered on metal catwalks, fire-ports creaked open. Grenade-launchers boomed and trees fragmented. Unmanned machine gun turrets, controlled by the computer, swivelled peevishly on their servo-mounts, chattering like monkeys. A tank bumbled up onto a dirt ramp set back behind the wall, traversed its main gun and destroyed one of the few intact water tanks left in the northern Embargoed Zone. The sentries in Lilac Three picked themselves off the floor, trembling, temporarily blinded, ears ringing, unable to hear the 'open fire' alarm which now blared from their computer terminal. And off to the south, as if on cue, the first terrorist rocket of the day rose up from the ground. Most probably on cue.

The rocket's exhaust fumes marked its trajectory, upwards and over, a white question mark in the pale morning sky. It soared over the long snaking wall and its canine-tooth watchtowers, over the rat-shack sprawl of the army base beyond the wall, over the straggling lines of the tank park. The rocket flew on, over the highway, the agricultural fields, the outskirts of the quiet little town whose peaceful citizens were still in their beds, and then its engine cut and its nose turned decisively downwards again, into the blare of the one-minute warning, gravity reeling it homeward, plunging ahead of its sound-wave. It fell onto a school's football pitch, ten feet from the corner flag, and exploded there, showering clods of smoking earth as far as the penalty box.

Machine guns stammered the length of the wall, harrowing the scrub on the edge of the free-fire zone. Overhead, the loitering drone changed course towards the orchard from which the rocket had been launched. Fifteen kilometres to the east, six artillery pieces barked in succession, firing on the rocket's radar trace, and seconds later the orchard vanished beneath a chorus-line of dancing light and earth and splinters. Fighter-bombers thundered in from the sea, rapid response teams piled into tanks and armoured personnel carriers, starting their engines, waiting for orders. And back where it had all started, in the base of watchtower Lilac Three, a small metal door creaked timidly open.

The door was made of six-inch-thick steel plate, painted gunmetal grey. It wavered on its hinges, and then a rifle barrel appeared around it, followed by a helmet.

From underneath the helmet, worried eyes considered the fruit trees, three hundred metres away across the track-churned dirt of the free-fire zone. Then they turned to look at the Rorschach blot of blood and crushed bone and offal which glistened on the otherwise unmarked surface of the wall. Beneath this viscous stain, mirroring it, was a crater full of gore and pulverized tissue, marking the spot where the donkey had dematerialized. It looked as if someone had folded the wall and the ground together, pressing the donkey between them like an insect in a book. Flies were buzzing loudly. There was a churning stench of blood and stomach contents, burnt meat and half-burnt chemicals.

The eyes' owner made a retching sound. 'I think I'm going to be sick,' he told someone behind him. 'This is horrible.'

He pushed his helmet back to wipe the sweat from his eyes, then winced as his chinstrap bit a rash of angry spots, relics of a shave two days before. Raising his rifle, the young soldier squinted at the tree-line through its optical sight.

'Hey, David,' he called. 'Aren't you going to cover me?'

A machine gun barrel emerged from the top of the tower. The barrel wavered back and forth a few times on its bipod then tipped towards the sky, crisscrossed now with the contrails of jet fighters.

'I *am* covering you!' said a voice from the firing port behind the barrel. 'Now stop wasting time, Johnny! Get out there and inspect the scene of the atrocity!'

Still braced in the shelter of the doorway, Johnny glared up inside the tower. 'Why don't *you* go?'

'Because I'm senior. I have to stay here at the post.'

'But we're both the same rank!'

David sighed. 'I'm still senior to you. Besides, that Daddy Jesus guy put me in charge when he posted us here last night. Remember him, Johnny? Do you want me to call Daddy Jesus and get him to explain it to you again?'

Johnny thought of the leering monster which had materialized in their billet in the dead hours, reaching under their blankets with huge, lingering paws. He shuddered, took a step towards the mangled remains of the donkey, then ducked back inside as two huge explosions shook the ground to the south. The air force engaging the Embargoed Zone from 20,000 feet.

'I really don't think I should be exposed out here alone like this, David,' he complained. 'I'm pretty sure I read something about that in the standing orders, or somewhere ... There could be snipers, or something, in that tree-line.'

Steel brackets, set into the concrete, formed a ladder up the inner wall of the tower's tubular stem. Leaning backwards, Johnny peered up through the hatch which gave access to the firing platform, twenty feet above. He could just make out David's left buttock, braced against the wall above the hatch. A black leather prayer book protruded from its pocket. 'Grow up, Johnny,' said David. 'Just do the job, okay?'

Johnny stepped clear of the door again, squinting at the scrubby tree-line through his sights. Moving sideways in a half-crouch he made his way quickly to the edge of the gore-pool, then lowered his weapon and studied it.

'Poor little donkey,' he muttered, and shook his head. A thought struck him, and he turned to the tower and shouted: 'Hey, David. Did we do this?'

David's face popped out through the firing port. It was round and freckled, with angry red eyebrows subverted by anxious blue eyes. 'I don't think so. I think the donkey just exploded.'

Johnny pushed his helmet back, slowly this time, so as not to trouble his spots again. 'Really? . . . Wow . . . Whoever heard of an exploding donkey?'

'Are you *serious*? . . . Everybody has, Johnny. This is something like the third bomb-donkey attack from the Embargoed Zone this month! Don't you read the terror alerts?'

Johnny slung his rifle and stepped closer to the curdled soup of blood and organs. His stomach was steadier now. It occurred to him that he was standing with his boots on the ground, exposed to a hostile tree-line, on a genuine combat mission, *inside the Embargoed Zone*! He felt himself grow taller. With the toe of one boot, with elaborate unconcern, he nudged a gelatinous blob that might once have been a hoof.

'Hey Johnny,' David called again. 'Can you see any sign of the mechanism?'

Johnny didn't bother to look around. 'What mechanism?'

'You know, for detonating the bomb . . . I saw this documentary on Discovery about how they always try to find the bomb's mechanism. That way they can work out who made it.'

Johnny chuckled. 'David, I think we already know who made *this* bomb. I think we're definitely looking at the work of terrorists here . . .'

He turned away from the wall and stared back towards the tree-line. 'Wait a minute, though – there *is* a wire! Leading back into those trees!'

David stuck his head all the way out of the tower. 'A wire? That doesn't make sense . . . They're supposed to use cell phones to set off bombs. That's what it said on Discovery.'

Johnny shook his head pityingly. 'This isn't TV or the internet, Davy boy. This is for real. This is war.'

And as if to underline his point another salvo of shells slammed into the shattered orchard, making the earth tremble beneath Johnny's feet. David's head jerked back inside the watchtower. He said nothing for a few moments, and then his machine gun yammered into life.

Johnny hurled himself face-down as steel-clad slugs zipped over his head and thumped into the free-fire zone. He was still trying to squirm into the dirt when the firing stopped. Slowly, carefully, he lifted his head, to see a cloud of dust hanging in the air thirty metres beyond him, where David's bullets had chewed up the soil.

'You bastard!' screamed Johnny. 'What the hell were you shooting at?'

The smoking barrel disappeared from the firing port and was replaced by David's face. 'Uh . . . Sorry about that . . . It just occurred to me that all the other towers have been shooting off their weapons ever since that donkey blew up. If we don't fire off some ammo ourselves, people will think we chickened out, just because we were the closest ones to the attack.'

Johnny rose to his feet and unslung his rifle. He put it to his shoulder, switched the selector to full automatic, aimed at the pool of gore in front of him, and emptied the magazine. Blood and dirt and gristle spouted into the air, until the bolt locked to the rear of an empty receiver.

There was a moment of ringing silence and then David spoke again.

'You're sick,' he declared flatly.

Johnny changed his magazine, watching a large blob of fat and nodules slide down the wall.

'Hey. You know what would be really funny?' he said, brightening. 'I should put my tag on this!'

'No!' yelped David, but Johnny was already rummaging in a webbing pouch. He took out a small can of spray paint.

'Don't do it!' David protested, as Johnny stepped up to the wall and uncapped the aerosol. 'Remember what happened when they caught you spraying C and TS onto the doors of those UN jeeps?'

'They let me off with a warning. The old man thought it was funny.'

'But defacing the wall is a really serious offence! They'll send us both to the military prison!'

Johnny shrugged him off. 'Don't panic. I'm not going to put my name on it, just some kind of cool enigmatic emblem . . .'

He stood there for a few moments, frowning, his arms crossed high on his chest and the aerosol held to one cheek. 'I've got it!' he announced, and he began to spray. When he was finished he extracted a cell phone from his pocket and snapped a few images, including one of himself with his new creation, taken with the phone held at arm's length.

'There,' he said. 'Pretty good, eh?'

David had to lean right out of the firing port to see what Johnny had painted on the wall. 'Nice one, Johnny!' he jeered. 'That's the ace of clubs – but the ace of spades is the cool ace. Even I know that.'

Johnny whirled to face the tower, his ravaged chin jutting angrily upward. 'This isn't an ace of clubs, you oaf! It's one of those Irish things – a shamrock. I saw it on that documentary the other night about prisons in Texas – all the really cool-looking prisoners had these things tattooed all over them, with lots of sick runes and stuff.' He snorted in contempt. 'And since when do you know what's cool, seminary boy?'

But David had already withdrawn into the watchtower. 'I'll tell you what I do know, graffiti boy,' came his muffled voice from within. 'Captain Smith's jeep is on its way over here. You'd better get back in here before he sees what you did to the wall!'

'Oh shit! Is that Daddy Jesus guy with him?'

'I can't see – they're still too far.'

Johnny sprinted back to the tower, slammed the door shut and bolted it behind him. Along the wall the gunfire was dying away. The jet pilots had shot their bolts and gone home again, but innumerable drones now haunted the sky. Shells were falling on the ruined apartment blocks still visible through the smoke to the south, inside the Embargoed Zone. Another terrorist rocket sighed up into the sky.

CHAPTER TWO

It was not the bombardment that woke Flora that morning – the shells were dropping well over a mile away, into someone else's life – but the measured argument of rifle fire, single shots in the middle distance, dulled by the gusty wind and by streets of crumbling concrete. Turning onto her back, she stretched her arms out from under the blankets, seeing them almost brown against the bare white walls of her bedroom. The cold air pinched her skin.

The pattern of shots told her, as clear as writing, that army sniper teams had infiltrated in the night, seizing family homes to make nests on their rooftops, gouging loopholes in their walls. Down below, families were being held at gunpoint while soldiers stole or smashed their valuables and pissed on beds and floors. And where the snipers and their support teams came, the tanks and armoured infantry would shortly follow.

I should probably take in the washing, thought Flora.

She reached for the clothes which she had left folded on a stool beside her bed. Several squirms later, she emerged from the blankets wearing jeans and a blue cotton hoodie.

Passing down the apartment's dark, ill-plastered

corridor, she saw that Gabriel's door stood open, and that her brother was gone. She hoped that he would not be drawn towards the shooting again, him and his giddy little friends.

He was not in the kitchen, either. Taking a plastic basket, Flora unlocked the back door and picked her way across the muddy yard to the clothes line. The apartment building glowered cracked and ugly above her, its concrete eaten by grime.

The washing shuddered in the wind, still wet, but she began slowly to gather it, ear cocked to the sounds from the streets. There was another sniper shot, off to the east, and resistance rifles began to answer, barking blindly from corner to corner like dogs in the night. Further east again, the bass thud of a heavy machine gun betrayed the arrival of the first tank of the day.

Flora hugged her hoodie tight about her, turned east and closed her eyes to concentrate. The wind hissed cold in her ears, stinging the back of her neck with fine grit. She pulled the hood over her long black hair and stood there motionless, eyes shut and head bowed, like a young pagan novice praying to the dawn.

Prayers answered, she opened her eyes again: the tank fire, she decided, was coming from beyond the low ridge which ran to the east of her neighbourhood, parallel with the coast. It was not, therefore, her neighbourhood's turn to be raided today. She began pegging the washing back on the line.

Her father appeared in the black rectangle of the kitchen

door, smiling uncertainly. His eyes flickered between Flora and the washing line as he tugged at his moustache. She pretended not to notice him, pegging up more washing. He cleared his throat.

'Are those clothes still wet?' he asked hopefully. Her back was turned to him, but she had to close her eyes before she could answer.

'Yes.'

'Ah,' he said, pleased. He took a few steps into the yard and then stopped, frowning, as his slipper slid on the wet dirt. His grey trousers had once been part of a suit; their cuffs, frayed despite all Flora's efforts at mending, dragged in the mud. He stood there puzzled, running a hand through his stiff grey hair, contemplating the ground beneath his feet, and then the wind, gusting through his cardigan, brought him back. He turned to Flora and smiled at her again.

'If you had something wet for me I could put it in that dryer I've been working on, to give it a test run. I've just finished fixing it.'

Flora shook her head, still not looking at him. 'There's no electricity.'

'No electricity?' His lips moved, and then his brow smoothed out again. 'Of course, of course,' he said, and turned to the door again.

Flora found herself calling after him. 'I can let you have something from this wash if you like . . . You can put it by, for when the power comes on again. They might give us some power later today, or maybe tomorrow.'

She took from the line one of her father's shirts, transparent now from over-washing, and followed him inside.

Her father's workshop was a bare concrete room at the front of their ground-floor apartment, with a floor-length metal shutter fronting the street. Light seeped in from two windows above the shutter, which had been rolled up a little way to let in the air. The room smelled of solder and oil, and was filled with household appliances scavenged from dumps and waste ground – washing machines, dryers, fridges and ovens. The appliances were arranged in rows on the floor, and stacked two or three deep round the walls.

Her father sat at the far end of the room, beneath shelves stacked with bins of spare parts, and tins of nuts and screws, and coils of hose and wire. He sat, fingers spread on his temples, gazing at a clothes-dryer set on the workbench in front of him. The bench was lit by an Anglepoise lamp wired to a car battery, its illumination now faded to a dull orange. Her father must have been up all night again, running down the battery.

'I'd better put this machine up with the others,' he said, his fingers still pressed to his temples. 'I need to make room on the bench for the next one.'

'I'll help you.'

He lowered his hands to smile at her. 'Don't be silly. It's much too heavy for a girl. Go find your brother. He's a big strong lad.'

'I'm much stronger than he is,' Flora protested. 'He's only twelve.'

'Twelve?' her father pondered, his eyes sliding away from her again. She realized where his thoughts would take him, and quickly put in: 'I'll look for him outside. He's gone out already: probably playing with his friends.'

Taking a scarf and a raincoat from behind the front door, Flora passed through the building's dark vestibule and emerged in the street outside her home.

A damp wind, blowing off the sea, rustled the grass that grew from the gutters. Rows of rusting cars lined both sides of the street, immobilized by the blockade and then crushed by playful tanks. Flora found a gap between two of the wrecked vehicles and stepped out into a shabby grey canyon that ran east and west between bullet-scarred cliffs of cancerous breeze-block. Tank tracks had torn away scabs of tarmac, exposing the soil beneath, and broken pipes and crushed bricks crunched beneath her sneakers. Raw sewage trickled down the gutters, sprouting grass and reeds in the pools where the kerbs had collapsed. The weeds were suppressed in the roadway itself by the UN trucks which still sometimes passed this way. Here and there, glaciers of rubble from bombed-out buildings nosed down to the edge of the street.

The working day would soon begin for those – UN employees, mostly, and aid agency workers – who still had jobs. Their bustling progress infected the street with a twice-daily sense of purpose, sweeping along, if only for a few minutes, all the others for whom clocks were now checked and re-checked merely to space out thin meals. Caught in the tramping rhythm, hunched figures in charity shop overcoats went about whatever business they had – mothers clutching their families' UN ration books; students meandering to bookless schools, children zig-zagging their own secret errands; all with their faces to the ground. On corners and in doorways, men – married and single, old and young – passed hand-rolled cigarettes, talking and smoking in short, angry snatches.

Three gunmen from one of the resistance groups came trotting up the hill, breathless in black cotton masks, burdened by rifles and home-made rocket-propelled grenades. A drone aircraft whined overhead, its tone sharpening suddenly as it entered, invisible, the patch of sky above the street. The gunmen flattened themselves against a wall, exchanging theatrical hand-signals, until the drone moved on. Then they continued on their way, trailed by the curious children who were following them to war.

Flora frowned as the gunmen dwindled in the direction of Mercyville; she recognized some of the following children, but Gabriel was not among them. Turning her back, she headed west, towards the sea. A few women and girls greeted her as she picked her way down the hill, past shuttered stores and burnt-out workshops. Men and boys pretended to ignore her. She had just reached the former petrol station when a tank shell exploded behind her, somewhere back beyond the crest dividing Hilltown from Mercyville, close enough to make heads turn sharply all along the street. But when Flora looked around she saw no smoke and no fire and no still or running figures, just the blank sky stretched between the buildings, their upper storeys turned to lace by years of flying metal. The children paid no heed, playing their games again. She would look for Gabriel in the park.

CHAPTER THREE

Flint Driscoll was having problems with his armour. He had been very pleased with his new flak jacket – a pixellated dispersal-pattern vest with outsized bullet-proof plates, purchased especially for this assignment – but when he folded himself into the front seat of Captain Smith's jeep he found that his posture forced the plates to ride up. The front plate was now jammed between his thighs and chin, while the one in the back grated the base of his skull, freshly shorn for the occasion. The jeep bounded and twisted along the track which ran, vertiginously, just inside the Embargoed Zone, skirting the base of the wall; each jolt was exquisitely painful.

Driscoll's helmet was also a worry. He had decided he would sit on it, to protect his vitals from improvised explosive devices. But should the helmet be placed rim-side up or rim-side down? It was so long since he'd seen those movies. Either way, the helmet jarred harshly whenever the jeep hit a pothole. It also lifted his bottom eight inches clear of the passenger seat so that, being a very tall man, he was forced to sit with his head tilted sideways against the metal roof. He couldn't avoid catching Captain Smith's eye whenever the captain looked at him; the captain's own helmet was discarded on the back seat, between the two young soldiers they had brought along as escorts. The escorts wore their helmets on their heads.

Captain Smith glanced at Driscoll again. 'First time in the Easy, Doctor?' he enquired. A round little man, rather old for his rank, he kept his poise as the jeep bucked and heaved around him, feet dancing on the pedals, hands stroking the wheel and the gear lever.

'Not at all,' snapped Driscoll. 'I've been here many, many times before, Captain. I was embedded with your armoured infantry when this place was abandoned to the terrorists. And I've also reported on many of the other embargoed zones set up since then – Cabinda, Peshawar, Lurgan, you name it. But for me this is still the oldest and the best: I'm proud to call myself an old hand in the Easy.'

'Me too,' said the captain, and he smiled.

The jeep hurtled along the pitted gravel track, yellow dust billowing behind it. A few feet to the left rose the sheer concrete slabs of the wall, while off to the right, across the free-fire zone, lay a wasteland of splintered fruit trees and overgrown fields, dotted with heaps of twisted steel and ruined concrete, the remains of bulldozed homes and farmsteads. To the south, three kilometres away on a line of hillocks, scarred towers marked the edge of a quarter which, Driscoll remembered, the terrorists called Hilltown. Several buildings had been set alight, not for the first time, by the morning barrage. Beyond the towers, dark flecks floated in a cold sky. Driscoll turned to the captain again.

'Are those drones engaging terrorists right now, Captain Smith?'

The captain glanced past Driscoll and then consulted a computer which was clamped to the jeep's dashboard. The screen showed a jumble of gridlines and topographical features and red and blue contact icons.

'Those aren't drones. Those are kites.'

'Kites?' Driscoll took out his notebook and pen. 'What on earth are the terrorists doing with kites, Captain? Signalling?'

Smith glanced at him again, then shifted down gears to race the jeep across a gully where a dry stream ran under the wall. The watercourse was blocked with a metal grille, and signs warned of mines and automated machine gun turrets and lethal electrical currents. The jeep bounced up the far bank and skidded to a halt near the base of a watchtower. A cloud of flies rose to reveal a donkey's severed head, tongue protruding, eyes wide with its last sudden grievance.

The morning was tranquil now apart from the rumble and thud of artillery, firing in support of a routine tank raid to the south. The sun had burned the last of the fog away. They got out of the jeep and stared at the slick of stinking offal smeared near the tower's base.

'Jesus,' said Driscoll, breathing though his mouth. 'Those sick bastards . . .'

He took a video recorder from his belt and shot some footage of the scene. Finished, he looked up at the captain.

'Captain, do you mind if I get you on camera now, for

my video-blog, talking us through what just happened here?'

Smith had been staring at a scorched fragment of carrot which lay in the dirt. His face assumed an expression of regret.

'I'm afraid I can't do that, Doctor. Briefings by intelligence officers must be unrecorded and non-attributable. If you want, though, I can talk to you off the record. But we need to be quick: I have a job to do inside the Easy this morning – servicing a ground agent.'

'I understand completely.' A notebook replaced the camera in Driscoll's hands.

'Well,' the captain began, 'basically, the terrorists dispatched a donkey loaded with explosives in an attempt to penetrate our defences and kill as many innocent people as possible. They were foiled by the courage and vigilance of the young men and women who guard the wall. Miraculously, no one was harmed.'

'No one but the poor donkey, you mean,' muttered Driscoll, scribbling. 'But Captain, could you tell us a bit more about the type of explosives employed, the delivery system, detonators, terrorist command structures – that sort of thing? My blog has a big following in the national security community, so don't be afraid to get technical.'

'Well,' Smith said slowly, 'from the smell I'd say the bomb was made from fertilizer and diesel oil. It was delivered by a donkey ...' His eyes narrowed as he noticed something lying in the free-fire zone. 'And to judge from that electric cable over there, I'd say the terrorists used a command wire.

They probably hid in that tree-line over there while the attack was going on.' He was frowning now.

'A command wire, eh? So that's what the terrorists used to control the donkey's movements?'

Smith raised his eyebrows. 'No, Doctor. That's how they set the bomb off.'

'Really? I thought they always used cell phones to set off bombs these days . . . So if they didn't use the wire to control the donkey's movements, how did they steer it to its target?'

Captain Smith lifted his arms a couple of inches clear of his sides, blew out his cheeks and let his arms fall again. 'I suppose they must have trained it somehow.'

'Tell me, Captain, did your forensics team find any of the mechanism?'

The captain's eyes fell upon the carrot, and he frowned again as he shook his head. 'This only just happened, Doctor – we're the first to arrive on the scene. Just think: if we'd set out on this inspection only a few minutes earlier, we could have been killed ourselves!'

Driscoll lowered his pen, eyes narrowed. 'You think this attack was aimed at *me*?'

'No no no!' said the captain. 'I only meant that we could have been in the wrong place at the wrong time. As it is, we're in the right place, at the right time – from the point of view of your story, that is.'

Driscoll looked disappointed. 'I guess so.' His eyes narrowed again and he pointed to the wall. 'Tell me, Captain, what does this symbol mean?'

Driscoll's finger hovered a couple of inches from what

looked like a large three-leafed clover, rendered on the wall in black paint. A capital A was printed underneath the symbol and there was a number 6 inside each leaf. The captain considered it for a moment, his face betraying no curiosity.

'I'm afraid I don't know, Doctor. It's probably just some old graffiti.'

Driscoll ran his finger along the stalk of the clover and then turned, a black digit held aloft.

'Look here, Captain! The paint is still wet! Yet you said that we were the first on the scene!'

One of the escorts coughed. 'Uh, sir, that's an Aryan symbol. Me and Lenny here and the rest of the guys from our tank crew were watching this documentary about prisons on Discovery the other night and we saw—'

'That's enough,' Captain Smith put in, smiling at the soldier. The youngster blanched and moved to the back of the jeep, aiming his rifle at the Embargoed Zone. His comrade sank keenly down on one knee.

Driscoll looked back and forth between the captain and the silenced soldiers, his blackened finger dropping to his side.

'Aryans, eh?' he mused. 'And still wet?' He smiled. 'Well, you must keep your own counsel, Captain – I can respect that in an intelligence officer. But I still need to record a quick piece to camera ... Damn it, though. I've forgotten to bring my tripod!'

Captain Smith reached a smooth hand for the camera. 'Not to worry, Doctor,' he said. 'I can hold the camera for you, if you like. It wouldn't be my first time.'

CHAPTER FOUR

Joseph West, face-down on an old sofa on the roof of his office building, was woken by a generator spattering to life on the balcony below. Artillery grumbled to the north, somewhere around Hilltown. To the east, beyond the windowless towers, a pale sun dissolved into dishwater overcast. He unwrapped his dew-soaked blanket and checked the front of his fleece for the holes left by burning seeds. Finding no new ones, he stood, stretched, scratched himself, then crossed the roof to the parapet overlooking the street, picking his way through satellite dishes and broadcast antennae and drifts of empty whiskey bottles. Six storeys below, the street was deserted apart from a few early carts on their way to a food distribution. The full complement of white armoured jeeps was parked along the kerb, each marked 'TV' in black gaffer tape. Things must be quiet this morning. Perhaps there'd be time for some breakfast.

Someone coughed behind him, and Joseph turned and saw an anxious young face in the stairwell, hovering above the top step. Tony had formed the habit of climbing the last few steps to a roof on all fours, which people thought eccentric until he showed them where a sniper had shot half his ear away.

'I've turned on the generator,' Tony said, and pushed his fringe from his eyes. He had grown his hair out to hide his ear and it did not suit him: he was otherwise neat, with the doomed, eager look of a young supply teacher.

'So I hear,' said Joseph, rubbing his jaw. He should probably shave today. He would do it in the office toilet, in the mirror fixed to the cabinet over the sink: the cabinet in which he kept his headache pills. He would not allow himself to take any of the pills until he had shaved, he told himself. That's how to get things done.

Tony was nodding quickly to himself, which Joseph recognized as a distress signal. 'Erm . . . Did you fall asleep up here again?' Tony asked.

'Yes . . . Why?'

'It's just that there's a lot of messages for you on your cell phone, down in the office. From the world desk in London.' Tony shrank back against the wall to let Joseph pass down the stairs. 'I'll put on some coffee,' he said.

Joseph found his phone lying on an edit suite which was grey with cigarette ash and sticky from spilled whiskey and sugary tea. The edit suite was seldom used these days: nobody wanted cut packages any more, just scraps of raw footage or – on those increasingly rare occasions when 24/7 sent in a staff reporter – one-minute two-ways, live from the Embargoed Zone!

He sat in a swivel chair and put his elbows on the edit suite, scratching his head. A couple of hairs alighted on the console. When did they start turning grey? His phone told him he had missed eight calls. It began to ring again, just as he reached for it.

'What,' said Joseph, and the phone exploded in his ear.

'Joseph! Where the fuck have you been? I've been trying to get hold of you for an hour now! New York is going apeshit about this pig-fuck story that you've got running there and I can't even get you on your cell phone? What the fuck are you doing to me?'

Joseph massaged his temples. 'Please calm down, Felicity. What story are you talking about?'

'What story? Jesus, fuck! There's been a major terrorist attack right on your doorstep and you don't even know about it? What the fuck are we paying you for, you local-hire twat?'

Joseph took the phone over to the window and looked down into the street again. There were more people about now, shuffling close to the walls, but all of the Land Rovers were still at the kerb.

'Well, whatever your story is, it's definitely not a pig-fuck,' he told her. 'None of the competition is out covering it.'

'Fuck the competition!' spat Felicity. 'Do me a favour: get online and take a look at blow-back dot net. Once again we're being done up the arse by a poxy fucking website! Take a good fucking look and then call me right back.' She hung up.

Tony came out of the kitchen with two cups of coffee. Joseph grunted and sat at a computer. The regular news wires made no mention of any major incident in the Embargoed Zone, but when Joseph clicked on blow-back.net the headlines jumped out at him.

'Fresh terror attack in the EZ – exclusive to blow-back.net. Award-winning author, security analyst and war correspondent Dr Flint Driscoll, reporting live from the front line.'

Joseph read the first few paragraphs of the accompanying piece then clicked on the video link. A bony face appeared on the screen, beneath a matt black helmet with 'Driscoll: blow-back.net' stencilled on its brim in rough, military-style lettering. In the background the tower blocks of Hilltown gushed columns of smoke. He must be embedded with the army, Joseph thought, just this side of the wall. The face mouthed excitedly for several seconds before Joseph remembered to switch off the mute control.

'. . . thwarted at the last minute by the vigilance of the soldiers guarding the anti-terror barrier,' boomed a gravelly voice from the speaker. 'And blow-back dot net understands that this time the terrorists may have employed a secret new technology to carry out this attack – more on that later. Reporting live, on the ground, from inside the Embargoed Zone, this is Flint . . .'

Joseph turned the sound off, swivelled his chair away from the screen and sighed.

'Oh dear,' he said. He picked up the office phone, pressed a pre-set and held the receiver away from his ear until the initial torrent of profanity had passed. Then he looked across the room at Tony, who sat – leg jiggling nervously – on the edge of a desk, and switched the phone to speaker.

'Felicity,' he wheedled, 'here's the thing – that story is bullshit. This kind of thing happens all the time here. No one else in the building is even bothering to cover it.'

'What the fuck do you mean, "it's bullshit"?' Felicity screamed. Across the room, Tony flinched. 'Flint Driscoll has just been involved in a real-live terror attack! By mid-morning he'll be all over Fox like shit on a sheep's arse, and by lunchtime the other networks will be running the story too, whether they want to or not. So don't tell me there's no story there!'

Joseph lit his first cigarette of the day. 'Here's the thing,' he said again. 'Even if the story is as big as you say it is, Tony and I still can't shoot it. If you want to shoot a story that close to the wall you need to get a camera crew from the other side to do it, embedded with the army, which is presumably how this Driscoll guy is doing it.'

'You think I don't know how to do my fucking job? I've been trying all morning to get permission for one of our crews from the other side to shoot the story, but the army won't allow it. This bastard Driscoll has got friends in high places, and he's using them to protect his exclusive. Which means *you'll* just have to get the footage.'

Joseph took another drag and smiled thinly at Tony, who was looking even more unhappy than usual. 'Felicity,' said Joseph, conversationally, 'you do know that if I or anyone else from the Embargoed Zone – man, woman or child – goes anywhere near that wall, we will be blown to bubbles by the army? It's the main reason why I'm still in this shithole.'

There was a long pause and then Felicity spoke again.

'I don't think I like your attitude,' she said quietly.

'What attitude? Not wanting to get killed trying to stand

up a bullshit story by some blogger who's embedded himself up the army's arse?'

Felicity gave a light little laugh. 'I'm not interested in nit-picking, Joseph. At 24/7 we need people with a can-do attitude. That's not what I'm hearing right now.'

'So what are you going to do, fire me?'

'I wouldn't rule it out.'

'Who else are you going to get to shoot for you in the Easy?'

'Oh Joseph,' she tinkled. 'With the technology we have now we could train a monkey to shoot for us. Don't fucking tempt me.'

'What do you think Bob Reilly would have to say if I got fired? Last time he came here he was still thanking me for saving his life back in Kinshasa all those years ago.'

'Fuck Bob!' Felicity was screeching again. 'Bob's retiring next year! He's taking the fucking package, like all of the other old relics around here!'

Joseph took another pull on his cigarette. 'And what about you, Felicity? Will you be taking a package before Bob does?'

There was another pause before she spoke again.

'Okay, Joseph,' she said wearily. 'Let's agree to this: I'll cover for you being too chicken to go to the wall today, but you have to get me something else instead. Something good. The Embargoed Zone is back in the news for once, thanks to this Driscoll cunt, so we need to show New York that you're still on the job.'

Joseph winked at Tony. 'We've run out of cigarettes and whiskey again.'

'Fine. I'll send you some more booze and fags.'

'And what about my ticket out of here?'

'I keep telling you. The army says you're a confirmed terror threat – you and your whole extended family. They won't say why.'

Joseph studied the tip of his cigarette, held point upwards in his hand.

'So what are you going to do for me today?' insisted Felicity. Tony spoke up.

'There's another tank incursion this morning, Felicity. Near Hilltown. Routine, but we can probably use a long lens to get some smoke and explosions and stuff.'

Felicity sighed. 'Fine, Anthony. That'll have to do then. Just go out and do your jobs, yeah? While we all still have one.' The phone went dead.

CHAPTER FIVE

After he failed flight school Gordie Moon was reassigned to a unit which appeared on the order of battle, for reasons of secrecy, as the Third Signals Logistics Battalion. Its members, and those few outsiders allowed to know of its existence, called it the Slob.

The Slob was an unacknowledged bastard of army and air force, banished at birth to its own lonely compound in the Easy Division's main depot, out near the perimeter fence, where the coastal scrub and sand dunes gave way to vast bleak fields of industrial wheat and barley.

Moon hated it there. By night, mosquitoes swarmed from drains and leaking irrigation lines. By day, crop-dusting planes used the Slob's billet lines as aiming points for their strafing runs across the fields, providing close air support for the drills of genetically modified cereals that marched across the croplands. Their engines whined like migraines, and the spray from their overruns shrouded the Slob in a sickly-sweet mist lit with herbicide rainbows, spoiling all attempts by the radar girls to prettify the post with flowers.

It was always the new girls who did the planting, in the first few weeks after they arrived from their specialist training at the electronic warfare school. Moon had watched four cohorts of these girls come and three cohorts go. He knew how it worked by now. For their first few weeks the girls would be self-conscious and giggly, eager to learn the unit's folklore and in-jokes. If you smuggled in some dope or some booze they might even come to your billet at night. But the older girls, who bullied the newcomers at first, would slowly warm to them during long hours hunched together over ground radar screens and tactical displays. By their patronage, the new recruits would be introduced one by one to the glamorous parts of the base that lay beyond the tank park, near the wall that sealed off the Embargoed Zone. There, along the beach, were the infantry cantons, the paratroop base, the armour and engineering depots and – holy of holies – the little square of sand-bagged tents which housed the reconnaissance commandos. Once the new girls found their way across the tank park they were lost to the boys of the Slob.

The wind caught Moon a wet slap in the face as he stepped from his billet that morning. Shivering, he turned up the collar of his tan air force jacket, then set off to work through lines of peeling wooden huts. The path had once been duck-boarded, but the planks had long since been prised up and burned to heat chilly huts at night, or to give a semblance of romance to couplings in the sand dunes. Moon, heavy and clumsy, sank with each step into the loose sand, his breath wheezing in his ears.

Clear of the huts, the path twisted up through clumps of shrub and thistle into a range of grassy dunes. The control room for unmanned aerial vehicles, where Moon worked, was housed in a bunker buried deep underneath them. High above, a winking red light topped a thicket of aerials, to warn off the crop-dusters, yet the bunker's entrance was hidden, in a ritual nod to secrecy, behind a stand of stunted pines. Guarding the iron steps was a sentry from the paratroop brigade, who cradled his carbine meaningfully whilst flirting with an off-duty radar girl. Moon pulled back his jacket to show the ID card clipped to his shirt, and the girl frowned and looked away from him. The paratrooper curled a lip and said nothing, and Moon – who outranked them both – scurried sadly down into his hole.

Safe in the darkness, he allowed his pace to slow as he descended to the dim corridor below. Rows of gunmetal-grey doors, with blinking slots for electronic swipe cards, controlled access to the mysteries beyond them: the UAV control room, the radar girls' operations centre, the intelligence liaison bureaux, and the workshops and offices of the private aerospace corporations which designed, built and exported the hunter-killer drones and missiles that were field-tested by the Slob.

Moon used his own card to enter the drone control room. It was a narrow, windowless rectangle, lit mainly by the banks of screens that lined the further wall. Inside the door, a trestle table bore an electric kettle and paper cups, and bowls stocked with sachets of instant coffee and sugar and powdered milk. The room was warm, smelling of statically-charged nylon carpet and adolescent sweat.

Moon's assistant, Gerald, had already logged on for the

shift and sat waiting at their usual workstation, checking the read-outs from a cruising drone. His frizzy red hair almost concealed his headset. Moon made himself a coffee then shrugged off his jacket and took his place beside Gerald.

'Anything doing?' he asked, putting on his own headphones.

Gerald pursed his lips and considered. 'There was another donkey bomb early this morning, and some rocket launches. Valkyrie almost got one of the launch teams, in an orchard in Easy Four. And there's a routine up-tit operation underway to the east of Hilltown, which we're flying top cover for.'

Moon stirred his coffee with his finger, watching the video feed from the cruising drone. Buildings, streets and cratered wasteland scrolled down the screen in front of him. There were figures too, men and women, walking close to the walls, hunched away from the wind and the daylight, their faces invisible, turned to the ground. Actual terrorists, Moon told himself again: how many other people of his age and non-combat designation had ever actually seen one? How many combat soldiers ever saw them this clearly, come to that? Every now and then an exposed face jumped into shocking focus, staring up into the camera, one hand reaching up as if beseeching mercy of the sky: children, out flying their kites.

Valkyrie and her assistant bade Moon and Gerald a sleepy goodbye as they clumped past on their way to the door. The two young women wore tan air force fatigues which, like Moon's, were frayed and crumpled, with no insignia apart from their lieutenant's bars. Gerald was the only pilot in the Slob who actually wore his unit flash and his drone wings – his mother had proudly sewn them on for him – but it was clearly some time now since the shirt had been ironed. He waited until the other crew had left the room and then he used his index finger to push his glasses back up his nose.

'I don't think that Valkyrie will catch up with you, Trollhunter,' he confided. 'She is still eight kills behind you, and you both have only one month to go.' He had forgotten to sniff, and a transparent tendril crept out of his nostril and across his pursed lips.

'Don't call me Trollhunter, Gerald. I've already told you: call me Gordie, or Gordon, or Moon – anything but my callsign.'

Round-shouldered, Moon hunched forward to study the computerized map. His face resumed the anxious expression that it always wore when he forgot that people might be watching. Little blue icons were stippled across the screen – transponder contacts, relaying the exact real-time positions of all the friendly tanks and armoured vehicles then operating inside the Embargoed Zone. Half a dozen flashing wings indicated the drones that were already circling over the area or en route to and from the airfield, thirty kilometres to the rear, where ground crews armed and serviced them.

Gerald snuffled again, running his left finger along his upper lip. It came away glistening. He wiped it on the underside of the console.

'Trollhunter,' he declared without preamble. 'I have decided to volunteer for the potential captain's course.'

Moon wasn't used to surprises from Gerald. 'Why would you want to do that? It means voluntarily extending your service, and your reserve obligations.'

'I'd like to learn to fly a real plane.'

Moon turned. He removed his headphones. 'You really think that if you sign up for the captains' course that the air force will put you on the *flight line*?'

'No,' said Gerald, 'I do not.' Then a voice crackled in his earphones. 'Roger,' he told his chin mike, and then he punched several keys in front of him. A little red question mark appeared on their map, blinking slowly. 'One of the tanks says it has found a possible target on the western edge of Hilltown,' he told Moon, 'but for some reason the crew can't register it on the computer themselves. They think it's a terrorist rocket cell. Shall I send a drone to take a look?'

Moon shrugged. 'Sure, why not? . . . So what makes you think that extending your service will help you to become a real pilot?'

'If I pass the course,' said Gerald, using his joystick to manually redirect a drone, 'the air force will help me to gain a private pilot's licence through the flying club. It's a new offer – they put it up on the notice boards last week. They're trying to promote voluntary re-enlistment amongst technical cadres such as ourselves.'

Moon found it difficult to imagine Gerald at the controls of a real aircraft; unlike himself, Gerald had not failed flight school, but had been assigned directly to the Slob as soon as he was enlisted. 'But why would you want to take up private flying? You can't go anywhere in a light aircraft any more, thanks to the terrorists. There's hardly any airspace left that isn't heavily controlled or outright forbidden.'

'I'd like to be a crop-duster.'

'A *crop-duster*? . . . Your folks told me you were going to be a physicist when you get out of this. All crop-dusters do is fly back and forth all day in geometric patterns.'

Their drone had moved into position, and a muddy wasteland appeared on the video screen, strewn with twisted cars and moulding rubbish.

'I'd like to fly in geometric patterns,' said Gerald, adjusting the image. 'I've been doing it for two years now, albeit vicariously. Geometric patterns help me to think.'

'Wow,' mused Moon. He opened a locker underneath the console and took out his customized joystick. 'So, you'll save crops whilst solving equations?'

'You're mocking me,' said Gerald, adjusting the controls. 'I don't think that my plan is unfeasible. You, to my knowledge, have no plan at all.'

Moon laughed. 'You've got me there, Gerald,' he said. He plugged in his joystick and put his feet on the console, crossing the ankles. He was just getting comfortable when the door from the corridor opened behind them. After a few seconds, sensing a brooding note in the silence, Moon turned his head and looked. Standing in the doorway, in the uniform of a full air force colonel, was a man whom

Moon vaguely recognized as the Slob's new commander. The colonel was of medium height and build but trim and wiry, with one of those chiselled, tanned, instantly detestable faces that they use to sell Swiss watches. He was glaring at Moon with an expression of cold loathing. Behind him in the doorway, peering over his shoulder, was a skull-faced giant in a helmet and flak jacket.

Moon goggled back at them for a few seconds, searching for the right form. 'Attention?' he managed finally, pushing his chair back and lurching to his feet. Gerald remained seated, his eyes fixed on the screen as he reached up to adjust his spectacles.

'Fuck off, Trollhunter,' he declared. 'I'm not falling for that one again.'

CHAPTER SIX

People called it 'the park' because there had been trees there once, even some flower beds, before the blockade. But the municipal wells had long since run dry and the grass, already sickened by the poisoned water, had turned brown and died. The flower beds dried up and blew away, and the last trees were chopped up for firewood. So now the park consisted mainly of piles of hand-tipped rubbish, some burning, scattered around a patch of dirt which still served sometimes as a football pitch. Near the north-west corner, by the road that led to the sewage lake, stood a little bank of sand and dirt, the remains of an obstacle which militants had bulldozed across the road a long time ago, in the days when there was diesel still for bulldozers. The next day an invading tank had driven right through it without changing gear, but what was left served yet as a fortress for children, worn smooth by their tumbling games.

It was here that Flora found her little brother. He was hunkered down at the foot of the bank with half a dozen boys from the neighbourhood, his straw-coloured head bobbing eagerly at the edge of their huddle, a little below and a little apart. One of the older boys was pouring fluid from a metal tin into a row of plastic bottles. The others were tearing foil into strips.

'What are you doing, Gabriel?' demanded Flora.

'We're working on something,' said Gabriel, turning to glower at her. 'Leave us alone.' He flapped his hand dismissively. She recognized the gesture: it had once belonged to their big brother, Jake.

The boy with the bottles noticed Flora. He was a few years older than Gabriel and already much broader and taller, with dark fuzz on his lip and his jaw.

'Hello, Flora,' he said, and smiled at her.

'Adam,' said Flora, not smiling back.

Gabriel looked from Adam to Flora, aghast. 'Go home, Flora!' he shouted. 'This isn't for girls!' He turned huffily away.

'Dad wants you.'

The boys were tearing the strips again, cross-wise, to make flakes of confetti-like aluminium. Adam finished filling the bottles and balanced their caps on their necks, loose, the threads not engaged. He peeked at Flora again.

'Tell Dad I'll be home in a few minutes,' Gabriel said crossly.

'He needs you now.'

But Gabriel had his eyes fixed stubbornly on the other boys. They pooled their aluminium flakes on a plastic sheet, then divided the heap into small equal piles. Flora spoke again.

'He *needs* you, Gabriel. He needs us both, to help him move a machine.'

'I said I'll be there in a few minutes.'

'Okay,' Flora said slowly, 'I suppose I'd better get back then ... I suppose I can help him lift the dryer, without you. I offered to already, but Dad said it was man's work.'

Gabriel pivoted on his heels.

'Please, Flora,' he pleaded. 'Can't you just wait a minute? I really want to see this.'

'See what?'

'I'll show you, Flora,' put in Adam. He smiled at her again, then scooped up a bottle and a fistful of foil, scrambling up onto the mound. 'Just stand well back, and promise you won't go all girly, and freak out on us.'

'I'm older than you, Adam. If I'm a girly, that makes you a child.'

The other boys guffawed. Adam flushed, then, collecting himself, he stuffed the foil into the bottle, quickly screwed its cap shut and gave it a few hearty shakes. Picking up a metal pipe which lay on the mound, he went down on one knee, balanced the pipe on his right shoulder and, with his left hand, pushed the bottle inside it. Then he froze, one eye closed and the other squinting along the pipe. Nothing happened for another second and then there was a thud and a whoosh, and two jets of white smoke burst from either end of the pipe. The shredded remains of the bottle went whizzing back twenty metres, narrowly missing Gabriel.

'Oh God!' yelped Flora. The boys jumped up and down,

cheering, then swarmed up the hill to crowd around Adam, who was beaming proudly down at them, the smoking pipe still balanced on his shoulder.

'Oh, that's really smart, Adam!' Flora shouted. 'What if that thing went off in your hand? Don't you know you could kill someone?'

Adam ignored her. 'Didn't I tell you it was sweet?' he told his admirers. 'Just like a real RPG, eh? I'll bet if you were fifty metres off you wouldn't know the difference!'

The other boys were trying to wrest the pipe from him.

'Here,' clamoured Gabriel, offering Adam a bottle and some tin foil. 'Do another one!'

Still flushed with success, the older boy surrendered the pipe to his suppliants. He stuffed the foil into the bottle and skipped clear of the scrum. 'And the other thing,' he shouted, 'is that you can also do hand grenades this way – you don't have to use the pipe!' He turned and hurled the bottle away from him. It spun, end over end, out into the empty road.

Except that the road was no longer empty. Flora clapped her hands to her mouth and bent, cringing, as the bottle tumbled towards the jeep which had appeared – it seemed from thin air – on the road beyond the barrier. The jeep braked and swerved, tyres screeching, but in vain. The bottle bounced off the bonnet and exploded on the windscreen in a splash of smoke and light.

Flora felt her heart stop. The jeep careered off the road, bounced over a dirt verge and lurched to a halt in the park, its nose buried in a mound of rubbish.

Smoke gusted from the windscreen. There was a moment's silence.

'Oh shit,' said Adam, and he turned and fled.

CHAPTER SEVEN

David pulled his face back from the rubber eye-piece of his periscope, wiped the sweat from his eyes and then leaned in for another look. As he did so, the top of his helmet snagged the underside of the commander's hatch, dislodging his glasses. He fumbled to catch them, but they bounced off his lap and fell into the void beneath his feet, disappearing in the jumble of pipes, wires and valves on the floor of the tank turret.

He put his eye to the periscope again, adjusting the diopter to allow for the loss of his glasses, but the image was now more blurred than before. Someone tapped his knee. Lenny peered up from the gunner's position in the base of the turret, a hand extended, proffering the missing glasses.

'Thanks,' muttered David. 'My other pair have a string on them. But I lost them . . .'

He put them back on, readjusted the diopter and hunched forward, taking care this time not to disturb his glasses.

'I still can't see it,' he said, after a few moments. His voice echoed back at him through his headphones. 'What can you see, Johnny?'

On the left-hand side of the turret, beyond the breech of the main gun, Johnny was squinting into his own periscope. 'I'm still pretty sure I saw a muzzle flash,' he said doubtfully over the intercom. 'What have you got on the video cameras?'

David looked again at the monitor mounted under the commander's hatch. The view from the rear camera showed the debris of the house through which they had just passed. The front cameras showed the dirty ghost of the next row of buildings, glimpsed through a clutter of crumbling walls. Beyond those buildings, the open stretch of rubbish and mud was still a featureless blur. 'I'm not seeing anything on the screens either,' said David. 'There's too much dirt and stuff on the camera lenses.'

'I told you not to take us through all those goddamn walls and houses,' said Johnny.

'Hey! I was following the manual! Go through, not around – the way around could be mined, remember?'

'Let me pop my head out of the hatch and I'll take a look for you.'

'No way, Johnny! Rule one in the armoured warfare manual: you stay buttoned down in the tank if you're in a built-up area and you don't have infantry to protect you. Otherwise people can throw grenades or molotovs in. There could be terrorists lurking out there right now, just waiting for a hatch to open!'

'What about the computer?' demanded Lenny's voice on the intercom. 'Maybe someone else has already registered this thing as a target. If they have, then we're allowed to shoot at it, right? Even if we can't actually see it?'

David said nothing.

'Oh, dearie me!' keened Johnny sarcastically. 'You'd better tell them, David: our computer isn't actually working today, is it? You used it to access a porn site last night, and now you can't get it back onto the tactical network, can you, David?'

'What?' shouted Lenny, incredulous.

'Hey! Johnny's lying! It wasn't a porn site!'

'Oh yeah?' said Johnny. 'So then what are those hippy chicks doing with those goats in that scene that the screen froze on?'

'They're milking them! And they aren't hippies! That's a scene from the life of Abraham! It's a religious website! And how the heck was I to know we'd be using the tank today? We haven't been in it since we finished basic training! How was I to know we were going to be taken off checkpoint duty and seconded to these intelligence guys?'

Johnny tutted. 'Listen, David; I already told you: if we get caught, you have to say you were looking at hardcore barn-yard porn. We'll never live it down if the rest of the guys find out what you were really looking at.'

'I'm having trouble believing this,' Lenny said slowly. 'You're saying that we're lost inside the Embargoed Zone and we can't see anything and we don't even have our computer online?'

'Yeah. What the fuck?' broke in a fourth voice. It was their driver, Harry, cocooned alone in his cockpit in the hull. Their bickering had awoken him.

Silence returned, broken by the beat of the big diesel and

the hiss of the air conditioning. Then Lenny tugged at David's knee again.

'So what shall we do? We can't just sit here all day. The terrorists might stalk us.'

David grabbed at one of the poor options that flapped around him in the confined, confusing turret. 'I'm going to radio that Captain Smith and tell him about our computer problem, and ask him what we should do about this contact.'

'For the love of God,' begged Lenny, 'please don't do that – if an officer finds out that we came into the Easy without a computer we'll be cleaning toilets for the rest of our enlistment. Let's just reverse slowly out of here, following our own tracks: they shouldn't exactly be hard to see.'

'He's right, David,' said Johnny. 'Me and Lenny will sneak out to the tank park tonight and reboot the computer. You've already radioed in the contact – whoever's in charge can deal with it now.'

'I don't know . . .' said David slowly, leaning forward to check his periscope again. 'The field manuals say – ow!' The eyepiece slammed into his forehead, dislodging his glasses again. Harry, unbidden, had thrown the tank into reverse.

The armoured personnel carrier reversed ponderously, tracks churning the damp sand, until its rear access ramp was directly opposite the workshop's doors. Hydraulics whirred as the armoured ramp groaned open, and Captain Smith strolled out into the Embargoed Zone. The engine cut, and Daddy Jesus followed him, a pump-action shotgun held loose in one hand.

Sniper teams had been inserted the night before to provide cover for Smith's operation, taking families hostage, nesting on rooftops. Their lieutenant, with two of his men, was waiting by a Judas gate set into the metal doors of the workshop. All three infantrymen were draped in armour and equipment, faces smeared with camouflage make-up. The two enlisted men knelt back-to-back on either side of the Judas gate, squinting left and right along their carbines. Captain Smith nodded to the lieutenant, and he and his men moved away a couple of paces as Daddy Jesus swung up his shotgun and blew out the lock. Then one of the soldiers kicked the Judas gate open and the other threw in a stun-grenade. There was a flash and a crash, and all three infantrymen plunged into the building.

Captain Smith and Daddy Jesus, waiting outside, looked at each other. Daddy Jesus raised his eyebrows, and the captain shrugged and sighed. They listened as boots scuffled around inside the building and then the three infantrymen re-emerged from the doorway. The lieutenant nodded. 'All clear, Captain,' he said, and led his men back to their nest.

The captain sighed again and stepped in through the shattered door. Daddy Jesus followed him, crossing his arms in front of his body to fit his shoulders through the gap. Inside was a dim loading bay, scattered with scrap and dismantled machinery. A pair of blackened lathes had been installed along one wall, and a welded steel frame hung by chains from a tripod. In one corner lay a pile of plastic shopping bags, their tops tightly knotted. Some of the bags had split open, releasing the stinging smell of chemical fertilizer.

Captain Smith strolled over to a door in the opposite wall, opened it, and passed into a bare concrete stairwell, lit by a window on a landing above. A plank partition shut off the space beneath the stairs. He looked at Daddy Jesus, who raised his eyebrows again, and then the captain rapped on the partition with his knuckles.

'It's only me,' he cooed. 'You can come out now, Cobra.'

A section of partition creaked open on concealed hinges. A grey-bearded face peered anxiously around it.

'God Almighty,' the beard muttered peevishly. 'Did you have to shoot the door off? You know I always leave it open for you.'

'Sorry, Cobra. But you know how it is – we have to keep up appearances. Speaking of which, can't you find a better hiding place than this? Your people are bound to get suspicious when they hear that we raided this place again but still didn't find you.'

Cobra crawled out of his cubbyhole and joined them in the stairwell. He was a short and rather fat man of early middle-age, and he wore grey slip-on faux-leather shoes, olive combat pants and a camouflage jacket too tight for him to fasten. 'You needn't worry about my people,' he muttered, brushing dust from his knees. 'You killed all the smart ones a long time ago.'

'All except you,' said Smith. Daddy Jesus guffawed. Cobra gave him a pained look before turning back to the captain.

'So did you bring my money?' he demanded.

Smith cocked his head winningly. 'All in good time,' he said. 'First, why don't you tell me what happened this morning?'

'What do you mean, what happened? You know what happened – I saw you there myself. We put a bomb on a donkey and we blew it up by the wall, at the place and time specified. Same as usual.'

'Yes, but this time you used a command wire, didn't you?' Smith tutted. 'Very sloppy. What if a drone had spotted the wire and followed it back to you? That's why we gave you those cell phones and those special detonators, remember? So you wouldn't get yourself killed?'

Cobra stared at him. 'You mean your people don't have standing orders to hold their fire when I'm working for you?'

'The sentries that I've posted myself have orders not to shoot you – I'm able to hack into the computer terminals of soldiers seconded to me. But I can't control what anyone else might do – the drone people, for instance. This sort of operation has to be kept on a strictly need-to-know basis. So do you mind telling me why you didn't use a phone detonator?'

Cobra looked shifty. 'I had to sell the phones,' he confessed. 'Well, what else could I do? You haven't been paying me, and I've got my men to feed. And donkeys don't grow on trees, you know – that one this morning cost me two hundred and fifty euros!'

Daddy Jesus laughed again and Smith shook his head.

'Two hundred and fifty euros? Come off it, Cobra. That was a skinny old gelding – a hundred and twenty, max.'

Cobra shook his head excitedly. 'Not so, Captain! The prices have doubled in the past month! Our own operations were driving them up already, because we've taken so many healthy donkeys off the market. And then some American lady from People for the Ethical Treatment of Animals showed up in the Easy a few weeks ago, and started buying up all the donkeys she could find. She says she's going to save them from the terrorists, though what she plans to do with them nobody knows. There's no way she can get them out of here.'

Smith pulled a face. 'Yes, I heard about the PETA lady. I didn't want to let her into the Easy, but the army press office insisted. They said she'd be PR gold – those poor innocent donkeys, murdered by terrorists . . . It's the best we can manage, now that you lot aren't using kids any more.'

Cobra leaned his back against the wall. 'Those days are over. Morale is gone to hell. Nobody wants to strap a bomb vest on any more, if they're just going to be killed before they even reach the wall. Maybe if you could let one of our bombers through every once in a while then things would pick up again – a taste of success would do wonders for recruitment.'

'No can do, Cobra my old friend. It's more than my job's worth.'

The group lapsed into a commiserating silence for a few moments and then the captain clapped his hands and said brightly: 'So. Anything else I need to know?'

Cobra rolled his eyes. 'No. Same old scene. If any of the other groups comes up with anything new I'll be sure and let you know about it. But seriously, Captain, what about some payment? My men are swapping their bullets for food. They're losing all respect for me.'

'Fear not,' said Smith, and he ushered Cobra towards the front of the building. 'The answer to your problems is in the APC.'

Cobra baulked at the front door, but Daddy Jesus planted a hand in the small of his back and propelled him out into the sunlight. The little man stumbled from the building, wincing, eyes shut and shoulders raised, as if expecting a blow to fall. Captain Smith stepped up to the rear of the APC and gestured within.

'You see it?' he asked. 'It's a beauty, isn't it?'

Cobra peered into the innards of the vehicle, where a large square object gleamed white in the gloom.

'What the hell is that?'

'That, my friend, is a Maelstrom Circe. It's state of the art, that. It practically talks to you.'

'It's a washing machine.'

'And a very good one.'

'What's it got to do with me?'

'It's worth two thousand euros, that,' said the captain, looking at it fondly. 'Brand new, straight out of the box.'

Realization came slowly to Cobra, followed closely by dismay.

'Please tell me you're joking,' he pleaded, slumping back against the building.

The captain and Daddy Jesus assumed sorrowful expressions. 'The thing is, Cobra,' Smith wheedled, 'we're having difficulty freeing up funds this month.'

'You mean, you're keeping my money for yourselves.'

Daddy Jesus stepped towards Cobra and raised a hand to strike him, but Smith shook his head. Cobra was so deep in his misery that he didn't seem to notice.

'Now, now, Cobra, it's not like that,' said Smith, putting an arm around his shoulders. 'It's just that times are changing . . . I've got a new CO back at the base and, not to put too fine a point on it, he's a bit of a cunt. I was actually his boss for a while, a long time ago, until he ratted me out over a little logistical misunderstanding, and now he's terrified that I'll do the same to him. So he's querying all my accounts, including payments to my own private agents.'

Cobra's head snapped back, his eyes widening. '*Private* agents? Oh, that's just great! So now you're telling me that even your bosses don't know about our relationship? I'm beginning to feel very lonely here.'

'Now, now,' soothed Smith. 'I'm planning to tell Colonel White that you're my number one star agent, but only when the time is right. He's an air force man, you see – they don't really do subtlety in the air force, they just do large amounts of explosive, dropped from a very great height. And your relationship with me is *very* subtle, Cobra. Luckily, we've found another way to pay you until we get our new commander house-broken – you can easily sell this beauty for a grand, eh? Am I right?'

Cobra was on the point of crying. He turned his face away from the two soldiers so they could not see his eyes. 'How the hell am I going to sell a washing machine inside the

Embargoed Zone?' he demanded, his voice muffled by his collar. 'Did you even think about that? You only let us have electricity for a few hours every other week, and hardly anyone has any money . . .'

The captain patted him on the back. 'Oh, don't be like that, Cobra. You'll think of something. You always do.'

Cobra turned his face. His mouth was still buried in his collar and he stared at Smith from one red eye.

'So what about next month, then? Are you going to pay me my cash then? And what about that new car battery you've been promising me? My old one is worn out – I can't even charge my cell phone fully any more.'

The captain patted his back again. 'I'll see what we can do.'

A walkie-talkie crackled and Daddy Jesus put his hand up to his earpiece and listened.

'Hold on,' he said, and turned to the captain. 'It's the drone room. They say that one of our escort tanks – I think it's the one that was clearly palmed off on us as a joke, the one with all those fucking clowns in it – reckons it's spotted something suspicious. They want to know what to do about it.'

Smith shrugged. 'Whatever they like. I don't care.'

Daddy Jesus spoke into his throat mike. The captain turned back to Cobra, beaming again. 'Come on,' he said, squeezing Cobra's elbow. 'Let's get this lovely piece of gear inside for you, eh? I'll give you a hand.'

CHAPTER EIGHT

Joseph rolled to a stop face-down in a pile of rotting cabbage stalks. The chug of a diesel engine, somewhere behind him, was punctuated by a series of short, high-pitched squeals: the sound, he realized, of his own whimpering. Beyond these was another layer of sound, the thud of explosions and rattle of gunfire. Then the engine died. Joseph held his breath and waited.

'Hey, Joseph, are you okay?' It was Tony's voice. Joseph watched a woodlouse brush past his nose. The sounds of battle resumed their proper station, a mile away in Mercyville, on the other side of the hill. Tony was staring at him from the front seat of the Land Rover, which was rammed nose-first in a heap of rubbish. Tendrils of smoke curled from the bonnet and the windscreen.

'Shit!' screamed Joseph, jumping to his feet. His eyes misted with rage. A couple of young heads peeped over a bank of sand and gravel, then vanished again when they saw him lurch towards them. A dark-haired girl, a little older than the boys, stood off to one side, wide-eyed, her hands clapped to her mouth. Her loose raincoat flapped in the wind.

'You little bastards!' screamed Joseph. 'I'm going to throttle you!'

The girl lowered her hands from her mouth. 'Hello, Uncle Joe,' she said. And then he recognized her.

'Flora . . .' A tactful howitzer shell filled the awkward pause.

'Are you okay?' she asked.

Joseph nodded. 'Yeah, sure, fine . . . I thought we were being attacked.' Tony was inspecting the jeep for damage. There was a scorch mark on the paint, and a little white star on the bullet-proof windscreen.

'It was just some boys, playing a stupid game,' Flora told her uncle. 'They really didn't mean to hit the jeep.'

'Right . . .' He felt himself deflating. 'How's your dad?'

'He's okay. The same.'

'Right . . .' Joseph took her hand and shook it formally. 'I've been meaning to call round, but you know how it is . . . It's been very busy lately.'

'Sure,' she said. He had never met another girl who smiled so seldom.

'And how's Gabriel?' he tried again.

'He's good too. He was here a minute ago.'

'Really . . . *What?* You mean *he* did this?'

And then she almost did smile. 'No. His friend did. But it was completely by accident.'

Reluctantly, Joseph surrendered the last glow of his rage. If Flora said it was an accident then an accident it was. Tony joined them, with the camera which Joseph had left behind when he abandoned the jeep. Tony smiled when he saw

Flora. 'Hey – where've you been? You haven't been to see us in ages.'

She shook his hand. 'I've been busy. Looking after Dad and Gabriel.'

Joseph inspected the jeep. 'So how do you think the kids did this?'

'It's a chemical reaction,' said Flora. 'Some kind of household cleaning fluid, I think, mixed with flakes of aluminium.'

'Right . . .' mused Joseph, rubbing the dirt from his hands. 'It certainly fooled me.'

He took a step towards the mound. 'Hey, boys!' he called, and halted. 'Hey, boys! I know you didn't mean it. I just want to talk. I'll stay right here.'

Three faces appeared at the top of the bank, just as a monstrous detonation rent the sky overhead, followed by the wuthering passage of a missile, fired by a drone unseen in the haze. The wuthering trailed off into the east and then erupted into a second explosion, invisible beyond the rooftops, which Joseph felt through his feet. The boys kept their eyes fixed warily on him.

'Are you all right, mister?' Adam called. 'I swear we didn't see you.'

Gabriel peered around the side of the mound. 'Hello, Uncle Joe,' he squeaked. 'Sorry. Didn't mean it.'

'Sure. I believe you. But you up there, the tall one: that trick – could you do it again?'

Tony was instantly at his elbow. 'Joseph,' he said urgently. 'No—'

Joseph flapped his arm at him. 'I was thinking,' he went

on, addressing the boys, 'what a really cool trick that is. I'd really like to film it.'

Tony grabbed his arm. 'No, Joseph! This is wrong!'

Joseph wheeled on him, suddenly livid. 'No, Tony – it's not wrong! What would be wrong would be me and you getting killed today just so Felicity could have something interesting to say at the morning fucking conference! *That's* what would be wrong!'

'Please, Joseph! If we get caught we'll be thrown out of this business.'

'Yeah? Well, getting killed will also put us out of business. Do you think 24/7 is going to look after your mother and sisters if you die on the job? Never forget, Tony, you're just local hire as far as they're concerned.'

Tony turned away. 'I'm going to wait in the Land Rover. I don't want anything to do with this.'

'Have it your own way,' Joseph shouted after him. 'Just move it around the corner. I don't want it fucking up my shot.'

Joseph turned back to the kids.

'Hey,' he called, 'I'd like to come up there so I can film that big plume of smoke on that hill over there, where that missile just hit. Could you boys set off a couple of your bomb thingies while I'm doing that? Not too close to me, mind. And try and keep out of the shot.'

Adam nudged his mates and they backed away.

'You have to film us too, mister,' called Adam. 'We want to be on the television.'

Joseph felt his temper rising again. Had it come to this? Was he now so burnt-out that he couldn't even manage a set-up? 'Okay, fuck it. I'll film you too, if that's what you want.'

Adam's gang spread out along the top of the bank, laughing and cheering, punching the air and brandishing their bottles. Several of the boys hurled themselves onto their stomachs and tiger-crawled short distances before leaping to their feet again, gazing bravely off towards the battle. Adam picked up the drainpipe and fed another bottle into it: this time it went off almost immediately, spewing gouts of flame and smoke from either end.

Joseph, cursing himself, shot all of it, even when the boys started fighting over the drainpipe. Then Flora appeared in the edge of his frame and grabbed Gabriel's arm.

'Come home now,' she insisted. 'You promised you'd help Dad.'

'Hey, mister, no fair!' Adam appealed to Joseph. 'We can't have girls in our movie. Tell her to go away or the deal is off.'

'Flora: go away!' shouted Joseph, the camera still raised to his eye.

'I'm staying right here until Gabriel comes home with me.'

'Go home, Flora, you're always spoiling my fun,' howled Gabriel, struggling to rip his arm free. 'I want to see more explosions!'

He began to cry. The other boys nudged each other and grinned, pointing at him, jeering his tears. Joe felt stirrings of sympathy.

'Let him stay a little longer,' he said to Flora, lowering the camera. 'It can't do any harm, can it?'

Another salvo of shells was crashing into Mercyville. Rifles spat and rattled in the distance. Closer – almost, it sounded, amid the broken buildings along the ridge line above them – a tank engine grumbled. Smoke rose in billows over the hill, where the motors of several drones had blended into a single spiteful whine. Flora considered all this, then turned back to her uncle.

'No,' she said. 'We need him at home, right now.'

'Then go with your sister,' Joseph told Gabriel.

'Yeah, go home with your *sister*, Gabriel!' hooted Adam. And the other boys laughed and jeered as their young comrade, weeping tears of mortification, was dragged from their midst. Just a kid, thought Joseph. So innocent. Innocence . . . I might be able to use a shot of that.

'Hey,' he called to the remainder of his cast. 'Why don't you kids all get together, with all that smoke in the background, and give me a big smile and a wave? Then we'll get on with the explosions, eh?'

The boys laughed and crowded together at the top of the mound, jostling and giggling, flashing thumbs up and victory Vs.

'That's good,' called Joseph, aiming his camera. 'Just stay like that a moment more.'

CHAPTER NINE

Driscoll felt his breath catch as he squeezed past Colonel White. The colonel had planted himself inside the doorway and was glaring at a tall, somewhat doughy youth who was swaying on his feet in what approximated to a position of attention. The other one, who was still seated, seemed to be dribbling. Driscoll decided to ignore this. He gave a low whistle and bounded over to stand behind the two drone jockeys, marvelling at their banks of screens and dials.

'So this is the nerve centre, the beating heart of the war.' He shook his head, grinning. 'You know, Colonel, I've blogged thousands of words about the crucial role of UAVs in modern warfare, so it's just so incredibly, I don't know – almost humbling? – for me to finally be in a room like this myself.'

'Carry on,' the colonel told the two drone jockeys. The one who was standing slumped back into his chair and began playing with some buttons. The other one seemed to scratch his nose, then rubbed his hand under the lip of the console.

Colonel White came over to stand beside Driscoll, assuming a salesman-like air of friendly condescension.

'Indeed yes, Doctor – nerve centre is right. Over the past

two months this drone room has killed more terrorists than the entire paratroop brigade has managed in the last two years. But there's more to what we do here than just scoring big body-counts, impressive as those are. As well as housing the drone pilots themselves, this room also provides the most high-powered and user-friendly interface environment for senior military and intelligence personnel who want to access our fully-integrated tactical computer network; basically, it gives them the god's-eye, real-time window that they need to fight and win this war. Now, as I'm sure you know, every vehicle and aircraft and infantry squad in our forces now has its own IFF transponder chip . . .'

'Identification Friend or Foe,' Driscoll put in sagely.

'Just so, Doctor. They all have their own IFF chips, video cameras and field computer equipment, which tell us their exact location and status at all times, along with information about any hostile forces they are in contact with. Back here in the drone ops centre we can use this information to build up a clear, real-time picture of the action on our 3D map of the battlefield. We then integrate that data with all our other data streams – intelligence reports, drone videos, the terrorist population register, electronic and audio surveillance, blueprints of buildings, and so on – and feed it all back to our commanders on the ground. Thus for the first time in history we have achieved the Holy Grail of the professional warrior: total real-time tactical awareness, allowing our commanders, going forward, to both define and dominate the digitalized battlefield.' He had finished his spiel, and looked pleased with himself.

'Amazing,' marvelled Driscoll. 'No more fog of war, no more unknown soldiers! A new breed of digital warrior . . .'

The red-headed kid was running his finger under his nose again. The other one was fiddling with what looked like a toy joystick.

'So,' Driscoll said loudly, addressing the youngsters. 'You guys are the famous drone jockeys, eh? I know your work is top secret, but let me tell you, in the circles I move in you guys are heroes. I'll bet your families are all really proud of you.'

The nearer of the two airmen, the one with the joystick, swivelled his chair round.

'Not me, sir. I'm an orphan. The rest of my family all died in a plane crash when—'

'Enough!' the colonel barked. He glared at the kid for a few moments, then turned back to Driscoll. 'Tell you what, Doctor, why don't we both take a seat at the console and maybe I can show you a few things . . . You there, Lieutenant, Lieutenant—?'

'Moon, sir. Call sign Trollhunter, sir. We've met before, sir.'

The colonel smiled unpleasantly 'I didn't ask for your *call sign*, Moon. Only *real* pilots are known by their call signs.' The colonel tapped the gold wings sewn above his own breast pocket.

'Sorry, sir.'

'Don't ever forget that, Lieutenant Moon. Now give us your situation report.'

The kid cleared his throat. 'Um, sir ...' He ran a quick glance across the screens in front of him. 'Um ... We have six drones over the area of operations right now, four of them still fully armed. We've had no confirmed contact with terrorists on this watch yet, and we're now flying cover for a ground operation in Hilltown. It's another up-tit, apparently.'

Driscoll had shucked off his flak jacket and was settling into a chair. 'An up-tit? What's that?'

'Uprooting The Infrastructure of Terror,' the colonel explained. He gave Moon another nasty look. 'A specialized type of precision operation, Doctor, carried out on pin-point intelligence, designed to write down the physical and human infrastructure of terror.'

'Ah.' Driscoll took a notebook from the thigh pocket of his pants and made a note.

'Put all the video feeds onto this screen,' ordered the colonel, and the kid called Moon tapped some buttons. A large monitor began to relay split-screen images shot from several different points, wheeling high above the ground.

Driscoll leaned forward to stare more closely. 'Incredible ...' he said. 'It almost looks like a normal city, apart from the squalor ... And look at all those terrorists, out walking in the street!'

'Indeed, Doctor. We find there's a marked increase in terrorist activity during daylight hours. Not that we need the sunlight to see them: with our new imaging technology and biometric software we can identify individual terrorists almost instantly, even by starlight. Provided they look up, of course.' He turned to Moon. 'Hey! You there – what's-your-name. Do we have any targets waiting for our attention?' He smiled at Driscoll. 'Perhaps we can put on a show for you.'

Moon looked at his computer. 'Uh, no, sir. We have a contact query sent in by an intelligence operation in Hilltown. But it's not confirmed as a target yet. We're just about to take a look at it.'

A sly expression appeared on Driscoll's face. 'Int op, eh? . . . Would that be Captain Smith, by any chance?'

The colonel looked at him sharply. 'How would you know about that?'

Driscoll waved a hand. 'The captain and I have worked together before. Inside the Embargoed Zone.'

The colonel gave Driscoll a long, conjecturing look, then lowered his voice. 'Tell me, Doctor, what do you think of Captain Smith?'

'I'm very impressed by him. A brave and shrewd officer. He handled himself very well when we were both involved in an ambush situation. I'll probably mention him when I meet your esteemed general this afternoon.'

Colonel White's face contorted in horror. He leaned towards Driscoll and lowered his voice still further.

'Between you and me, Doctor, Smith's a disaster,' he confided urgently. 'He has no sense of discipline – he'd be a colonel himself by now, perhaps even a general, if he hadn't been demoted twice for reasons I can't go into. The man's a neanderthal: his background was in the artillery, and as an intelligence man he's also stuck in the past – far too much running around on silly comic book adventures inside the Embargoed Zone. How can you trust anything that anyone tells you there? They're all a bunch of terrorists!'

'Ah,' said Driscoll. It pained him, profoundly, when men he admired, good men, spoke ill of each other. He needed to change the subject.

'Colonel,' he said, lowering his own voice, 'tell me something, please. Off the record, of course. Have you picked up any information in recent days that would suggest a new Iranian presence inside the Embargoed Zone?'

'Iranians?' the colonel said with a shrug. 'Well, obviously, Iran is flooding the Easy and all the other quasi-autonomous terrorist entities with weapons and money and propaganda, and all that. If it weren't for Iran and all the other instigators of hate there wouldn't be any terrorism - we've gone out of our way to be nice to these people.'

Driscoll nodded quickly. 'Of course. But what I mean is, have you heard reports of actual Iranian agents inside the Easy?'

'Oh, good heavens, no! We'd never let them in!'

'I see . . . Because I have to tell you confidentially, Colonel, that I have solid information that Iranian agents are indeed operating inside the Embargoed Zone. And I have very strong reason to believe that they were behind this morning's atrocity.'

White bristled. 'I suppose Captain Smith told you that, did he? Well that doesn't mean any—'

Driscoll held a hand up to still him. 'Oh no, Colonel. Captain Smith told me nothing. Or almost nothing; I have my own sources, and I make my own assessments ...' He glanced at the two drone jockeys sitting nearby, apparently busy about their tasks, then lowered his voice to a murmur. 'Tell me, Colonel, what do you know about the US Navy's top-secret cetacean warfare programme?'

White looked puzzled. 'Only what I saw on the Discovery channel,' he admitted.

'Colonel, could we go somewhere private?'

'No need,' said the colonel. He raised his voice, jerking his thumb at the door. 'You two – out. Go stand in the corridor until I call for you.'

Moon stared at him anxiously. 'But sir, regulations say we can't both leave this post unless we're properly relieved by a qualified—'

'I *am* a qualified ... whatever it was you were going to say!' barked the colonel, jabbing his thumb at his pilot's wings. 'Now go!'

When the pair were out of the room Driscoll leaned close to Colonel White.

'You may not be aware of this, Colonel, but for many years now the US Navy has been using dolphins and small whales to protect vessels and port installations from hostile frogmen, and to recover experimental weapons systems lost at sea.'

White made an effort to look surprised. 'No. Really?'

'Oh, yes. All highly classified. More recently, the navy has also experimented with using marine mammals in a

75

counter-terrorism role, to deliver payloads against terrorist ports and shipping ...' Even though they were alone, Driscoll was almost whispering. 'Initially this proved unsuccessful. Although supposedly highly intelligent, the trained animals kept shaking off their warheads and swimming away before they could be detonated. But then the scientists found ways of combining top-secret neuro-mechanical synapse interfaces with the very latest in autonomous drone technology. The result was a powerful new weapon – the remote-controlled anti-terrorist bomb-dolphin.'

'Amazing,' said the colonel, politely. 'And do these bomb-dolphins work?'

'To a point, Colonel ... What I'm telling you now is known only to the highest circles in the Pentagon, and to a few trusted insiders and opinion-formers like myself. But I'm sure I can rely on the discretion of a loyal ally such as yourself ... Anyway, the first dolphins worked fine on the test range in Florida, but the entire programme was compromised, perhaps fatally, during the first operational sea trial in the Shatt-al-Arab waterway. The operators had guided a prototype to within one hundred metres of the chosen target, a terrorist fishing boat, when contact with the weapon was suddenly lost.'

'The terrorists jammed the control signal?'

'No. Worse than that. It seems that the operators had misjudged the distance to their target, thinking it closer than it was. When the dolphin came to the end of its control tether its momentum pulled the umbilical jack from the animal's cerebro-cortical data port, severing contact with its operators on a nearby undercover research vessel.'

'You don't mean to say the dolphin had to be *plugged in* to work?'

'That is correct – it was a wire-guided dolphin. The navy concedes that it may have been a mistake to field-test the prototype in this configuration – they should have waited until they had fully debugged the radio controls intended for full operational use . . . Unfortunately, the dolphin used in the Shatt-al-Arab test was last seen swimming towards the Iranian shore, and the Pentagon and Langley are both very concerned that the Revolutionary Guard may have recovered it . . . So do you see, Colonel, what I'm getting at here?'

'No,' he said, almost wearily.

Driscoll smiled thinly. 'I think you do, Colonel. That dolphin was controlled by a command line – just like the bomb-donkey deployed by the terrorists this morning. And to clinch it all, I found an Iranian calling card at the site of the attack – a secret Aryan symbol, freshly painted on the wall!'

The colonel looked pale.

'Colonel,' continued Driscoll. 'Let's be frank with each other: we can both see the writing on the wall.' He smiled urbanely. 'Let me ask you this one question, completely off the record, hypothetically if you like, on deep background: is it possible that this morning's terror attack was carried out by an experimental explosives-packed bomb-donkey, controlled by top-secret neuro-electronic synapse technology stolen by Iran and then smuggled for testing here in the Embargoed Zone?'

The colonel closed his eyes again for a long moment and then slowly opened them again. 'Yes,' he said solemnly. 'It is *possible*.'

'Ah,' said Driscoll, and he made a jot in his notebook. 'Good ... Now, you said something about a target?'

The colonel went over to the door and called the two drone pilots back to their posts. 'Right, boys,' he said. 'Let's see that target you were telling us about.'

The one called Moon looked unhappy. 'It's not a target yet, sir – it's just an unconfirmed report. Even the tank crew who reported it weren't that sure about it.'

The colonel took a cigarette box from his tunic, removed a cigarette and then, realizing where he was, stuffed it angrily back. 'Never mind that,' he said testily. 'Let's just get this done. Put the area on screen. And get ready with that joystick.'

'But sir—'

'That's an order!'

CHAPTER TEN

The university at which Flora was taking her pre-medical year had no anatomical dummies, so her knowledge of first aid was almost entirely theoretical. But 24/7 had sent Joseph abroad on a survival course once, years before, when the wall was still somewhat porous, and he remembered enough to be able to clear the boy's airway, and get him breathing again. The heavy jeep bounced and wallowed as Tony hurled it into the bends, sending Flora and Joseph sprawling across the body on the blood-slick floor between them. The blood seemed to be coming from everywhere, not just from the mop of fibrous meat which sprouted where the boy's arm and shoulder had once been joined, the white ribs gleaming through it. The jeep's medical kit contained two field dressings and four bandages and a vial of some kind of opiate, and there was also a tourniquet and a packet of sticky plasters. When the field dressings were both tied to the chest, already heavy and dark and glistening, Joseph took off his shirt and tore it into strips and began applying the tourniquet to the knee-length leg-wound. Flora, kneeling in the blood, tried to think of something useful to do. Unwrapping a sticking plaster, she fixed it over one of the little blue-mouthed entry wounds created by the plastic, X-ray-proof flechettes. And then it occurred to her how silly she was being, and she stopped, bracing herself against the side of the jeep and forced herself to lean over the boy's face. His lips were blue, and his eyes had rolled up behind half-closed lids which fluttered like insect wings. A low groan came from his mouth, like an exclamation of puzzled annoyance, and the eyelids stopped fluttering. Flora touched the boy's throat, inexpertly seeking a pulse. She couldn't find one, so she tried a wrist, and then she lowered her cheek over the gaping mouth, hoping for a breath. After a time she sat back on her heels and tapped her uncle on the shoulder.

'Adam's dead,' she shouted above the engine noise. And then she turned back to her brother, who lay across the back seat. His eyes were tight shut and he was breathing fast, but he was no longer screaming.

A doctor stood outside the entrance to the emergency room, smoking a hand-rolled cigarette. The Red Cross ambulances, being unarmoured, had reached the hospital before the heavy Land Rover, and Flora saw the paramedics open the back doors and show the doctor what was inside. He puffed on his cigarette a couple of times then jerked his thumb towards the ramp which led round the back of the hospital. The ambulance drivers let their clutches out and drove down the ramp, no longer in a hurry, and Tony eased the Land Rover into the space they had left. The doctor plastered Gabriel's broken arm and cleaned up his cuts and gave him an injection which put him to sleep.

The child lay motionless on a grey, sour-smelling sheet stippled with little balls of loose cotton. The sheet was too small for the mattress, exposing wedges of dirty yellow foam in which bored little fingers had picked so many holes that it now resembled a cheese. The hospital had run out of bed gowns a long time ago, so Gabriel was still dressed in his own underpants and T-shirt, smeared with the blood of his friends.

Plaster flaked from walls which were damp from lack of heating. Fragments of broken glass and cardboard sagged from the gaffer tape which criss-crossed the windows. There was the sweet, horrid smell of generic body fluids. Over in the corner nurses were fussing around a four-year-old boy who was, for some reason, slowly dying. A couple of older kids watched from their beds.

'Come on,' Joseph said to Flora. 'We need to get you home, so you can wash and change, and get some pyjamas for Gabriel. Do you want me to tell your father what happened?'

Flora rounded on him. 'We're not telling Dad!' she shouted, and then she controlled herself. 'Dad doesn't need to know. Gabriel is going to be fine. He's hurt his arm, that's all. I can look after him.'

Tony waited for them out in the Land Rover. Adam's body was gone, and someone – presumably the morgue attendants, who were used to such work – had hosed and mopped all the gore from the back; the wet metal floor plates were steaming. Flora sat on the damp bench behind the front seats where Gabriel had lain. Horns blared, and two other armoured Land Rovers swept into the hospital car park, tyres singing on the tarmac.

'We really beat the competition on this one,' said Joseph. 'Felicity's going to be delighted.'

'You're not actually going to send her that stuff from this morning, are you?' demanded Tony.

Joseph sneered at his own reflection in the windscreen. 'Why not? Felicity will love it. She'll be a big star at this morning's conference.' He turned to Flora. 'Sorry,' he said.

'There's an obvious set-up on that tape, Joseph,' Tony warned.

'So what? I'm not going to send London the set-up. I'm only going to send the other stuff, the stuff that came later. The stuff I couldn't have set up if I was Steven bloody Spielberg.'

They passed by the park. Another group of boys were playing on the mound.

Flora slumped against the wall in her building's dark vestibule, considering her next move. If she moved quietly enough, she should be able to sneak to her room and change her clothes before her father knew she was back. Holding her breath, she opened the front door and tiptoed along the passage towards her bedroom. To her left yawned the open entrance to the workshop. Deliberately not looking, Flora glimpsed her father in the corner of her eye; he was contemplating a large washing machine placed before him on his work bench. She was reaching for her bedroom door

82

when the sound of voices halted her. Her father was not alone.

'It's a beauty, that!' said an admiring voice, a man's, low and ingratiating, furred by tobacco. 'The Maelstrom Circe! The most advanced automatic washing machine yet built. It's so smart it practically talks to you. Brand new.'

'Right . . . So why does it need fixing?'

The stranger chuckled. 'It doesn't, my friend. It's right out of the box, that. Perfect working order.'

'So why are you here?' Her father sounded even more bewildered than usual. Flora wanted to go to his rescue, but first she had to change her clothes.

'It's worth two grand, that,' the stranger went on. 'But I'll let you have it for fifteen hundred. On account of your son Jake. He was a good kid. One of our best.'

'I don't want it.'

'Yes, you do.'

'No, I don't. I fix old appliances. I don't sell new ones. Anyway, this is the wrong kind of washing machine.'

'What do you mean, the wrong kind?' The stranger was indignant. 'It washes clothes. What more do you want?'

'It's an American washing machine – a toploader. Most of the world uses frontloading washing machines, like all the other ones here in this workshop.'

'What difference does that make?'

'A very big difference.' Flora felt a pleasant pain: her father was beginning to sound professorial again. 'For a start, American machines can wash a load much faster, and you can also pop open the door in the top here to take stuff out, or put more stuff in, while the machine is still working. You can't do that with a frontloader because the door is holding all the water in – you have to be patient, with frontloaders.'

'So the toploader is better, then.'

'Oh, no. Not when it comes to economy. Clothes washed in toploaders wear out more quickly, because they rub off this spindle here that comes up through the middle of the drum. Also, they use a lot more electricity and soap than frontloading machines, and they need an external hot water supply. The costs quickly mount up. You'd struggle to give this machine away, in most parts of the world.'

A sudden metallic crash made Flora jump. The stranger must have punched or kicked the side of an appliance.

'And there's another thing,' her father went on, as if he hadn't noticed his visitor's eruption. 'When you have a frontloading machine you can stack other appliances on top of it – a lot of people put their dryer up there. It saves a lot of space if you live in a small house. Of course, that's generally less of a problem for Americans, so they can afford to stick with toploading machines, like this one of yours.'

There was another crash of metal. Flora turned the handle of her bedroom door as quietly as she could. She had a foot inside the room when the stranger spoke once more.

'Not this one of *mine*: this one of *yours*,' he said menacingly. 'You've just bought it.'

'No, I haven't.'

'You're buying it from me for fifteen hundred euros.'

'I'm not. I haven't got fifteen hundred euros.'

Flora heard the stranger chuckle again. She stepped into her room, leaving the door open so she could still eaves-drop. Moving as quickly and quietly as she could, straining her ears so as not to lose track of the conversation, she stripped off her stained clothes and kicked them under her bed.

'He was a brave lad, your son Jake,' mused the stranger. 'I felt terrible when that drone killed him. Him and your poor wife, too, as I recall. Martyrs, the pair of them . . . But you've got a couple more kids, don't you? I remember once, a little boy followed Jake all the way to training one night, and there was a sister who had to come and drag the little fella home again . . .'

Flora's father didn't answer. Dim light filtered into Flora's bedroom through her orange nylon curtains. She eased open her wardrobe to pull out clean jeans and a sweatshirt. Glancing down, she saw that Adam's blood had seeped through her clothes as she cradled him. It lingered now like a dark rash on her forearms and stomach. There was no time to wash it off.

'I've seen the girl around since, mind you,' continued the stranger. 'I've been keeping an eye on her. Pretty thing. She'll make some lucky man very happy some day . . . Let's hope that day doesn't come too soon, eh?'

Still her father said nothing, and the stranger went on. 'There are some pretty nasty types around these days. No respect for common decency. And they've all got guns, mind.

Even for a strong leader like me, it's getting harder and harder to keep my boys on a leash. Especially when I've got no money to pay them.'

Pulling the sweatshirt over her head, Flora heard her father speak again.

'I could maybe get one thousand euros,' he said.

There was a loud rattle from the workshop as the metal door slid open. Flora sat on her bed to pull on her jeans.

'One thousand euros . . .' the stranger mused, and from his tone Flora understood that he would have settled for much less. 'Okay, it's a deal – I'll let you off with the other five hundred on account of poor Jake. One of my men will call around tomorrow to pick up the cash. See that you have it – or he might look for payment in kind.'

Flora was rushing barefoot down the hall when she heard the metal door slide down again. She caught another glimpse of her father as she dashed past the workshop. Skidding on the tiles, she slammed into the front door, fumbled it open and ran through the vestibule, her bare feet cold on the rough concrete.

Out on the stoop, blinking in the daylight, she recognized a small bearded head gliding off towards the park. There was a sound of hooves, and as the head passed a gap in the crushed cars she saw that its owner was perched on a wooden cart mounted on car axles. He wore a camouflage jacket, pulled back just far enough to reveal the butt of an automatic pistol protruding from the waist of his combat trousers. From the way his mouth worked, he seemed to be singing to himself. Something made him glance back at the building and he saw Flora, glaring from the stoop. Cobra raised a hand and grinned at her.

CHAPTER ELEVEN

Following his most recent demotion Captain Smith had been posted to the Slob as a ground intelligence liaison officer. His predecessor's office had been located in the main command bunker, but soon after his arrival Smith moved his operation to a disused billet far out in the dunes on the edge of the compound. The hut in question was part of an isolated group of billets and store rooms which had become the haunt of the Easy Division's fringe elements – the shirkers, dopers, prostitutes, black marketeers and internal deserters. Justifying his move, the captain explained that his work needed privacy.

Shortly afterwards his new neighbours, roused before dawn by a one-minute rocket warning, found that an expensive padlock had appeared on the door of their bomb shelter. It was a particularly large bomb shelter, designed for storing fuel and ammunition, and its metal doors were wide enough to admit a two-and-a-half-ton truck. Captain Smith hinted that he and his personal orderly, Daddy Jesus, needed the space for interviewing the clients they extracted unwillingly from the Embargoed Zone. Why they also needed their own forklift truck was never explained. The most popular theory was that it played some unspeakable role in their interrogation method: a theory which caused several of the more squeamish local residents to relocate to other parts of the base. Before long, the remaining hold-outs were also gone, having been forcibly evicted by the Easy Division's commanding general. Captain Smith had sadly informed his office that, contrary to standing regulations, personnel in this area no longer had access to a bomb shelter.

Sand blew into the abandoned huts through broken windows and ill-fitting doors. Plywood shutters worked their nails loose and drummed in the wind. New drafts of soldiers and airmen rotated in and out of the base, until there was no one left who remembered seeing lights in those windows, or footprints in that sand. Senior officers never visited these crumbling huts, so it was with some surprise that Captain Smith – alerted by a blast of cold wind – looked up from his desk to see Colonel White glowering from the door of his office. Raindrops had spotted the colonel's tan uniform, and his shoes and trouser cuffs were red with wet sand. Seized by a fit of coughing, the captain beckoned his visitor inside with jerks of his right hand, while his left eased a sheaf of freshly signed receipts into an open drawer. The drawer slid closed when, in standing up to greet his visitor, the captain's knee deftly nudged it.

'Hello, sir!' said Smith, pulling a chair over for the colonel. 'How nice of you to come all the way out here to visit us! Please forgive my appearance – I'm just back from a ground op, inside the Easy.'

The colonel's lip curled as he looked around the office.

It had been formed by knocking two sleeping rooms together. A plywood partition, pierced by a shut wooden door, isolated it from the rest of the long wooden prefab, and the walls were decorated with yellowed printouts showing the faces of wanted terrorists, most of them long dead. The captain's desk was scattered with ash and chewed pens and grey military paperwork, amidst which the glossy, supersaturated colours of a used-car magazine shone like the gold in a panful of mud. A tactical computer terminal had been pushed aside to make room for a fancy new fax/copier, from which sheets of paper – invoices, order forms, and direct debit authorizations – spilled across the linoleum floor. The colonel sat down, frowning.

'Inside the Easy?' he growled. 'Are you trying to impress me, Smith? I've flown more combat missions than you've had hot dinners.' He tapped the row of ribbons on his chest.

'I don't doubt you're right,' Smith answered smoothly. 'I've missed a lot of hot dinners, being a humble ground soldier. Our missions, unlike yours, frequently last longer than half an hour. And our clients, unlike the air force's, are still able to shoot back at us. It can play havoc with one's meal arrangements.'

'Don't forget who you're talking to, Smith. I'm *your* commanding officer, now. And I haven't forgotten how things were when the boot was on the other foot.'

Smith seemed not to hear him. 'Only this morning, for instance, I was on the ground in the Embargoed Zone. Terrorists everywhere. And what was my commanding officer doing at that time? He was sitting in a concrete bunker ten kilometres back from the wall, using a robot to kill children. Are they giving out medals for *that* yet, Colonel?'

White smiled. 'Those were *terrorists*, Smith, not children. And you of all people should be very careful what you say about that. The computer logs will show that the air strike you refer to was carried out in support of *your* operation and with *your* authorization, following a request by a tank crew seconded to *your* control. So when the investigators ask about it I suggest that you don't say anything more about children.'

Captain Smith took out a packet of cigarettes and lit one, without offering one to his boss. 'I get investigated all the time,' he said, exhaling with precision. 'Some twenty-one-year-old military police sergeant knocks on my office door, so timidly I can barely hear it, and I let her come in, and tell her to stand where you're sitting now. She asks me in a very little voice if I did anything wrong and when I tell her no she gives me a big smile of relief and makes a tick in her notebook and then I let her sit down and I give her a cup of tea and a biscuit and then she goes away again. It's all rather sweet.'

The colonel grinned. 'It might not be so sweet this time, Smith. There are complicating factors.'

'Such as?'

'Such as the fact that live footage of the attack has already gone viral thanks to 24/7 News. And that's not the worst of it. Flint Driscoll from blow-back dot net was with me in the drone room when it happened. He watched the drone-strike live on the video feed, and he immediately put out an eye-witness report describing it as a pin-point strike against heavily armed terrorists. Because that's what I told him he saw. But then less than an hour later 24/7's footage went out across the globe, so now Driscoll looks like a fool or a liar, or both. He is very, very unhappy about that. And if he turns sour on us then the general is going to make someone pay for it. And don't kid yourself, Smith: that someone is going to be you.'

Smith blew out another plume of smoke. 'Why me, Colonel? Why not you? I'll bet you ordered that drone strike, just to show off to your new best pal Driscoll.'

The colonel smiled again. 'That's an interesting allegation, Smith, but I doubt if you'll find any evidence to support it. If anyone is going to take the fall for this it's going to be you. Unless, that is . . .'

'Unless what?'

'Unless you make the whole thing go away.'

Smith studied the colonel along the length of his cigarette. The colonel leaned back and laced his fingers behind his head. 'I want you to talk to Driscoll as soon as you can,' he went on, gazing at the ceiling. 'The usual sort of thing: explain to him why 24/7's footage doesn't actually show what everyone thinks it shows. It shouldn't be too hard to persuade him of that – he'll want to believe you. And if we can get Driscoll back on-side he'll rubbish 24/7's story for us.'

'I don't know,' said Smith, '24/7's footage is pretty good. You can see the expressions on their faces when the first rocket hits. We'd be better off kicking for touch on this one – announce an internal inquiry, and all of the other standard evasive procedures.'

The colonel shook his head. 'Not this time. The main problem right now is keeping Driscoll sweet on us – as for the rest of it, if the worst comes to the worst we can always say the air strike was an honest mistake.'

'You'll blame it on the tactical computer?'

The colonel was standing, preparing to go. 'Hell, no! The computer system has to be infallible: it's already cost us a billion to develop, and we're on the verge of selling it to both India *and* Pakistan ... No, if I have to, I'll pin it on those drone jockeys who were there. They're the most expendable component.'

The colonel, having reached the doorway, halted, one hand raised to his forehead. 'Oh! Yes! Silly me: I almost forgot ... There's something missing from the strong-room in the bunker. I wondered if you'd know anything about it?'

'Missing, sir?' Smith's eyebrows migrated northward. 'What would that be?'

'A washing machine. I put it there myself yesterday, and it wasn't there today. I assumed you'd know something about it, since you have the only other key to that room.'

Bewilderment and innocence skirmished for possession of the captain's face, then sensibly called it a draw.

'On no, sir. I've seen nothing like that.'

A muscle twitched in the colonel's jet-pilot jaw. 'You don't know anything about it?'

'No, sir. But I can ask around if you like. Perhaps I left

94

the door open, and one of the quartermasters took it away. They're probably using it already; washing machines wear out very quickly here, on account of all the grit.' A thought seemed to strike him. 'Come to think of it, sir, it has probably been stolen. Why don't we indent for another one? If you'll sign a requisition for me I'll send it off right away to the Supply Corps.'

The colonel had trouble speaking. 'I don't want another washing machine,' he said finally. 'I want that one. It's special.'

'Surely a washing machine is just a washing machine?'

The colonel's cheek squirmed like a freshly-sliced worm. 'This one is American. A toploader. They don't import them here.'

'I'm sure we can get you a frontloader that will wash just as clean.'

The colonel exploded. 'Listen to me, Smith! That machine was left in a secure room for which you are jointly responsible! I want it back at all costs, or by God there'll be trouble!' Mastering himself, he continued: 'You're already on thin ice over this air strike business, and don't think I've forgotten our personal history. So get that machine back, or by God I'll let them crucify you!'

The wind caught the door and slammed it shut behind him. A few seconds later the interior door creaked open and Daddy Jesus's hideous face appeared around it. The wreckage of a hamburger oozed through his huge, discoloured fingers.

'Trouble, boss?'

Captain Smith stood. Sliding open the window behind his desk, he stuck his head out and peered down at the weedy, butt-strewn ground six feet below.

'Daddy Jesus,' he called over his shoulder. 'Can you guess who I'm imitating?'

Daddy Jesus looked back at him, stony-faced.

'Well?' demanded Smith. 'Who am I being? Go on – have a guess.' He turned away and stared theatrically down at the ground again, raising one hand to shade his eyes like a story-book explorer.

'Sorry, boss.'

'I'm being an air force intelligence officer. This is how they gather air force intelligence ...' Smith closed the window and slumped behind his desk again, waving Daddy Jesus to the chair which was still warm from the colonel. He sat back and sighed, his eyes wandering over the dead yellow faces staring down from the walls.

'Remember the old days, Daddy Jesus? Remember when you had to look a man in the eye before you stabbed him in the back? We're the last of an old breed ...' He shook his head sadly. 'Tell me, Daddy Jesus – were you listening to me and the colonel?'

'Yes.'

'Good ... So what do you think?'

Deep in thought, Daddy Jesus eased the last gloopy scraps of his burger into his mouth, then wiped his fingers on one sleeve and his lips on the other.

'We could have a fire in a quartermaster's store-room, then say the washing machine was in it.'

Smith shook his head. 'No good. That scam goes back to the time of the legions. Besides, I've already used it once this year.'

'Then we should get that washing machine back from Cobra.'

The captain picked up his pen and drummed pensively on the desktop. 'Yes ... I was afraid you'd say that ... But Cobra's going to want something in return if we take the washing machine back from him. He's being a real pain in the arse about money lately.'

'We could give him his money.'

The captain laid his pen down, sighed and stood up again, turning his back to Daddy Jesus. Isolated raindrops were spattering against the window.

'My wife had a surprise for me last night,' he told the rain. 'Not only are we paying for my eldest daughter's wedding in the spring, which I already knew, but now it seems that she and my wife have decided that they need to shop for the wedding in Paris. And they're taking my youngest girl with them, just so she won't feel left out. And I have to pay for it all ...'

Daddy Jesus thought again. 'So we pay him only some of his money. Five hundred should do.'

The captain turned back to him, grimacing. 'Five hundred euros? ... Dear me ... I suppose we could low-ball him on two hundred, and go up to four or five if we really had to ...' He patted his pockets. 'But dear me ... I haven't got any cash on me.' For a few moments he stared hopefully into Daddy Jesus's expressionless eyes, then gave up.

'Oh, all right,' he said, and reached inside his jumper. 'Here – take my card down to the highway service station. See if the machine there will give you five hundred – I'm close to my limit. On the way back, stop by the tentage depot and see if you can lift a few of those canvas eight-man tents. There's an open-air trance festival up north next weekend: hippies pay big money for anything army surplus.'

Daddy Jesus took the card but stopped just short of the door, apparently deep in thought again. 'I'm still hungry, boss,' he decided. 'Do you want another McDonald's?'

The captain had retrieved his receipt book from the drawer and was preparing to start signing again, his pen held awkwardly in his left hand.

'Dear me, no. I couldn't eat another thing – I don't have your appetite, my friend . . .' He put the pen down again. 'Oh, go on. But I don't want a hamburger. Get me a coffee, and something to go with it.'

'How about an apple pie, boss?'

'Yes! Just the thing! I love those apple pies they do . . . so lovely and hot on the inside . . .' A fond smile spread over Smith's face. 'You remember that time, Daddy Jesus, when you accidentally squirted some of your pie filling on that terrorist, and he thought it was part of your technique?'

A strange, heaving gurgle filled the room, like the sound of a gut-shot sow. Daddy Jesus was laughing.

'We're the last of a breed,' the captain said again, shaking his head ruefully. He reached for his cell phone. 'Hang on –

I'd best give Cobra a call before you go. We should agree a price before you take out the cash.'

The captain pressed a speed-dial, waited a few moments, then beamed at Daddy Jesus.

'Hello, Cobra? I hope you're still having a nice day . . . Yes, yes, so are we. But listen: it's about that washing machine. Something's come up, and we need to get it back from you.' His smile broadened as he heard the reply. 'Sold it already, eh? . . . Of course you have, Cobra, of course you have.' He winked at Daddy Jesus. 'Well, you'll just have to refund your customer and get the machine back. We need it for something.' The captain rocked with silent laughter as he listened to the reply. 'Oh, I see. So you've already given all of the money from the sale to your men, and they've already spent it, so you won't be able to get the money back from them. I suppose that means you'll need us to give you some more money now, so you can buy the machine back?' Daddy Jesus shook his head and tutted. The captain continued: 'And how much did you sell the machine for, Cobra? . . . Fifteen hundred euros, eh? Well, that *is* a good price. I congratulate you.' His face became sorrowful. 'But here's the thing: I can't come up with more than three hundred euros right now. And I want that machine back, right away, or there will be some very unpleasant consequences.'

He replaced the phone. 'Unbelievable, Daddy Jesus! Cobra actually thinks he can play me! Sold the washing machine indeed – inside the Easy! We'll let him stew for a while, and then he'll be happy to give it back for whatever we offer him.'

'Yes, boss. McDonald's now?'

'By all means. But first pass me that computer; I have to deconstruct and recontextualize a narrative that I need.'

CHAPTER TWELVE

New York was pleased. Bob Reilly was very pleased. And Felicity in London was so very, very pleased that she gave Joseph and Tony the rest of the day off. As if she normally knew, or cared, whether they were working or not. Joseph decided to visit the BBC bureau downstairs which, rumour had it, had received some supplies that day. Tony took the Land Rover and drove back to the hospital.

Gabriel, still sedated, was unattended in the children's ward, so Tony left some sweets by his bed and departed. Shadows were lengthening as he parked the jeep outside Flora's building. The apartment door was unlocked, and after a series of timid advances down the hall, calling softly, he came upon Flora's father alone in his workshop. Tony had to address him twice before the old man turned to look at him. His expression, Tony saw, was even more distant than usual.

'Hello, Sam,' Tony managed. 'I was just wondering, has Flora come back from the hospital yet?'

'Hospital?' asked the old man, frowning, and Tony realized his mistake.

'Did I say hospital? I meant university. I've brought a couple of things to help her study . . . Joseph sent them. There's a new car battery, so she can run her computer more often. And I've printed out the full game-play manual for that flight simulator she likes so much.'

Sam smiled suddenly. 'She used to want to be a pilot when she was little. But now she's going to be a doctor.'

The late sun shone yellow through the dirty panes above the door, picking out the fine dust which lurched aimlessly about the gulf between the two men. Tony found himself taking a step backward, out of the workshop.

'I tell you what, Sam,' he said. 'I'll just leave the stuff for Flora in the hallway. When you see her, please tell her I said hello.' The old man's smile became uncertain, and Tony realized he was now invisible in the darkness of the hallway.

'Is there anything else I can do for you, Sam?' he called, and when there was no reply he went on, 'Well, goodbye, then. See you soon, I hope.'

He went out to the jeep to fetch the things. Returning, stooped, with both hands straining beneath the heavy battery, he used his shoulder to nudge the front door. To his surprise, Sam was waiting just inside, frowning at him.

'Anthony, I could use a favour, if your offer still stands. I need a lift in your car, with one of my appliances.'

The jeep's rear door was just wide enough for them to slide in the washing machine tipped on its side, but the bench behind the front seats prevented the appliance from going in all the way, leaving ten centimetres of white casing protruding into the street. Tony improvised a cradle from the jeep's tow-rope, so that the machine wouldn't slide out when the Land Rover moved off. As they started up the hill, the noise of the exhaust pipe blattered in through the open rear door, deafening them.

Cobra lashed his donkey as hard as he could, but even on level ground it would never do better than a trot, and the road to Sam's home sloped steeply upward. A hundred metres short of his goal, he could see, quite clearly, the washing machine sticking out of the Land Rover's back door. But then the jeep was moving off, its driver deaf to Cobra's shouts and threats, blind to his waving pistol. As it turned a corner and vanished he gave up the chase, dealing his donkey a flurry of blows to reward it for its failure. Then, after a few moments of reflection, he drove on again, turning his cart into an alley across from Flora's building. Tipping his cap over his brow, he settled down to wait.

CHAPTER THIRTEEN

It had been full daylight when Moon staggered away from the truck stop, but by the time he reached the base's perimeter fence it was already so dark that he struggled to find the gap in the wire. Crawling through it, a barb snagged his carrier bag, ripping it open. Both bottles of vodka spilled into the gloomy bushes along with – unnoticed – his cell phone. As he gathered the two bottles, Moon saw that one was already a third empty. Stumbling up a low dune, he unscrewed the top and took another gulp.

The crest of the dune gave a view across the small-arms range to a further line of sand dunes – higher, built anew each day from wind-blown sand – which masked the beach. Dusk had blown the sky clear, the stars had yet to appear, and the sun lingered low in a vacant horizon.

In front of Moon, the path continued down the face of the dune then split left and right. The Slob's billets lay along the path to the right, and beyond them reared the high dunes which entombed the command bunker. Above them a hard red eye, the light on the radio mast, winked at Moon knowingly. There were people over there, he remembered, who would want to congratulate him for having set the unit's new high score that day. He saw again the scenes from that morning – real-time on his computer screen, or later, in slow-motion, on the foreign news channels – and was again gripped by nausea. The vodka wasn't working yet.

So Moon turned left, away from the Slob, onto a path he had never taken before, rising steeply away towards a patch of pine forest. Beyond that forest, he knew, lay the camp's eastern gate, and the infantry cantons. It was fun to go exploring. But the sun soon dipped behind the dunes, shadows welled from the ground, and Moon had only gone a short way before he could no longer see the pine trees. Instead, he found himself twisting and stumbling through a maze of sandy humps and overgrown wet hollows. And was that still a path beneath his feet, or merely dirt too fine for weeds to root in? He tried to retrace his steps, steering by the light in the west, but the ground baffled his already vague intentions. He had always assumed, having seen it only from a drone's video feed, that the terrain around here was flat and featureless. But it threw ditches in his path, and banks of loose soil, and it scratched him with thorns and snared him in bushes. His bottles, clutched in either hand, hampered him further. Branches lunged at his eyes from the gathering darkness, and he was already beginning to panic when, on the crest of another sandy ridge, his heels flew suddenly out from beneath him. Crashing through branches, Moon slid on his back, feet-first, down a near-vertical bank of sand. Then his shoes planted themselves in loose dirt, jarring his knees painfully, and he found himself on the edge of a wide, gloomy plain of sand and gravel, shaken, but still somehow upright. All was silent apart from the hiss of the breeze in the bushes above and, closer to hand, a melodic gurgle; vodka escaping from an open bottle, held tilted in his hand.

Moon decided that he must have been traumatized by his fall, and took another big hit from what was left in the bottle. He was lucky not to have been injured. But where could he go from here? Behind him was an eight-metre bank of dirt, bulldozed almost vertically from the dunes, stretching north and south until it vanished in the gloaming. He was, he realized, standing on the edge of the base's vast sunken tank park, where ranks of canvas-shrouded hulls loomed out of the dusk. To Moon, in his impressionable state, they seemed to be alive but sleeping – fat, carnivorous larvae, their olive cocoons splitting to expose segmented tracks, bristling aerials, the probing stingers of their guns. Perhaps his intrusion would wake them. Terror seized Moon, and he dropped his bottles and tried to claw his way back where he'd come from. It was no use: he might make it one metre, perhaps two, up the bank, but then the soft, yielding dirt would bear him back down again, sweating and gasping, his nails clogged and raw. He lay there, panting, face-down in the soil. Then one of his hands found a bottle – the unsealed one – and, turning on his back again, he unscrewed it and took another slug. The armoured vehicles were as he'd last seen them, motionless.

There must be a way out of this place. He levered himself

to his feet, swaying. Carefully, so as not to make too much noise, he began to make his way around the edge of the tank park, keeping the bank to his left.

It was not too much later, probably, that he finished what was left of his first bottle. He hurled it expansively off into the darkness, where it smashed against a metal hull, tinkling pleasantly. The bank still rose, an unbroken rampart, on his left-hand side. Somewhere ahead, he supposed, perhaps very close now, would be the quarters of the combat units, and beyond them the border with the Embargoed Zone. Perhaps, the vodka whispered, it was time to make his pilgrimage to the wall.

It was a suggestion worth considering, at least, and Moon stopped, unscrewing the top of the second bottle, and leaned back against a tank track. His eye was caught by a dim blue light which flickered from a hatch that stood, half-open, on the next tank.

He heard muttering voices, and then one of those harsh, flat splashes of sound which computers make when refusing an order. Somebody cursed. A dark shape appeared in the turret and a match flared, replaced moments later by a red point in the darkness.

Moon took another nip of vodka to help concentrate his thinking: it was time he sought some help.

'Hello?' called Moon to the figure on the turret. 'I'm sorry to bother you. I'm just looking for directions.'

There was a yelp, and the red point flew off into the night. A beam of light sprang from the turret and wavered in the darkness. 'Who's that?' hissed a voice.

Panic seized Moon again. He saw the torch beam stab-
bing towards him. Then, just as it fixed him, his brain
dredged up something he had heard long ago, in his brief
basic training.

'Erm . . . Friend?'

'What do you mean, friend?' demanded the man in the
turret. 'I've never seen you before!'

'Friend, as in, not foe. You're supposed to ask me, "Who
goes there?" and I'm supposed to say, "friend". It's what you
do when a sentry challenges you.'

'*Challenges* you?' The light clicked off and Moon heard the
stranger mutter: 'It's just some idiot who's got himself lost.
He thinks we're on guard, or something. Thank God: I
thought it was Captain Smith, or that Daddy Jesus . . . Isn't
that thing back online yet?'

'It's rebooting now,' another voice whispered. 'Go and
find that little number you rolled before it burns down any
further. I'm wise to your tricks, Johnny – when you roll you
always supercharge the first couple of inches, because you
know you'll be smoking first.'

A dark figure plummeted down from the turret and
landed beside Moon. The torch clicked on again and the
tanker spoke, almost in his ear. 'So who are you, pal?'
The torch searched in vain the bare cloth of Moon's tan
sleeves, then up to his lieutenant's bars, then winked out
again.

'Oh, sorry, sir. What are you, some kind of pilot?'

Moon thought of the events of that morning. 'Yes. That's
right. Some kind of pilot.'

'Hey, Lenny,' said the tanker, raising his voice, 'guess what: it's a pilot!'

Another figure thudded to earth on the other side of Moon. 'No way, Johnny! What would a pilot be doing way out here in the tank park at night?'

Moon straightened his back and hooked both elbows behind him so they were supported by the tank track. The open vodka bottle, still almost full, was clutched in his right hand. 'I'm out for a little stroll,' he declared. 'A spot of ground liaison. My own personal inspection.'

There had been quite a few Ss in that speech, Moon reflected. Too many, perhaps. There was a silence and then Lenny spoke again. 'Is that a bottle you have there, sir?'

'Indeed it is, soldier.' Moon's new companions had a pleasant, herbal smell. 'But you don't have to call me sir,' he went on, passing the bottle to Lenny. 'Why should we let differences of rank spoil a nice evening? . . . By the way, I can see that thing you're looking for. It's still burning, just over there.'

CHAPTER FOURTEEN

Stifling a yawn, Captain Smith moved his computer so that its screen was visible both to himself and Flint Driscoll, seated on the other side of his desk. Driscoll hunched forward in his chair, notebook open.

'Before we go any further, Captain,' he said, 'I take it that this alleged footage was produced by a local-hire camera crew, and not by regular 24/7 staff from outside the Embargoed Zone?'

'Of course. We've complained about them countless times, and asked 24/7 to shut down its Easy bureau in view of its clear pro-terrorist bias. But something tells me that this latest incident might be the final straw.'

'It will be, if I have anything to do with it.'

Captain Smith rubbed his eyes and then, supporting his cheek with an elbow propped on the desk, reached out to activate the computer's media player.

'It really is hard to know where to begin, there are so many issues to address . . .' Smith fast-forwarded through the first few seconds of 24/7's broadcast, then stopped. 'Now here, you see, is the first big question mark. As I'm sure you'll know from the movies, air strikes produce large explosions of orange and black flame, and big eruptions of dirt and debris.' Driscoll nodded and made a note.

'But here the so-called explosion' – the captain played it through again – 'looks nothing like that. All you have is this puff of smoke and dust and a ring of flying dirt.' He replayed it again. 'Now, if it had been a real air strike, you'd also expect to see these bodies catapulted twenty or thirty feet through the air, but instead they just fall over and lie around. It's not very convincing, is it?'

Driscoll lowered his pen. 'I think I can see where you're going with this.'

This time the captain did yawn. 'I'm sure you can, Dr Driscoll. You're a very shrewd man.' He reactivated the media player.

'Now as you'll see here, in the second after the explosion the camera zooms in so that you can see nothing but the dust-cloud. The jerkiness of the image and the garbled soundtrack – the apparent sound of the cameraman whimpering, above a background of purported screams – make this seem authentic. But watch closely.' He played a few more frames of the clip. 'Now, there you saw the camera zoom out again from the dust cloud, and as the cloud clears you can see dead terrorists lying together, mutilated and covered in blood. And all in one continuous shot. Right?'

Driscoll stared back at him expectantly. The captain waited, measuring the appropriate pause, and then plunged ahead. 'Right? Well, let me sketch out a little scenario for you, Doctor: when Alfred Hitchcock was making *Rope* he wanted the movie to look like it was filmed in one long continuous shot. But in those days a film camera could only go ten minutes before it had to be reloaded. So in *Rope* the camera zooms in, every few minutes, for no apparent reason, on somebody's jacket, or on a blank wall, or whatever, and then zooms out again. Of course, these zooms were used to conceal the edits made when the film had to be reloaded. Just as the terrorists could have used the dust cloud in this shot to hide their own trickery.'

'I want you to spell it out for me,' said Driscoll grimly.

Smith shuffled his hands, miming a conjuring trick. 'Consider this scenario: the terrorists film a shot of some of their younger cadres, posing as children. Then they detonate a large concealed firework to create the first dust cloud. Then they shut off the camera and rearrange their youth members – heavily made-up, or perhaps actually killed and mutilated by their own leaders, for extra verisimilitude – lying on the ground. Then they start the camera again and set off a second firework, so that when the dust clears the bodies are seen lying there, as if stricken by one of our missiles. Then, hey presto! all the terrorists have to do is edit the two dust clouds together, remove any footage that was shot between them, and they are left with what looks like the before and after of a missile strike!'

'Why, the dirty lying scum!'

'They hate our freedoms, Doctor. I've been fighting terrorism for more than twenty-five years now. I guess in your own way you have too . . .' Driscoll nodded. The captain leaned forward and frowned. 'But you know, I still some-times have to ask myself, Doctor … Where does this evil come from? This hatred? These lies? …'

He fixed his guest with a look of grim resolution. 'But evil and lies will not prevail, will they, Doctor? The terror-ists are smart, yes, but they always slip up, as they did again today.' He played back the footage. 'To give only one glaring example, here you can hear the cameraman screaming, "They're dead, they're dead, they're all dead." Yet when you look more closely you can see that this one here – the one pretending to have had his legs blown off – is twitching. Which proves that the whole incident was fabricated. And it gets worse: I want you to pay particular attention to this actor here, the midget, who is being dragged off by this young female terrorist. In the corner of this later shot' – he clicked forward – 'you can even see her embracing him. They are probably congratulating themselves on their part in this charade.'

Smith pulled the computer screen around to face himself, with something like a flourish. 'But now, Doctor, we come to the absolute clincher … As you probably know, our tactical computer network incorporates the most sophisti-cated biometric software on the planet. I can isolate a screen-shot of a terrorist's face, and the database will instantly generate a pop-up display showing me not only that terrorist's true identity but also their place of residence, personal history, family ties, medical records, known contacts – everything. Now, let's have a look at the girl and the midget here.' He tapped at the keyboard, then turned the computer around to Driscoll, who hunched forward to study it.

'I'd like to you to note these names. As you can see, the midget terrorist and the female are – guess what? – brother and sister! Now, what kind of terrorist brings his sister along on an operation? She has clearly been planted there for dramatic effect, playing the part of an innocent bystander. And by whom?'

The captain whipped the computer around, tapped it again, then turned it back to Driscoll. 'By this man – Joseph West, 24/7's cameraman in the Embargoed Zone. Who also happens to be – tah dah! – their uncle!'

Driscoll slumped back in his seat, slapped his notebook on his knee and gave a loud guffaw. 'Oh, man,' he gasped. 'Hitchcock could not have done better himself!'

'You're quite right, Doctor. Hitchcock could not have done better. But I can. Look!' He proffered the screen again. 'How are these siblings related to West? Through their mother, his sister, who was killed two years ago, along with their elder brother, in a surgical counter-terror strike on the vehicle in which they were travelling. And who was their older brother? Hey presto! None other than a senior leader of Cobra Force, a deadly Hilltown-based terror group!'

Driscoll scribbled some information from the screen, then slapped his pen on the desk with an air of finality. 'I have to hand it to you, Captain, you do know how to tell a story, saving the best to last. Of course, we journalists have to write it the other way around: put the best stuff at the top;

in the shop-window, as it were. Can you give me a couple of quotes, just for polish?'

The captain blew his cheeks out regretfully. 'Alas, no, Doctor. As I told you this morning, I'm not allowed to speak to you with any attribution – not even as a "military spokesman" or a "security source".' He tapped his desk a few times, frowning, and then his face brightened. 'You know . . . it just occurred to me, Doctor . . . It might be best in this case, in the interests of discretion, if you let it be understood that you uncovered this plot by yourself. And of course, you have done, really. You asked all the right questions.'

Driscoll pursed his lips. 'Yes. That might be best. But while I'm still here, Captain, can you tell me any more about this family? Who is the children's father, for example? Is he an active terrorist too?'

The captain tapped the computer again, frowning as he read. 'No, strangely enough. He's a physics professor, or at least he used to be, it says here. He fixes old appliances now . . .' A smile appeared on the captain's face as he stared at his laptop, then he snapped its lid decisively shut. 'The professor is nobody,' he said. 'Forget about him, Doctor. I suspect you already have quite enough villains for one piece.'

Driscoll stood, checking his watch. 'A physicist, eh? Well, I guess you're right: too many characters muddle the plot . . . Anyway, I must be off, now. Colonel White is giving me a lift back to my quarters – they've put me right beside him, in the VIP compound. He should be waiting outside.'

'Then please give the Colonel my warm regards. Tell him that I'm still working on the toploader project. Tell him I've got my very best field agents on the job. We'll soon retrieve it.'

Smith showed his guest to the door then walked back to his desk and sat down again. He picked up the land phone and pressed a button.

'Daddy Jesus? . . . Yes, he's gone, thank God. Sycophantic git – you're lucky you haven't had to meet him. Now listen: get on the computer and see if you can fix Cobra's present position, from his cell phone signal.' The captain waited for a few moments and then smiled. 'Great! That confirms it: he's right outside the place where I think he left the washing machine. It's a kind of amateur repair shop, in Hilltown: he must be keeping an eye on the machine, now that he knows it's worth something to us. Poor old Cobra: he should have closed the deal with us earlier; now that we know where it is, we can nip in and pick it up for free under cover of the next up-tit operation; it's right on the edge of Hilltown, only a dash from the wall. It isn't going anywhere in the meantime. Not in the Embargoed Zone.'

CHAPTER FIFTEEN

Flora sat on the third stair of the steps which led to the roof of the media centre, her raincoat folded beneath her to protect her from the grime. The steps were made of bare metal, and the wooden handrails had long since been wrenched from the wall and chopped up for firewood. The walls of the landing – dressed with oddly cheap-looking slabs of green marble – were decorated with images, most of them rather gruesome, grabbed from 24/7's own video footage. Flora had to will herself not to look at them; she wished she had brought a book. Finally, she took pen and paper from her bag and scribbled a short note.

'Dear Uncle Joseph,' she wrote. 'I am sorry to bother you, but I need your help with a very urgent matter. Somebody is trying to extort money from my father, and I am afraid that he will give in to them. He does not listen to me, but you might be able to talk to him. I know it is short notice, but if you receive this note today could you please come and see us at home?

Best wishes, Flora.'

She dated the note and slid it under the door, then made

her way to the street again, down six flights of greasy, unlit stairs.

The street murmured with the sounds of early evening; lucky people walking home from their aid jobs; mothers with trophies of rice or cooking oil; donkeys stamping, heads down at the kerb, their drivers hoping for one last fare before the curfew. Down here the sun had already set, yet high above the street dozens of kites wavered red and white and gold in the last rays of sunshine, each the focus of a child's tethered dream. Flora checked the alley beside the building, to see if Joseph's Land Rover had reappeared in its usual space: it had not. Wearily she turned her steps homewards again: perhaps, she consoled herself, Uncle Joseph would soon read her plea, and follow after her. If he saw her on the road she wouldn't have to walk all the way home. And then she remembered what she had forgotten to put in her note, that she wasn't taking the direct route home, that she would be going via the hospital, to check on Gabriel. The hope of a lift, however fond, must have meant more to Flora than she had realized, because she found herself abruptly on the edge of tears. What could she do? ... She stood there for a few moments, head bowed, oblivious to the glares of those forced to step around her, and then she came to a brisk resolution. She was thirsty and hungry and tired. She would buy a glass of lemonade and a piece of cake from the stall across the road, and then she would pay for a seat on a donkey cart and travel to the hospital in style. The donkey cart would cost even more than usual, so close to the curfew, and the money would have to come from the housekeeping, which was already short for the month. But this was an emergency, another emergency. And of course everything, everything, depended on her.

CHAPTER SIXTEEN

There was no moon that night, and no electricity, so Cobra was almost invisible in the alley where he lurked. Only the occasional scuffle of his donkey's hoof, or the quick flash of a match, betrayed him to the blackened street. Cobra smoked furtively, with the tip of his cigarette cupped in his palm, not so much to hide the glow from snipers as to disguise the fact that, unlike most people in the Easy, he still somehow had access to factory-made cigarettes. For the same reason, he always kept his cell phone concealed in an inner pocket, its ringtone muted. But he did not know how to mute the phone's low battery alarm, and he heard it again now: a loud, tell-tale beep that broke the silence and lit up the phone's dormant screen. Fishing it out from his shirt pocket, he saw that the battery was down to the last flashing bar. There was a new text message too, from the civilian service provider on the other side of the wall, warning him that last month's bill was now overdue: Smith had clearly failed to pay it again. How long, Cobra wondered, did his handlers think he could carry on like this? It was almost as if Smith no longer cared what Cobra thought of him, or did for him ... He put the phone away again, shivering for a moment, although he did not feel cold. And then, as his eyes readjusted to the dark, he became aware of a figure standing in the rectangle of grey light at the mouth of the alley, staring straight at him.

The back of Cobra's head struck the cart as he hurled himself backward, reaching at the same time for his pistol. But the donkey was startled by Cobra's yelp, and as he fell backwards it leaped forward, jerking the cart out from under him. Cobra spun onto the alley's filthy floor, his pistol flying off into the blackness, as the donkey and cart clattered off down the hill. Stifling his breath, Cobra flattened himself against the darkest part of the wall and tried to make himself smaller. Then his phone beeped again, and looking down he saw with sick horror that his jacket had come open in the fall, and that a bright rectangle of light shone through the cotton of his shirt, over his frail, fluttering heart. He moaned and bowed his head, waiting for the assassin's bullet.

A cat mewed, wind fussed in the rubbish, and a girl's voice said loudly: 'Leave us alone! We don't have any money!'

Cobra opened one eye, and then the other. He pushed himself away from the wall, brushed himself off and sauntered to the alley's mouth. 'Oh, it's you, is it?'

He was trying to sound casual, but his breath came with a lingering shudder. He took a couple more steps until he was close enough dimly to see her face. She was as tall as he was: he had hoped to be able to leer down at her.

'Why are you sneaking around like that in the dark?' he demanded. 'I could easily have shot you.'

He took another step towards her but she stood her ground. 'I heard what you did to my father earlier on. We haven't got any money and we don't want your machine. Take it away again.'

Cobra took another step forward, until he was close enough to touch her if he wished. 'Why, that's just why I'm here: to take it away again. I've found a buyer for it. But there's a problem: it's not here any more.'

'Of course it's still here. Where else could it be?'

'Don't play games with me. It was carted off in a jeep earlier, by one of those cameramen from 24/7. The younger one. I saw it go with my own two eyes. Where has he taken it?'

She seemed confused. 'I really don't know. I thought it was worthless.'

'Oh no, not at all. In fact, I've found a buyer who's willing to pay you five hundred euros for it. So here's what we'll do: I'll pass the machine on to the buyer for you, the buyer will give me the five hundred, which I'll keep, and then your father will only owe me another five hundred, to make up the thousand euros we agreed when I sold it to him. Everyone's a winner.'

Flora took a step forward and Cobra found himself back-pedalling. 'We owe you nothing!' she hissed in his face.

He made a show of lighting his cigarette. 'Look, dear: if you overheard me talking to your father earlier, then you'll know how our deal is structured.' He shook the match out and held the tailor-made cigarette openly, where she could see it. 'I'd have thought that you of all people would be keen to see the deal, well, *honoured*. Besides, the money isn't for me. It all goes to the cause.'

'Our family has already paid enough for what you say is your cause!'

Cobra pulled on his cigarette. 'Not quite enough – you're still five hundred euros short. And one washing machine. Get them for me by tomorrow or there'll have to be payment in kind. From you. Or your brother.'

Flora turned and walked away. Cobra watched her go, puffing on his cigarette. And then he remembered his errant donkey, swore, and set off down the hill to search for it. He had gone fifty metres when he remembered the even more pressing matter of his missing pistol. Wearily he retraced his steps and entered again the dark mouth of the alley. No glimmer of light reached its rubbish-strewn floor. He stood there, despairing, until he remembered the cell phone in his pocket. Taking it out, he unlocked the key-guard, and a faint but useful cone of light sprang from its screen. Congratulating himself, he bent low to start sifting through the rubbish. Then the phone beeped at him again, three times in quick succession, and its screen went dead.

CHAPTER SEVENTEEN

The stolen tents had been lying in the back of Daddy Jesus's jeep all afternoon compacted together by their dead crushing weight. Captain Smith and Daddy Jesus had to use all their strength to unload them, tugging them free one by one, puffing and sweating in the darkness, their feet slipping in the loose oily sand at the entrance to their bomb shelter. They did not notice Colonel White's jeep until its head-lights swept across their tableau and stopped fixed on the contraband.

'Oh dear,' said Captain Smith to himself.

The jeep's door exploded open and Colonel White came flying towards him, the sand spurting from his heels. He grabbed Smith by the shirtfront and slammed him hard against the side of Daddy Jesus's jeep. Stars flared in Smith's head, but he had the presence of mind to lift both hands and wave frantically behind the colonel's back. As the stars faded Smith could just make out the sinister bulk of Daddy Jesus, only a foot behind the colonel but backing silently away again. The colonel's face was inches from his own.

'Smith!' it hissed wetly. 'What the fuck did you just say to Driscoll about that washing machine?'

The captain blinked the spit out of his eyes. 'Driscoll? I just thought you'd like to know how that business was going, that's all. It seemed so important to you earlier on.'

'Really? So to keep me informed you decided to entrust a *blogger* with top-secret military intelligence?'

'Intelligence? It's a washing machine. It's for cleaning clothes with.'

The colonel wasn't listening. 'And what in the name of holy fuck did you mean when you said you have "your best field agents" looking for it? Where the hell are you looking for this thing, Smith? Because it doesn't sound to me like you think it's on this base any more.'

Captain Smith became aware of a pain in his lower back, dull now but throbbing, where the Colonel had bashed his spine against the jeep's door handle. The pilot's face loomed over him, eyes flashing arrogance and contempt. Usually a man of quiet passions, the captain felt a hard, hot knot forming just behind his eyes.

'Oh no, sir,' he said, his voice quite calm. 'You're quite right, sir – your washing machine is not on the base any more. I'd been meaning to tell you, sir – it's in the Embargoed Zone. Sorry about that.'

He braced himself for a blow. The colonel was a combat pilot, and therefore both quick and stupid enough to get a punch in before Daddy Jesus maimed him.

Instead, the colonel spun on his heel, brushed past the lurking Daddy Jesus and marched off into the night beyond the cones of the headlights. Baffled, Smith watched him go. There was a long silence, and then the colonel spoke again.

'I see ... It's in the Embargoed Zone ...' His voice was strangely quiet. 'How did it get out of the store-room and then through the wall?'

Smith rolled his eyes in the darkness. 'Oh, gypsies, I should think. You know what they're like, sir – they can get in anywhere.'

The colonel gave a little laugh. 'Gypsies? ... Is that really what you think? Oh, dear God ...'

And to his great surprise the captain heard a sob. Followed by Daddy Jesus, he sprang away from the jeep. They found the colonel slumped to his knees in the sand, staring into the encircling darkness. An uneasy feeling began to trouble Smith: cowards, thieves, bigots, perverts, addicts, liars, sadists – even heroes and idealists: these he knew how to handle. But madmen were another matter.

'Oh don't take on so,' he said soothingly. 'I'm sure we'll get the washing machine back for you, if it means so much to you ... It just might cost us a little bit extra, that's all.'

Daddy Jesus laid about ten pounds of fingers on the Colonel's shoulder and raised and lowered them a couple of times, murmuring 'there, there', as gently as his nature allowed.

The colonel's voice seemed to come to them from the bottom of a very deep and narrow well; they had to lean forward to hear him.

'You don't understand. That was no ordinary washing machine. And now we've lost it. And not only have we lost it, but we've lost it in one of the very last places on earth that we would want it to be. That is, if it's not already on its way to somewhere even worse ...'

Behind his back, Smith and Daddy Jesus exchanged baffled glances. 'I don't know what you mean, sir,' Smith ventured.

The colonel got to his feet. His face, caught by the diffused rays from the headlights, wore a ghastly grin.

'Tehran, Smith! Tehran! There are Iranian agents in the Embargoed Zone right now – it was confirmed by top-secret sources today. Now we know what they're doing there – they must be after the washing machine, if they haven't got it already ... When the brass find out about this, they'll cut our balls off!'

The Colonel lurched away, dragging his feet through the sand with the shambling gait of a newly broken man. His subordinates exchanged another glance, then Smith went after him while Daddy Jesus darted back to the bomb shelter. The colonel was fumbling at the door of his jeep when Smith caught up with him.

'Now, now, sir,' he wheedled. 'Perhaps we're all being a little bit over-emotional tonight. It's been a long and trying day. Tell you what: let's all have a little drink and talk it over. See if we can't find out what the problem is, and how to sort it out.'

Daddy Jesus emerged from the shelter with a bottle of Scotch and three plastic cups. He set them down on the bonnet of the colonel's jeep and poured three large doses. The colonel took one and threw it back, then signalled for another. The other two tasted their drinks, and waited for him to begin.

CHAPTER EIGHTEEN

Joseph took another swig of gin and orange juice. The others in the room had fallen silent, and Joseph was aware of them watching him, but he kept his own eyes on the TV screen fixed to the wall of the BBC's bureau. A long, cadaverous face, crowned by a ludicrous helmet, was building to the peak of its jeremiad.

'. . . *Yet another example of the systematic fabrication of stories by terrorist sympathizers in the liberal media . . .*'

'My fat sweaty arse!' declared Joseph. An AP producer raised his glass to him.

'. . . *Once again, the bias of the self-styled gatekeepers of truth has been exposed in an on-the-ground investigation by your own independent watchdog, blow-back dot net . . .*'

'On the ground? Bollocks!' sneered Joseph. 'You've never been on the ground, matey! Day-tripper embeds don't count.' There were ironic cheers from his colleagues.

'. . . *And so we say to 24/7 News: if you have nothing to hide, why don't you release your footage? . . .*'

'We already did, bugger-lugs! It's on the news tonight – all over the planet!' There were whoops around the room.

'. . . *Why don't you lay all doubts to rest,*' continued the face on the screen, '*by releasing for independent scrutiny the full, unedited digital files of all of the footage that your crew shot today? And let the world judge for itself if your story really is what you say it is?*'

The room filled with jeers and guffaws and catcalls. Somebody patted Joseph on the back, and ice and liquor tinkled into his glass. 'You show him, Joe!'

But Joseph wasn't listening. 'Oh no,' he murmured softly to himself. 'Oh no, oh no.'

In his pocket, his cell phone was buzzing.

CHAPTER NINETEEN

The colonel set his cup down, a little unsteadily, on the bonnet of the jeep. Daddy Jesus had switched the headlights off: the three men could see each other's faces in the faint light from the sky. The colonel's mouth had a bitter twist to it. He leaned his chest against the fender and put his elbows on the bonnet, cupping his face in his hands.

'I'm taking it for granted,' he began, 'that neither of you knows anything about the branch of mathematics which is known as "fuzzy logic".'

Daddy Jesus cleared his throat. 'I do,' he said, and when they both turned to stare at him he added, defensively, 'I saw a programme about it on Discovery.'

The colonel clapped his hands ironically. 'Well done, Sergeant! You *are* a clever one ... Well, for your benefit, then, Captain – and I'll try and keep this simple for you – fuzzy logic is a branch of mathematics that concerns itself with shades of truth. Whereas binary logic defines any given proposition as either true or false, as 1 or 0, fuzzy logic allows for degrees of truth, or falsity. Something can be 0.1 true or 0.9 false, for instance ... Am I losing you already, Captain?'

'On the contrary, Colonel. For me that's just another day at the office.'

The colonel smirked mirthlessly. 'Think so? I did say I was keeping it simple for you. Now, one of the things that fuzzy logic is good at, which traditional "crispy" logic doesn't do so well, is to allow you to set up mathematical systems which can handle vague concepts like hot and cold, empty and full, heavy or light. It's easy to state how much someone weighs, for example – that's just a figure in kilograms. But is that person therefore to be considered heavy or light? That depends on subjective judgements, and on such factors as age, gender, geographical origin, health and so on. These are valuations which human beings and even quite simple animals find it easy to make, but which baffle traditional computers, which need everything to be either one thing or another . . .'

'. . . That all sounds very interesting,' put in the captain. 'I might even Wikipedia it when I get home tonight, if I remember to. But can you please tell us what it has to do with our problem?'

'It has everything to do with our problem, Captain! A computer which is able to run on fuzzy logic can mimic the kind of basic operational judgements that people and animals make a million times a day without any diffi-culty. We feel a little warm so we walk a little slower. We feel very warm so we stop and find some shade. But we're able to feed other factors into the decision – are we in a hurry, for example, and if so, how much of a hurry, and why? We don't simply come to an abrupt halt as soon as the temperature reaches exactly 25 degrees centi-grade . . .'

His hands groped the air in search of understanding. 'Look, I'm not a mathematician either, or even an engineer. What's important is that fuzzy logic is already widely used to run machines that can, to an extent, think and act for themselves. It's used to control anti-lock brakes for automobiles, for example, and in digital imaging, and to power the artificial intelligence engines that run most computer games and simulations.'

The colonel paused and drank again, and then he smiled crookedly. 'Fuzzy logic chips allow modern washing machines to determine how much detergent and water they should use for any specified type and weight of load. And the same fuzzy logic, built into almost identical chips, is now being used by the Pentagon to drive the next generation of fully autonomous aerial drones and unmanned tanks and combat robots. Soon we'll be seeing entirely new types of war machines, able to operate alone on ground, sea or air, and self-fuelled by dead biomass found on the battlefield. And, of course, immune from prosecution for so-called war crimes.' He raised his glass to his listeners in mockery of a toast. 'I think, Captain, that perhaps by now you are beginning to see where I'm going with this.'

'Yes,' said Smith. 'I'm afraid I am.' He nodded, and Daddy Jesus refilled the colonel's drink.

The colonel went on: 'Now, our friends in Washington are wonderful people, of course, but every now and then they get it into their heads to try and keep secrets from

us, which isn't very nice. Fortunately for us, the manu-
facture of prototype fuzzy logic chips is a very specialized
matter, and the Pentagon has outsourced its production
to a small semi-conductor laboratory which also makes
chips for civilian industry. Once we found this out, we
arranged for a number of the military-grade chips to be
accidentally switched to the neighbouring production line,
which makes chips for commercial washing machines . . .'
He grinned. 'Not long after that, the Maelstrom Home
Appliance Corporation was forced to recall a whole batch
of its brand-new Circe line of de luxe washing machines.
They were making a terrible mess of any laundry put
through them. Particularly the whites: everything came
out all grey and streaky, and sort of furred. Naturally,
when the manufacturers realized why this was happening
they were horrified – this was potentially a major breach
of homeland security! But upon mature reflection, they
decided that it would be better not to mention the matter
to the government. After all, no harm had been done, really.
They'd got all the missing chips back, on the quiet . . . All
except for one that was in a machine that happened to
fall off a truck which was crossing a bridge over a deep
and turbulent river. And why should they worry about
that one?'

'I still don't quite get it,' interrupted Smith. 'If all you
wanted was one chip, why did you bring the whole washing
machine all the way here from America? Why not just take
the chip out of the machine and smuggle it by itself?'

'First, because you need a very skilled technician to remove the chip without damaging it. And second, for reasons of camouflage. It would have been very embarrassing for us if, by some remote chance, federal agents had caught our spies red-handed with the stolen microchip. But if the chip was still in its washing machine, well, that would be a different matter. Our people had an elaborate story prepared about how they were on a fishing trip and they happened to find a second-hand washing machine, slightly flood-damaged. You know how it is: so long as you maintain the barest veneer of deniability you can get away with just about anything.'

'So long as you keep things nice and fuzzy.'

The colonel sarcastically touched Smith's glass with his own. 'Quite so.'

'Another thing I don't get is why you brought this treasure here, to the Slob. Why wasn't it sent to a government laboratory, or locked away in a vault at headquarters?'

The colonel glanced away, towards the blinking red light on the radio mast. 'Oh, camouflage again,' he said. 'If we're spying on our allies, we have to consider that they might be spying on us. It was felt safer to tuck the machine away out of the limelight. The Slob was the perfect place – it's highly secure, and far away from HQ, but it's also visited a great deal, in the normal course of things, by the kind of aerospace scientists who would be qualified to remove and study the chip. And no one would ever think to look for it here.'

'No one except for the gypsies.'

The colonel, who had begun to regain some of his old

arrogance as the whisky worked on him, wilted again.

'No, you fool – except for the Iranians!' He turned a stricken face to them. 'You still don't get it, do you? You think it's just a coincidence that a weapons-grade washing machine was spirited into the Easy at exactly the same time that Iranian agents were detected there for the first time? *Real* Iranian agents, Captain, not the made-up ones we brief the security correspondents about every couple of weeks to frighten the public, the ones who we say are about to give the terrorists anti-tank weapons that actually work and anti-aircraft missiles and bombs filled with anthrax and all of the rest of it . . .' He broke off, overcome.

Captain Smith considered his commander's back for a few moments then put a hand on his shoulder. 'You know, sir . . . It occurs to me . . . There might just be one way that we could—'

The colonel whipped round and grabbed his forearm. 'What are you saying, Smith? Finish what you were going to say!'

'Well, sir, it's just that . . .'

'Spit it out, man! That's an order!'

'. . . If the Iranians really are now operating in the Easy, it occurs to me that there's only one terrorist leader there who is smart and ruthless and high-powered enough to be working with them.'

'Really? And you know this man?'

Smith smiled grimly. 'Oh, yes, sir. He's an old adversary. A true fanatic, covered in blood. But I think that maybe, just maybe, we could get to him.'

'How?'

'The old-fashioned way: money. My guess is that the Iranians won't have told him why they want that washing machine; I've heard that those Persian bastards play their cards close to their chests. If we come over the top at him with a big enough offer, maybe we can get him to double-cross them, and give us the machine instead.'

'What? . . . Splendid! Do it, Smith! That's also an order!'

'We'll need money, sir. A lot of money. We'll have to honour any pledge we make to the terrorist, you know. In this line of business it doesn't do to get a reputation for welching.'

'How much will you need?'

'Ten thousand euros, I should think . . . No, wait. Better make it twenty.'

The colonel scarcely seemed to hear him. 'Twenty thousand euros, eh? Whatever. I'll go and get it from my office. Meanwhile, you set the wheels in motion.'

Smith waited until the colonel's jeep had disappeared behind an abandoned billet, and then he turned and looked at Daddy Jesus.

'Well, fancy that,' he said. 'He keeps that kind of money in his office . . . If only we'd known that before, we wouldn't have had to steal that darn machine in the first place, eh?'

'No, boss.'

'Come to think of it, stealing the washing machine and palming it off onto Cobra was *your* idea, wasn't it? . . .' He considered his sidekick. 'You're not an Iranian agent, are you, Daddy Jesus?'

'No, boss.'

'Thought not ... Still, I'm getting a little nervous about all this talk of Iranians in the Embargoed Zone. Driscoll was hinting at it too, and he can't be wrong about everything ... No, I think we'd better finish this thing right now, just to be on the safe side. Get me Cobra on the phone. We can offer to bung him a grand of White's cash, just to make sure it all goes off smoothly.'

Daddy Jesus dialled his cell phone, listened, then cut the connection.

'His phone's powered off, boss.'

'Off? ... Oh, well, get me a fix on his phone's position. We can do that even with the phone switched off, so long as he still has the battery in. Then at least we'll know where to find him.'

Daddy Jesus went to his jeep and tapped at the computer clamped to its dashboard.

'No good, boss,' he called, a few moments later. 'His phone's completely dead – he must have taken the battery out.'

Captain Smith raised his eyebrows. 'But I told him to keep his phone on at all times ... He's deliberately gone stealth on us! I'm beginning to smell a rat, Daddy Jesus. Go and round up those idiots from our armoured detachment. They're going to have to escort us back into the Easy tonight: we need to pick up that washing machine while we still know where it is. Better safe than sorry with all these Iranians about, eh?'

CHAPTER TWENTY

The general who commanded the EZ Division had political ambitions, and he liked to host distinguished guests. So shortly after he assumed command he had decreed the construction of a new VIP compound on a bluff above the camp. There, visiting politicians, arms dealers, rivals and journalists could be briefed and flattered by his elite teams of whispering aides and shiny-eyed press officers, their beds made, meals served and laundry washed by a special cadre of young female soldiers, chosen for their high curves and low self-esteem. Driscoll was given the best of the guest quarters, a private chalet with its own living room and kitchenette and an en suite bedroom with a big double bed. All was clean and correct but, in that uniquely military way, just a little bit dingy: the ever-so-slightly damp bed sheets were ever-so-slightly grey, and the plastic lamps and linoleum floor tiles had faded a shade from their prime; the armchairs and sofa were made of a dull mustard vinyl which matched, almost, the laminate bookshelves and the unstocked, stale cupboards in the windowless kitchenette. The best thing about it, Driscoll decided, was the view: a picture window in the sitting room allowed him to gaze proprietorially out over a magical kingdom of tents and huts and aerials and jeeps and latrines, where ley-lines of grey-green duckboards criss-crossed the track-churned sand.

Inside, the bedroom was smaller than Driscoll had expected, square and cell-like, with only one small window of very thick glass set high in the wall. The door was made of one-inch steel plate and opened outwards into the living-room; the bedroom, it had been explained to Driscoll, had been reinforced to act as a bomb shelter, so its guests could sleep soundly at night.

Still wearing his kevlar jacket and his helmet, Driscoll paced back and forth across the little bedroom, a phone clamped to his ear.

'So, 24/7 won't play ball, huh? So where do we go from here?' He listened and yawned. 'I don't agree, Cass. If we give them more time then we lose our momentum. We have to go in for the kill now, while we still have everyone's attention.' He glanced sideways at the mirror and met his own gaze. He looked tired, he saw, tired and grim. He shucked his shoulders, and felt the lovely burden of his armour bear down on his back. A dangerous idea, planted during his jeep ride with Colonel White, burst thrillingly into flower.

'Listen, Cass, there is one way that we can guarantee to keep 24/7 off-balance, to keep this story going and, above all, to keep it to ourselves. Why don't I chase the story down myself, in person, no army escort, on the ground, *inside the Embargoed Zone?*'

There was a moment's stunned silence, and then a tinny babble filled his ear. Driscoll waved it away. 'No, seriously,

Cass, think about it: I could go and visit the scene where they staged the incident. I could talk to people who took part – they'll probably confess freely enough, if they think I'm just another sympathetic foreign journalist. I could doorstep the cameraman: why dick around with 24/7's PR people in New York when we can go straight to the source? Let's face it, this West is probably just another stupid tripod-humper, who'll give up the grift for a fistful of nuts. And there's another lead I can follow up as well – I have names and a home address for some of the actors–'

His editor interrupted him again. Driscoll shrugged. 'Sure, Cass, sure – it's dangerous. Okay, some TV and newspaper correspondents still go alone into the Embargoed Zone, but let's face it: they're all either terrorist supporters or else too scared of the terrorists to tell the truth. But it'll be different for me: if the terrorists work out who *I* am, and what *I* stand for ... Well, let's just hope they don't, eh?'

Again Driscoll ignored the reply, his idea skipping on ahead of him. 'There's something else too, Cass,' he confided. 'Something big. I caught wind of it this evening: something known only as "the Toploader Project". I don't know exactly what it is, yet, but it ties in, somehow, with the faked footage, or the Iranian agents, perhaps both ... The local intelligence boys are dedicating all their resources to it, which means it must be a very big deal indeed. And when I mentioned this "Toploader Project" to one of my top-secret private sources this evening – you might know the guy, Colonel White, he was military attaché in Washington until a couple of months ago – he nearly crashed the jeep he was driving! He actually started to shake!'

Cass sounded impressed. Driscoll nodded at the mirror. 'Yes, it must be something really hush-hush,' he mused. 'Toploader . . . Probably some kind of mortar, I guess – with mortars you load the round in through the top of the tube.'

His face began to frown at him. 'But here's the thing that puzzles me, Cass: the terrorists in the Easy already make their own mortars – I'm in mortar range of them right now, by the way, they could fire at any time. So why is the army suddenly so upset about them having mortars? . . . Unless this is some kind of new mortar – a really, really big one, maybe. Some kind of mortar of mass destruction. Maybe firing those new terrorist pig-flu bombs one of my sources briefed me about this morning . . .'

He flipped open the lid of his laptop computer, which was set on the dresser in front of him. 'Goodbye, Cass,' he said briskly. 'I have to get online, right now. This is big – way bigger than I'd thought. If I'm going into the Easy tomorrow I need to find out all I can about what's really going on there, and about this mysterious "Toploader Project". It's time I consulted the blogosphere.'

CHAPTER TWENTY-ONE

Moon woke on a canvas stretcher, and wondered where he was. He seemed to be in some kind of tiny metal room, which was spinning around him. Beyond his feet, a light glowed red above what might have been a door, revealing cream-painted walls cluttered with pipes and wires and valves, and strange green tubes and metal boxes secured by buckles and straps. His throat ached, and when he closed his eyes bad cannabis dreams slithered across his lids, forcing him to open them again and deal with the spinning. A line from a song that he hated was playing in a continuous loop in his head, whining through a jagged hole in his left temple, sawing back around behind his eyes and then emerging again on the right, slicing at his frontal lobe. Try as he might, he could not stop it. Deep in his stomach an ancient evil was stirring, impelled by the centrifugal force that whirled the little room. There was a heavy smell of diesel oil. 'What is this place?' Moon asked himself, and then had just enough time to turn his face sideways before the vomit erupted. Some of it pooled on the stretcher but most vanished into the darkness, spilling, he guessed dully, to the floor. There wasn't that much of it: he had eaten nothing that night except a Twix bar and a bag of crisps which he'd bought at the service station; he found himself regretting this as he twisted half off the stretcher to cope with the dry, racking heaves. A long time later he laid himself flat again, heedless of the rising stench around him. 'Well,' he said to himself, almost soberly, 'that's that . . . and I'm glad that it's over.' As he gave himself up to sleep he noticed that the room had at least stopped spinning. True, there was still a rhythmic thudding in his ears, and his body was shaken and jarred by mysterious external jolts, but compared to what he'd already been through this seemed little cause for worry.

It was silence and darkness which woke Moon again, he could not say how much later. His head pulsed as he sat up and swung his feet to the ground. The metal floor of the compartment felt horribly slick and slimy. Despite the surging pain in his forehead, he could now make out the word 'exit', printed on the red light which glowed by the hatch. He reached a hand out to touch the sign, then snatched it back as it gave to his touch. There was a whining noise and the door split in two, like a clam-shell, and slowly opened. Of course: a tank; he must have crawled into a tank's cargo compartment – the space used to store extra ammunition and weapons, or to transport stretcher-cases or infantry dismounts – and passed out there.

As he stepped down from the hull his feet sank into loose sand. Beyond the loom of the tank, half-remembered from the night before, he saw another line of metal shapes stretching off into the dark. Where, he wondered dully, had his new friends Lenny and Johnny gone? It wasn't very kind of them to abandon him here in the tank park. They might at least have left him some water, or told him how to get back to his billet.

He took another uncertain step clear of the tank, peering about him. There was a hot, fresh stink of diesel exhaust, which almost made him gag again. And why was the tank's engine ticking, as if cooling down? His eyes were just adapting to the night when a torch switched on in front of him, shining into his face just long enough to blind him again. A huge shape reared over him, seized him by the shirtfront and slammed him back against the tank.

'Where the fuck are you going, soldier?' the shape hissed, swatting Moon's head around to face it. The light flicked on for another half-second. 'Were you *asleep* in your tank, you dozy cunt?' The giant snuffled at his face. 'Have you been *drinking*?' The torch beam flickered towards the open hatch behind Moon's shoulder. 'Holy fuck, you've thrown up in the back of the tank! What the fuck is the matter with this crew? I warned the boss, I told him: ask an officer for his best men and he'll always give you his worst . . .' The stranger began to shake Moon back and forth like a rag doll, and Moon decided he didn't really care that much, so long as he wasn't sick again. Then a meaty hand came out of the darkness and slapped him hard across the mouth.

'Listen, shit-bucket,' hissed the stranger's mouth, right by his ear, so close and so vicious that Moon was afraid it would bite him. 'When we get back to the other side, me and Smith are going to *do* you for this, in ways that you've never even heard of. But right now you're going to do your fucking job and get out there with the other dismounts and watch our perimeter. Your place is over that way.' Moon saw a finger jab at the darkness, towards where he guessed the Slob must be. 'Now go!'

Moon dragged himself to his feet, too terrified and nauseous to say anything, and staggered off in what he thought was the indicated direction. He'd only gone a metre when he felt himself yanked back by the collar, so hard that he crashed to the ground.

'What the fuck do you think you're doing?' the giant hissed at him. 'You forgot to take your stuff!'

Moon heard his assailant rummaging in the back of the tank. The ground was soft, and despite his terror Moon felt his eyelids steal together again. Then a boot crunched in the sand beside his ear and Moon grunted and jerked upright, in agony and shock, as a jagged bundle of steel and fabric crashed onto his midriff.

'Take that and fuck off!' hissed his assailant.

Wriggling over onto his throbbing stomach, Moon dragged the parcel with him as he crawled off into the darkness. After what felt to him like a great distance his head bumped into something very hard, which turned out to be the wheel of a truck. Moon lay still for a while, listening to his breath as it steadied and slowed. There was no other sound apart from the hum of a drone a little way off, and the scuffle of wind in the weeds. Of his attacker there was no sign. And then Moon noticed that the wheel he had struck was half-buried in the ground, and that under the truck, between its front wheels, drift-sand lay soft and clean as a new-made bed. He yawned convulsively. There would be time enough in the morning, he decided, to deal with this hangover, and to find his way home.

CHAPTER TWENTY-TWO

As tired as she was, Flora did not think that she could sleep. The events of the day kept mobbing her. Instead of going to bed she took off her shoes, keeping her coat on; she lit a candle, and settled in a chair in the hallway to await her father's return. She tried to calm herself by reading the flight manual that Tony had left for her; she knew it could only have been him. But the candle was made from poorly rendered goat lard, and it guttered and danced in the draughts in the hallway, until, some time later, Flora realized that she was dreaming. It was her favourite dream, the clear, waking one where she could fly − not like an aircraft but like a bird, a lark or a swallow, one of those tiny, tumbling birds that seem to fly just for the joy of it. With an effort only of the will, Flora could now soar high into the air then swoop vertiginously down again, almost grazing the rooftops. It was, as always, her own house which turned slowly below her, her own neighbourhood, shrinking rapidly now as she rocketed up for hundreds then thousands of metres. She could, she knew, go on for ever, but the cold up here was beginning to sober her, and the winds of the jet stream wanted to sweep her away. She had no wings, she knew; only her illusion supported her, and there below her, so small that she could barely see it now, was all that was left that was real to her … Wet clouds were blowing past, thickening beneath her, trying to block her return. She would have to make her choice soon, as always, as the wind called with its wild frozen roar.

There was something new in the dream this time, a dull rhythmic thud, which began to rock her as she hung, poised, in mid-air, disrupting her balance and trim. The thudding grew louder, stalling her dream, plunging her back to wakefulness. That was a diesel engine, she thought, sitting up in her chair, cold and groggy and stiff – perhaps it was Tony, bringing her father home. But when she checked outside she saw that the street was dark and silent. She looked across to the alley where Cobra had lurked – where he might be lurking still – then went back into the apartment, bolting the front door behind her. The draught from the door had extinguished her candle, and she was trying to relight it when another strange noise stayed her hand. It came from the rear of the apartment, a faint, barely audible scraping.

On her stockinged feet, Flora walked silently down the hallway and into the kitchen. The noise sounded again, closer and louder now; it came from the locked back door. Her father, fearful of disturbing her, must be trying to sneak in though the backyard. Flora's heart surged. But as she reached for the doorknob it suddenly vanished in a spray of splinters, flying out from under her hand, as the door sprang open and smashed into her head. She was hurled backwards, the room flashing off into white ringing silence.

CHAPTER TWENTY-THREE

Captain Smith stepped through the wreckage of the door into a room lit by his own darting torch beam.

'Your men can wait outside this time, Lieutenant,' he said, speaking over his shoulder. 'I'm afraid this mission is extra-top secret, ultra hush-hush and all that sort of thing. As for you, Daddy Jesus, you owe me twenty euros: I told you I could pick that lock!'

Smith scratched his right ear with the muzzle of his un-holstered pistol. Daddy Jesus followed him inside, his carbine dangling from one hand. 'But you didn't pick it, boss. I broke it with my shoulder!'

'Not so, dear boy: it wouldn't have given like that if I hadn't already loosened the dead bolt ...' Smith's torch picked out something on the floor. 'Oh, hello – who's this?'

Daddy Jesus bent over the body on the floor, which was groggily trying to raise itself, then flipped it over so they could see its face.

'Ah ...' said Smith. 'The girl from the news report. I'll keep an eye on her while you go and check the other rooms, Daddy Jesus. If the place is clear, go and look for the machine. The computer says that the professor's workshop is in the front of the apartment – it should be through that door over there.'

Captain Smith helped Flora to her feet and then, supporting her elbow, he steered her down the hallway to the chair she had dozed in. Smith pulled up another chair so that their knees were almost touching, his torch beam probing her face.

'The place is clear, boss,' said Daddy Jesus as he clumped past them from the bedrooms. 'No one else home. I'll go and check the workshop.'

Smith leaned forward and studied Flora's face. She had a red mark on her right temple which, he knew, would soon turn into a bruise. She turned her face away from him.

'Are you all right?' he asked. 'I'm sorry about your door. But it could have been much worse, you know: we usually use a shotgun slug for that sort of thing. And the commandos in my escort wanted to throw in a stun grenade – in the middle of the night!'

She did not speak, keeping her face turned away from him. Smith recollected himself, and swung the torch beam away.

'Silly me! That light must be quite painful for you, after that blow to your head.' He placed the torch on its end, on the hallway credenza beside Flora's dead candle, so that its beam washed off the ceiling, bathing the hallway in soft yellow light. Smith saw the girl peep at him and gave her a reassuring smile.

'We'll just sit here together, shall we, while my friend

takes care of business? Then we'll go on our way, and we won't bother you any more.'

Daddy Jesus reappeared in the hallway, shaking his head. Smith noticed the girl winding herself up in her chair, as if preparing to spring away from them.

'It's not there, boss,' said Daddy Jesus.

Smith rocked back in his chair, staring up at him. 'Are you sure?'

'Most of the washing machines in there are old, and none of them was made by Maelstrom. And there isn't any toploader.'

'Oh dear . . .' mused Smith. 'Oh dear . . . That does change things . . .' He turned sad eyes to Flora, who was pretending to ignore them both. 'Well, my dear. Where is it?'

'Where's what?'

'You know. What we came for.'

'I don't know what you're talking about.'

The captain sighed 'Right. Have it your way, for now . . . Then can you tell me where your father is, please?'

'I don't know.'

Daddy Jesus's bulk stirred in the gloom. 'We haven't much time, boss. Let me take her into one of the bedrooms. I'll soon get her talking.'

'For shame, Daddy Jesus! I have a daughter her age! And don't you prefer boys, anyway?'

'She's skinny enough. At night all cats are grey.'

Smith noted that the girl, though still glowering, was also trembling.

'Well, I'll bear that in mind, Daddy Jesus. But let's try

explaining the situation to our young friend here – Flora, right?' She gave a start at the sound of her name. 'Daddy Jesus, please go out to the APC and fetch my computer. And the bag too.'

Smith waited until Daddy Jesus had disappeared down the hallway, and then he reached over and switched off his torch. The hallway instantly went black. He sat there, eyes closed, and listened to the girl as she tried not to breathe, to the little rustles of her clothes as she fought her rising terror, flinching away from all the groping hands and smashing blows that her blindness conjured from the dark. Sometimes you have to be cruel to be kind, Smith consoled himself: it was this or a hood, and all that other unpleasantness.

A pale blue light appeared at the end of the corridor, the screen of a computer which Daddy Jesus bore before him. Smith switched his torch back on, and the girl gave a jump as he rematerialized: she had already lost her bearings in the darkness, and was looking for him in entirely the wrong direction.

'Set it down there, Daddy Jesus,' said the captain. 'On that little credenza. Now, Flora: please give me your full attention.'

Smith struck a key and the blue screensaver was replaced by a clutter of lines and colours and tiny printed legends. Smith watched the girl as she struggled to make sense of the shapes on the computer and then, when her face turned impassive, he began.

'Now this, as you see, is a three-dimensional map of

your neighbourhood. And this' – he clicked to zoom in – 'is your building, and this' – click again – 'is your apartment. Now if I just go up here and pull down this little tab, you'll see . . . here, now . . . okay, there – your name, and the name of your father, and your little brother, and also the names of your mother and older brother, although their names are in a grey font, because sadly they're no longer with us.'

Despite herself she was watching now.

'Now, if you look beside your family's names you'll see a figure, and you'll notice that each one of you is listed as a number four. This is a scale which we in the security services use to designate how much of a terrorist any given terrorist is, on a scale of one to five. For obvious reasons, everyone born in the Easy is automatically assigned level three, which means they are considered to be collaborators in terror. Level four' – he waved a hand at her – 'means you are considered to be active in the support of terrorism. Level five indicates that you are an active terrorist who is possibly implicated in committing atrocities. Your late brother was of course a level five terrorist.'

For the first time the girl spoke. 'My brother was a resistance fighter,' she said coldly.

Smith smiled politely. 'Oh, I daresay he thought so too.'

She leaned towards him, points of red on her cheeks. 'None of the rest of us has ever done anything to you. Why are you calling us terrorists?'

'You all became number fours on the day we killed your brother and your mother. The computer automatically promoted you. You see, once the army has killed any member of your family, even if they weren't involved in anything, even if it was just an accident, then we have to assume that if the rest of the family ever gets the chance they'll seek revenge against our own people. So we rate them as level fours, which are never allowed to leave the Easy, ever.' He shrugged. 'Of course, what with all the trouble we've had down the years, by now just about everybody in the Embargoed Zone, and in all of the other autonomous terrorist entities under our supervision, is rated at four or above.'

'So just because somebody might conceivably be able to attack you, you treat them as if they already have?'

'I suppose it might seem a little unfair, to some people, but what can we do? We can't afford to take any risks with the well-being of our own people.'

'And what about our well-being?'

The captain tapped the screen sadly. 'It says here that you're all terrorists.'

The girl was silent again, staring at the computer. Smith leaned forward, rotating the image on the screen.

'Of course,' he said, 'our computer model of the Easy is constantly being updated. Let me show you how that works . . .' He frowned at the screen, then brightened. 'Ah! Now what would you say that is?' He pointed to a small hut in the backyard of Flora's building.

'It's a chicken coop. It's where we get our eggs from. Some of the children keep rabbits in it.'

Smith clicked on the image and a little tab popped up

160

beside it. 'Correct!' he said. 'That's what it says here too! Of course, if further information came to light that description could easily be changed.' He began to type, two-fingered. 'Terrorist ... structure ... weapons ... storage facility ... There! Finished.' He clicked on the image again.

'So you see how easy it is to change things,' he told Flora. 'You'd be surprised how many people in the Easy have quietly managed to work their way down from four to two, by being cooperative. Level twos can be allowed to leave here, when they're no longer needed, so long as some third party country will take them in. But people who are asked to cooperate and who refuse ...' He paused, for effect it seemed, and then he paused a little longer, and the pause was becoming just a little awkward when a clap of thunder tore the stillness of the night, followed by a howling, whirring moan. There was an explosion just behind the building, flashing red through the broken kitchen door, and the concrete walls lurched and settled. The girl clutched the arms of her chair.

'Ah,' said the captain, pleased. 'That will have been that weapons store you used to have out the back. Shame about those rabbits and chickens. But if anyone in the outside world should ever ask about them, which is highly unlikely, we'll just point out that it was the terrorists' fault, for using them as shields.' Daddy Jesus guffawed in the shadows.

'What do you want?' she asked quietly.

'You know what we want: we want the washing machine. We want to know where they took it.'

'I don't know where anyone took anything. I already told you.'

'You must know something. Or do I have to show you our computer model of Hilltown hospital, and the list of patients currently admitted there, and who's in which bed?'

She was silent for a while, and he knew then that he had her. 'It's Cobra you want,' she said finally. 'He's the one behind it all. He brought the machine here. We didn't want it.'

'So where has Cobra taken it?'

'Cobra? He hasn't taken it anywhere. He was here earlier, trying to get it back from us. But it was gone already. Somebody must have taken it while I was out.'

'Gone? You mean *someone else* has it?'

Captain Smith began to wonder whether, for the first time in his career, he might have stumbled into matters too deep for his comprehension. Were there really forces at work in the Embargoed Zone that he could not command? Iranians? Venezuelans? Nigerians? Koreans? *Were the legends true?* He steeled his voice. 'Who has it, Flora? And where has your father gone?'

Smith leaned forward and stared into her eyes. She looked scared, but held his gaze. 'I don't know where he is. I wasn't here when he left. Perhaps whoever has the washing machine took my father with them. Perhaps they kidnapped him. I don't know.'

Smith stared at her for a few moments, then looked at Daddy Jesus. 'We'd better get out of here,' he said. 'It'll be dawn soon. Go and round up our escorts.'

His face resumed its earlier kindly expression. 'Flora,' he

said, 'you seem like a nice girl. I don't know why you would refuse to help us – I suspect that loyalty to Cobra would not be among your reasons.' He lifted the flap on his bag and held it open before her.

'There's five thousand euros in here,' Smith told her. 'That's the reward for helping us to recover the washing machine. And this' – he pulled out a wad of notes – 'is an advance payment. Five hundred euros, to show I mean business, and to help with expenses. If you hear anything – and I think you will, Flora – you give me a call on this.' He took a cell phone from a pocket in the bag. 'Here's a power adaptor to go with it. Do you have any way of keeping the phone charged when the power here is off?'

She nodded.

'Good. Keep the phone on you at all times so I can get hold of you. Switch it to vibrate – you don't want it to ring when strangers are present.'

'No,' she said. 'I wouldn't want people to think I'd become an informer.'

CHAPTER TWENTY-FOUR

Colonel White sat alone at a drone console, smoking a cigarette, while the fingers of his free hand caressed the shaft of a joystick. Smoking was banned in the drone room, no matter how exalted one's rank, but so too were computer games, even on the graveyard shift. As the evening dragged on, however, he and the two duty drone jocks had come to an unspoken truce. He could do whatever he liked now, as far as they were concerned; engrossed in their online multiplayer game of *Bitchslapper III – Curb Sandwich*, they hadn't even noticed when he blew up that chicken coop.

His cell phone buzzed. 'Yes,' he said, and heard the hiss of static and the rumble of an engine. 'Have you got it?'

'Erm, no.' Smith's voice crackled in his ear. White shut his eyes tightly and allowed his forehead to sink into his cigarette-bearing hand. 'Then where is it?'

'Don't know yet. We have a couple of leads, though. Won't be long.'

Colonel White opened his eyes and looked back over his own career. From the age of eighteen onwards it had never seemed anything less than glittering. For it all to end here . . . Over in the corner of the control room, their faces grey in the light from their screen, the drone jocks were garrotting a rival pimp, so they could make off with his Bentley.

'What about this terrorist mastermind of yours? What have you got from him?'

Smith's reply had the squared-off, modular distortion of a voice that has been scrambled well and then badly reassembled. 'We're still trying to contact him, sir. But he has deactivated his cell phone. As soon as he puts the battery back in we'll know where he is.'

'What's his name and phone number?'

'Dear Lord, I can't tell you that, sir! Even if we weren't on the radio! He's going to be my confidential agent – his identity is need-to-know only!'

White had to think somewhat harder than he was used to. 'Don't worry about being overheard, Captain,' he managed. 'This is a specially scrambled line we're on now – air force encryption, the best there is. If you give me his number, I might be able to trace his phone even if he has taken the battery out – through its electromagnetic resonance, that sort of thing. It's a new technology we have in the air force. Very secret. You won't have heard of it.'

There was a long pause, during which Colonel White listened to the APC's tracks grinding through some structure or other, and then Smith spoke again. 'Oh, all right,' he said. 'Have you got a pen?'

Cobra's donkey was a clever beast, with a nose for the weeds that sprouted, unseen, in the hidden corners of bombed-out lots; it had taken Cobra half the night to find it again.

Wearily, he locked the massive, gunmetal-grey door of his lair, then plodded down the damp concrete steps that led to the damp concrete floor of his cellar. Reaching the bottom, he dropped his keys and his pistol on a walnut occasional table, then took out his lighter and lit a fresh candle. Its flame revealed a corridor which stretched to the far end of the basement, set on either side with half a dozen metal doors. The walls were stacked head-high with cases of expired military field rations and with boxes of plastic shoes, out-of-date antibiotics, Chinese batteries, weevilly flour and condemned baby formula. Above this hoarded wealth, the candlelight flickered on posters of Cobra's martyred heroes, the early ones, boys and young men who had died when there was still paper and ink left to spare for them. Once glossy, the faces in the posters had become dull with dust and age, and the light failed to catch in the blacks of their eyes.

The nearest door opened into a small, low-ceilinged room which Cobra had made as cosy as a former interrogation cell could hope to be. There was a single bed dressed with a cotton quilt with yellow flowers on it, and on the wall above it hung a hyperrealistic, supersaturated image – whether photograph or painting it was difficult to tell – of a lake with green trees and snowy mountains. Cobra put his candle on a dresser by the bed, beside the photograph of his exiled wife and children, and stripped down to his underwear, sighing and grumbling. He put on his pyjamas, then fished around on the floor for a phone adaptor which was attached, via an inverter, to an old truck battery under the bed. Plugging his phone into the charger, he attached another cable to the phone's data port, then pressed the 'on' button. No sooner had the phone flickered back to life than it began to beep angrily at him, again and again, as text messages and missed-call notifications jostled onto its screen.

It's late, thought Cobra. I ought to let that bastard stew. It would serve him right. But when the last beep had echoed off the concrete walls he pressed the call key and sat back on the bed.

'Hello, Captain? Yes, it's me . . . Now calm down, it's not my fault. My phone was dead – the battery ran out, and I only got home a minute ago . . . Never mind where I was, we have to be quick – this battery I've plugged into isn't going to last long either. It's knackered; I told you to get me a new one . . . Look, if it's about that washing machine then I don't know where they took it . . . What do you mean, "who is they?" . . . Well if you don't know who "they" is, what's it worth to you to find out? . . . Now calm down, Captain. I'm not trying to hustle you. I just want to get paid, for a change . . . A hundred euros? You must be joking! I want five. I saw them taking it away this evening, before I could stop them . . . Calm down, I'm getting to "who"; I saw them myself this evening, at Sam Miller's repair shop in Hilltown – you might remember Sam's son, Jake Miller? He was one of my mine; I set him up for the drone-strike myself. Anyway, I persuaded old Miller to buy that junk you foisted on me. But then you asked for it back so I went to collect it this evening, only to see old Miller carting it off in the back of a Land Rover . . . No, I'm not talking nonsense, they really did have a Land Rover; it was one those armoured press jeeps. That Tony guy was driving it – I don't know his surname; he's a cameraman or producer or something, for 24/7 News.'

It could have been his tired nerves, it could have been the dancing candle, or the ectoplasmic residue of all the screams and prayers that had soaked into the walls of that dark little room, horrors to which Cobra was normally indifferent, but he was sure that he heard a ghostly howl on his cell phone, keening across the ether, over the spectral rumbling diesel and the grinding of the gears. 'Hey, was that you, Captain? Did you hear it too? . . . No, it wasn't me, either . . . Strange.'

Not for the first time that night, Tony cursed himself for his foolishness. Here they were, past midnight, driving around the northern fringes of the Embargoed Zone, the only vehicle moving in the black, curfewed night. The streets here, what was left of them, were laid out in a grid pattern, and every hundred metres or so the Land Rover had to cross the yawning mouth of a cross street, covered in enfilade, Tony knew, by machine guns on the wall. It was less than a kilometre away, here. The cross streets presented themselves to Tony, not normally a fanciful young man, as dizzy concrete chasms, toppling away towards the hard certain death of the wall. He had to fight the urge to accelerate wildly through each junction to the relative shelter on the other side. But this could be interpreted as suspicious behaviour, and fatally penalized. He imagined fingers tightening on bored and sleepless triggers, and forced himself to stay calm.

Flora's father half-lay in the passenger seat, his face pressed against a window, sleeping peacefully. They could have been home hours ago, but Sam had insisted on waiting for the boss man to return to the camp, so that he could be paid in cash in full. Tony had a very strong notion, as he turned into the street where Flora lived, that she was not going to thank him for keeping her father out in the drone-haunted night. He reached over to shake him.

'Hey, Sam,' he said, 'wake up.' And then Tony saw Flora running out into the cone of the headlights, and the joyful expression on her face, and he left Sam where he was, still stirring groggily. His foot was just pressing on the brake when his cell phone rang. Tony picked it off the dashboard.

'Hello?' he said. 'Hello?'

Cobra was drifting into his first true dream of the night when he was lifted a foot off the bed. He fell back again, his heart racing and his lungs coiled up into his throat. For a moment the terror was absolute, an injection of neat adrenalin right into the brainstem, and then he fell back on the mattress, his heart still stuttering. Sonic boom, he told himself. Few people would sleep properly again in the Easy that night – man, woman or hysterical child. The booms always came in pairs, like shoes being dropped on the ceiling: at some point, between now and the dawn, it would amuse the air force to rip the sky open again, right over their heads

... Well, it might traumatize the children, but he, Cobra, was too old a campaigner to let it bother him. He could sleep from one boom to the next. Still, he thought, let's not make it hard on yourself. He reached out from under the bedclothes, switched off his cell phone, then settled down to sleep again.

Flora halted in the roadway, waiting for the jeep to coast up to her. Then its headlights twitched, as if it had been stung, and its back wheels slid out from behind it and it lurched broadside to a stop. Flora saw Tony open his door, quite slowly, and then he took one step away from the jeep and fell to the ground and started to crawl; only then did she hear, or perhaps notice, or remember, the brisk sound of metal punching metal, and the hiss of air escaping from blown-out tyres. Dust lashed her eyes, and gravel stung her face. There was another crack – and this time she heard the whirr that preceded it – and the Land Rover lurched again and settled down on its belly with an air of finality, like a poleaxed bullock, its headlights staring in mute dismay.

Sobbing, choking on grit, Flora scrambled on her hands and knees towards the lights, and the smoke which now trickled from the Land Rover's engine. Her hand sank into something soft and hot and wet and she heard Tony gasp, and then he spoke to her.

'Get away from here,' he murmured, as if from another room. 'Run.'

Tony's right leg and the right half of his pelvis had been

171

replaced by a thick bloody fringe of shredded cloth and skin and flesh and vital organs. With a strength she had not suspected in herself, Flora managed to heave and tug him another four or five metres from the Land Rover, into the partial shelter of a flat-bed truck which sat rusting by the road. She cradled his head on her shoulder, as what was left of his blood pooled black and oily in the dirt around them. She could think of nothing good to say to him.

Figures were converging on the scene from all sides, flashing in and out of view in the zig-zagging torch beams. Candles flickered in windows up and down the street, and hands pulled her away from Tony, though she tried to fight them. She was looking at the Land Rover again, lit by the flames that licked out from under its bonnet. A little two-inch hole had appeared high in the armoured hull, just behind the cab. Orange in the light of the flames, a human figure was sprawled in the passenger seat. Blood dribbled from the open door onto the sand, meandering on for a few feet to make a common pool with Tony's. It seemed incredible to her, almost funny, that no one else had noticed this yet. And just as she launched herself towards the stricken jeep there was another concussion in the sky, louder this time, a throatier whirr, and then the Land Rover, the torch beams, the shouting rescuers, the clamouring boys, were erased from the scene, screen-wiped into oblivion by a sunburst, which flared, blossomed and died, fading to a new tableau of smoke, burning debris and carbonized bodies and rancid soot. The white Land Rover was now black, its armoured hide peeled open like a banana. Savoury blue flames licked the mass on the passenger seat.

Flora picked herself up from the stinking earth and slowly raised both hands to her face. Then she turned and picked her way – thoughtfully, a witness might have said – off into the darkness.

'Where's Colonel White?' Smith asked from the doorway. The two drone jockeys looked up, startled, from their illicit computer game.

'Uh, don't know, Captain,' said the older of the two. 'He was here until a little while ago ... Then I guess he must have left.'

'Well I suppose that's a good thing. Must have been a quiet night?'

'Yes, Captain.' The drone jockey glanced at the monitors, and then he looked again more closely, and frowned. 'Uh, actually, Captain, that's not quite true ...' He punched a few keys. 'It says here in the log that the Colonel took out a terrorist weapons factory tonight. Wow – they were making some new kind of Ebola bomb, according to his notes.'

'Right,' Smith grunted, and turned to go.

'Oh, and there's more, sir. He also destroyed a terrorist's headquarters that was disguised as a residential apartment block. He must have been a major terrorist – the Colonel sent a fighter-bomber to drop a one-ton smart bomb to home onto his cell phone signal.'

'*What?* Are you sure?'

'Yes, sir. And there was another drone strike too. On a Land Rover that the terrorists were using to move weapons.

It says here that the Colonel used two kinetic missiles to immobilize it and then a hellfire, one of the new thermo-baric ones, to sterilize the scene. All targets confirmed destroyed. Do you want to see the videos?'

But Captain Smith had already vanished, leaving the door to swing slowly shut behind him.

CHAPTER TWENTY-FIVE

The sand blew in from the seashore, day after day, year after year, pushing its fingers inland. There were places, gaps between the rusting cars and crumbling walls, where it pooled, so white that it seemed to glow in the darkness. The sand was better than nothing, Flora told herself, over and over again, until, not long before daybreak, she began to wonder what she meant by that. You could use the sand to clean your hands: perhaps that had something to do with it. She thrust her blood-caked fingers into it, repeatedly, until they felt raw. Perhaps that too was better than nothing. She could not feel the pre-dawn cold, but she noticed how it shook her, as if she were still sobbing.

She was sitting on a patch of wasteland that ran behind her street, a tongue of the no-man's-land that stretched from the edge of Hilltown north to the wall. Her back rested against the cold steel of a truck's wheel, half-buried in the sand. Stars shone through the holes in the low cloud. Before her she could see the back of the building where she and her parents and brothers had lived. The family washing still flapped on the clothes-line, where she had pegged it the morning before. Weeds nodded at her from the garbage.

There was still Gabriel. If she could focus on him, perhaps this could be managed. She had been able to cope with this sort of thing before; she had known then that she was needed. She had not given in, as had some others she knew, and put on her best clothes, and walked towards the wall. She was still needed now. That was something. Gabriel lay in the hospital, five kilometres away, and knew nothing about any of this. In the morning she would have to go and fetch him. And where would she take him? She crossed her feet at the ankles and rocked back and forth.

They could not stay here. They could not escape.

Flora did not understand the plump little soldier with his money and his computer and his evil giant. She understood that she did not understand him. What his motives were, what he really wanted and why, were beyond her. He was from another plane of existence, a circumstance that afforded him, in her world, the powers of a god. And he had used those powers against her, and her father, and – for all she knew – her brother, that morning. Perhaps it was also he who had taken her mother, and Jake.

She began to rock harder, the wheel-studs now hurting her back.

One could not endure under such a brutal and capricious god. Not for long. He would be back for her and for Gabriel, when it suited him. She knew nothing, but somehow still she knew too much. A click of a mouse key was all that it would take: he had shown her that already. And their murder wouldn't even warrant an army press release, or a routine denial. They wouldn't see it coming. Flora started to cry again, not so much for herself and Gabriel, who were yet to die, but for her mother and father and Jake, whose love would soon be forgotten for ever.

She stopped rocking. This thought was unbearable. They would have to be remembered. She would free Gabriel and herself from the Embargoed Zone: there could be no more lingering here. But how to escape? The soldier had hinted that they might be allowed safe passage to some other part of the world, if she helped him, but that was only a hint, not a promise. And even his promise would have been meaningless: you can't hold a god to account.

But then, he wasn't really a god. A real god wouldn't wheedle, or deal ... If the little soldier needed something from her, then his powers must be finite. So what powers did he really possess, and how were they derived?

The sky was brightening now; the dawn would be somewhere behind the ruins of Hilltown. And then she became aware of something which she had long ago learned to ignore, the sneer of a drone aircraft, circling high and slow above her. She searched for it in the morning haze, finally glimpsing a flash of light as an early ray lit up its underside. It occurred to her that it might be the same armed drone that had killed her father, and Tony. Then she lost sight of it again.

The soldier's power, she understood, was that he could see them and they couldn't see him. And thanks to the wall and all the myths that went with it, the rest of the world – the real world – couldn't see Flora and Gabriel and all of the rest of them either, not as people. They were members of a lower order, one to which bad things just happened, out there in the darkness and dirt.

But she *had* seen the little soldier. She had looked into his face. She knew that he existed. And she and Gabriel existed too. Not only in the Embargoed Zone, but in the real world also: they would have been seen on television that day – Uncle Joseph had told her so. Just faces on the edge of another scene of violence, but for a brief moment they had flickered into a wider existence. Couldn't she use that somehow to extort some measure of humanity for Gabriel and herself? Once they became human beings they would not be so easy to kill.

Uncle Joseph must help her. She would go and look for him again when the sun came up. Together, they would find an angle. She was too tired now to think what it might be; that would be her uncle's department, she hoped.

And then she realized, with surprise, that for an hour or two she might even sleep, despite everything. After that, she could look for her miracle.

She stood, then almost fell as numbness pinched her legs; she had been sitting there for a long, cold time. Leaning against the cab of the dead truck, she waited for feeling and strength to come back to her limbs. There was a cough close behind her. Please God, she thought, turning slowly, don't let it be a caring neighbour ... But there was no one there. There was another cough, a male one, coming from under the truck. Some kind of tramp, she decided, and she was stealing away when it came again, a terrible, convulsive, retching cough. Flora found her conscience stirring. Whoever it was, they were clearly in a desperate condition. She peered into the shadow between the wheels.

'Hello . . . Are you okay under there?'

There was a flurry of movement and then a dim face raised itself towards her. 'Er . . . hello,' said the man under the truck.

'Are you all right under there?'

'Erm . . . no.' There was a scrabbling sound, and a young man crawled out from under the cab.

Using a mudguard for leverage, he pulled himself to his feet and stood swaying there, hunched miserably in on himself, squinting as he tried to make her out. Flora took in his smeared uniform, and the rifle and magazine pouches which hung listlessly from either hand, and she turned and fled. But the sand sucked at her feet as they sought to pull clear of it, forcing her to lean forward, and she had only gone a couple of metres when a wire snagged her ankle and she fell face-down in a clump of scratching weeds. Footsteps crunched behind her, and she closed her eyes and balled her fists up, waiting. She heard the cough again.

'Erm, excuse me?' muttered the gunman. 'I'm sorry if I scared you, but I'm rather lost. Could I please borrow your cell phone, just for a local call? I can't find mine, and I need to ring in sick.'

Flora remembered then the phone that the captain had given her. It felt heavy in her pocket. Shuddering, she rolled over and sat upright, her back to the soldier, shielding her hand as she fumbled in her pocket. She felt a click, and the battery fell away from the rest of the handset.

'I'm sorry,' she said, turning slowly. 'I don't have a phone.'

CHAPTER TWENTY-SIX

The first rays of day were spearing the dunes as Captain Smith rapped on the door of Colonel White's chalet. He waited, rapped again, and when there was no reply he turned to Daddy Jesus: 'Break it in.'

'Aren't you going to pick the lock first, boss?'

'Do it, Daddy Jesus. This is no time for finesse.'

They found the colonel in the bedroom, stuck half-way out of the narrow window, his legs flailing inside the room. He yelped as Daddy Jesus hauled him back inside, then spun him around and pushed him against a wall.

'Good morning, sir,' Smith said breezily. 'I'm so glad we found you here. Your voicemail message said you'd gone back to headquarters for the night. Just a little mistake on your part, I'm sure.'

Colonel White took a moment to rearrange his shirt, which had bunched around his armpits when Daddy Jesus wrenched him from the window. Finished, he seemed to assume that he had also reasserted his dignity.

'What's this about, Captain? I've been very busy,' he barked, trying to slide away from them. Daddy Jesus turned and leaned smoothly into the wall so that his shoulder blocked the colonel's escape.

'We need to have a little talk about what I've been hearing on the news,' said Smith. 'About how the air force dropped a one-ton bomb on a residential building in the middle of the night, and how a drone attacked a clearly identified press vehicle, killing one accredited journalist, and then fired a hellfire into a street full of rescuers. Do you mind telling me, sir, what you were playing at last night?'

Colonel White smirked. 'Read the operational notes, Smith: the building was harbouring a known terrorist leader. The vehicle was smuggling weapons, or acting suspiciously, I forget which. And who cares? They were only terrorists.'

Smith blinked slowly. 'There were families sleeping in that building. You killed fourteen people, most of them women and children.'

The colonel shrugged. 'I acted in full accordance with the rules of engagement. As usual, great care was taken to minimize civilian casualties – I could have dropped lots of bombs, but I only dropped one.'

Captain Smith stared at him. Then he collected himself. 'All right, Colonel. Be that as it may: what exactly were you trying to achieve by all this?'

The colonel stuck his jaw out. 'I was tidying up, Smith. You were dicking around in the Embargoed Zone, letting the situation slip away from you, so I had to step in and put a stop to things.'

'And how do you presume to know what I was up to in the Easy? Were you listening in on my communications?'

The colonel looked smug. 'Afraid so, yes. Commander's privilege.'

'And you were also eavesdropping on my phone call with Cobra, too, right? That's why you wanted his number? And then for some reason you went totally mad, and started flinging explosives around!'

The colonel's chin had climbed back to its cruising altitude. 'The situation was spiralling out of control! It's as important for us to stop the Iranians from getting that washing machine as it is to get it back for ourselves – imagine what they could do with that kind of technology! They'd sell it on to everyone, at half the market price! So I took some precautions. Whoever had the machine is probably dead by now, buying us more time to find it, if it hasn't been destroyed. And even if it was caught in the air strikes, your ground assets can still go and pick up the pieces.'

Smith surprised himself by smacking the wall hard with the flat of his hand. 'You idiot! The machine could still be anywhere, and so could the Iranians! I had two good leads and you've just destroyed both of them! Tell me, Colonel, is there any problem that you won't try and solve by throwing ordnance at it?'

'I played a percentage!'

'No you didn't! You panicked and lashed out blindly! You stink of fear!' Smith's voice abruptly resumed its habitually mild, conversational tone. 'Am I right, Daddy Jesus? You know a flop sweat when you taste one.'

Daddy Jesus teased a curl of Colonel White's hair around

a discoloured, spatulate finger. Then he put his finger in his mouth and slowly sucked it. He smiled.

'You're right, boss. He's shitting himself.'

The colonel shrank away from him. 'Leave me alone, goddamn it! I'm a full colonel!'

'Indeed you are,' mused Smith, 'which makes me wonder, what was it that scared a full colonel so much?' Daddy Jesus let his hand drop from the colonel's hair, brushing his cheek as it fell. The colonel turned pale but said nothing. Smith fixed him with a shrewd look.

'So what was it that spooked you? . . . The Iranians? Well, perhaps. But it wasn't them that made you snap so suddenly, was it, Colonel? You already knew about them. No – you went to pieces right after you heard Cobra tell me that a TV crew had got wind of this thing. That's what pushed you over the edge, wasn't it?'

'Don't be silly.'

Smith carried on as if he had not heard him.

'Yes, it was the media involvement . . . You were frightened that this business might somehow go public. Which would be pretty bad for us, of course. But freak-out-screaming, spit-the-dummy sort of bad? . . .' Smith shook his head. 'There's something you haven't told us, isn't there, Colonel?'

'I told you all you need to know for this mission! Everything else is classified, on a strictly need-to-know basis.'

'Of course. So tell me: who else needed to know about this operation, Colonel? If I were to pick up that phone over there and call our general, or the head of military intelligence, say, or the chief of staff's office, or the industrial espionage division, and mention this amazing new technology which we've just stolen from the Americans, would they know what I was talking about?'

The colonel was aghast. 'You wouldn't dare call them!'

'Oh, but I'd have to, sir: it's arse-covering time, thanks to your antics last night. So let's be honest with each other: our commanders don't know anything about the toploader, do they, Colonel? You're flying solo on this one.'

Daddy Jesus began to chortle, like a compressor running on dirty diesel. The colonel sagged against the wall. Smith sighed and turned away, reaching for the bedside phone. And then the colonel spoke.

'Please don't call anyone,' he said.

'I beg your pardon?'

'I'll cut you in on the deal. If you can somehow help me find that washing machine, and keep your mouth shut, I'll make you rich.'

'Tell me more.'

The colonel drew a heaving breath and, looking meekly up at Daddy Jesus, turned and sat on his unmade bed. He placed his elbows on his knees and buried his face in his hands.

'It's like this,' he said. 'That chip is extremely valuable, not only militarily but commercially. Apart from the military-industrial applications – weapons for our own services, and for retail abroad, of course – there will be all kinds of civilian spin-off benefits for computer gaming, mobile phones, control systems – even for washing machines.'

Smith nodded to Daddy Jesus, who sat beside the colonel and patted his back. The colonel cringed, then continued.

'Obviously, we planned to give the chip to one of our own domestic tech companies to exploit, both for our own military and for export abroad – a lot of countries will still pay top euro for the first look at new American technology, especially if we let them think that the Chinese are ahead of them in line. But which of our companies should we give the chip to? Whoever got to decide that would be very popular with some very wealthy and influential corporations. Normally, of course, a secret committee of politicians and generals would thrash out the decision, but that's a very inefficient way of doing things: it takes a lot of time and money to buy off an entire committee of big shots. So I thought, wouldn't it be much cheaper and more efficient for the lucky arms company – and therefore, better for our national interest too – if that company only had to pay one person for access to the chip? And what if that person was me?'

'So you set up a freelance operation to steal the chip, and you didn't cut in your bosses.'

The colonel nodded. 'My team in the States will be well looked after, of course, to keep them quiet. And so will you, if you help me.'

'What's your end of the deal? A highly paid consultancy post when you retire, heading up some big aerospace project, with a team of engineers to do all the work for you?'

White curled his lip. 'That's chicken feed. I'd get that anyway – all the senior air force officers get aerospace jobs when they go into the reserve. But if I had this chip on the table I could buy my way in at the top of any corporation, with a golden hello and a seat on the board.'

Smith nodded thoughtfully. 'And of course, you'd need your own highly paid specialist staff. People with a background in human intelligence and ground operations, that sort of thing. And they'd have to be on very handsome iron-bound contracts, so they'd have the focus and security they'd need to do their jobs properly.'

The colonel nodded reluctantly. 'Yes . . . I daresay they would.'

Smith clapped his hands together. 'Right, Daddy Jesus, it's time we got cracking. Cobra should be awake by now: let's try and get him on his cell phone.'

'You're forgetting,' said the colonel, mumbling into his hands. 'I dropped a bomb on him last night.'

Smith smiled fondly down at him. 'No, you didn't. You dropped a bomb on his cell phone signal, which is not the same thing at all. Cobra lives in a cellar; it's actually one of our old interrogation centres; I gave him the keys myself, when we disengaged from the Embargoed Zone. But there's a very poor cell phone signal down there, so when he's at home Cobra has to plug his phone into a booster aerial, which is attached to the roof of the building next door. That's what your smart bomb homed in on last night.'

'Oh, really? . . . So who did I bomb last night?'

Smith shrugged. 'The press office hasn't decided yet.'

The colonel relapsed into gloom. 'Still,' he said. 'Cobra

will hardly be in touch again. He must have figured out by now that we tried to kill him last night.'

Smith lit a cigarette, then offered the colonel one. 'I wouldn't count on Cobra figuring out anything – he's one of our most useful assets . . . But the girl, on the other hand, seemed rather clever. I doubt if we'll be hearing from her again, after you blew up that jeep outside her house, together with half of her neighbourhood.'

'What girl?'

Smith exhaled a plume of smoke and turned towards the exit. 'That, Colonel, is on a need-to-know basis. If you reflect on what you did last night I'm sure you'll understand why. And another thing – from now on I'm in charge of this operation. It's just an informal arrangement, but I think you'll find things work more smoothly this way.'

The colonel nodded. Daddy Jesus followed his boss outside.

Smith paused at the front door. 'Mind you don't panic again, Colonel,' he called back. 'So long as we keep our nerve those Iranians don't stand a chance against us in the Embargoed Zone: we know every last inch of it. We'll get that toploader back – and before it reaches the spin cycle, eh?'

Incredible, thought Driscoll, as he watched Smith and Daddy Jesus drive off in their jeep. There it was again: the Toploader Project! And his surmise had been correct – it really was linked to the Iranians! Who really were inside the Easy!

He closed the bathroom window and stepped down from his vantage point on the toilet bowl, rubbing his eyes. What a night. One wiki fact had led to another, one chatroom to the next, until he had looked up from his screen to see pale morning in the window. Time to pack his gear, shave his face and scalp, and then – the urgent voices from the next bungalow, and the captain's indiscretion!

He would cross now into the Embargoed Zone. He didn't really need to, if truth were told – he had found enough material on the internet that night to stand up half a dozen features about long-range mortars and Iranian anti-tank rockets and mutated swine flu aerosols. But he still had the chance to strike another blow against 24/7. And it would be nice to be able to put an Easy dateline on his pieces, to give them that extra shine. He wiped the lather off his head and gave the mirror a cynical smile. Going somewhere dangerous just to get a dateline – if he wasn't careful he'd soon turn into an old-school hack.

Something was still nagging him, a phrase the captain had used when parting from Colonel White. What was it? 'Spin cycle?' What could that mean? What kind of spin could possibly interest men like Colonel White and Captain Smith?'

And then it came to him. 'Centrifuges!' he cried aloud. 'And Iranians! The physicist! Here, in the Embargoed Zone! Oh my God!'

CHAPTER TWENTY-SEVEN

Flora's lungs fluttered, her legs were liquid with fear. Yet still some part of her stood aloof from the terror, taking stock. She had panicked and tried to run and yet the soldier had not shot her. She had fallen, and was at his mercy now, yet still he did nothing. He loomed over her, brandishing his rifle, a stinking, hulking, wild-eyed brute, his face contorted in hatred or rage, and yet his voice – when he spoke – belonged to someone else. He was sick? He needed a telephone? And he seemed to be finding it hard to see . . . Daring to raise her head, Flora saw no sign of any other soldiers. But didn't scouts, or commandos, whatever they were called, always work in teams? What were those hideous stains down the front of his uniform? Why was he trembling? Could he have been wounded during yesterday's invasion, and abandoned on the battlefield? Carefully, she sat up and moved a few feet further away from him, scooting along on her bottom. Then she raised her arms slowly.

'I'm going to stand up,' she said, managing to keep her voice level. 'Please tell me if that's not okay.'

'What?' he demanded, squinting. 'Um . . . Would you have

191

any aspirin, or something like that?' He spoke very carefully. 'I have a terrible headache.'

Flora rose to her feet, watching for his reaction. There was none. Her knees shook a little, and she had to fight not to glance at the rifle, machine gun, whatever it was, that he held by his side: her stomach lurched in fear of it.

And then a thought came to her that was so shocking, so perfect, so much more terrifying still than the soldier and his rifle, that she almost vomited. Lost? What if he were lost? And she had found him . . . She swayed for an instant, dizzied by the notion, but even as her balance brought her forward again she knew, with sick certainty, what she must try to do.

She cleared her throat. 'Don't worry,' she said, glancing about. 'I can do better than aspirin, if you like – my father has some prescriptions.' She cleared her throat again. 'Tell you what, why don't you come for a cup of tea? I live right over there, in that building.'

He looked at her more closely. 'Um . . . Thanks. That's very kind of you.'

The soldier followed Flora as she led him to the back of her building. She kept as far as she decently could ahead of him, half-turned to flee in case his true nature asserted itself. The soldier had slung his rifle over one shoulder and used his free hand to squeeze his temples between thumb and index finger. Eyes half-closed, he stumbled a couple of times on unperceived snags.

They reached a jagged gap in the wall that gave entry to Flora's backyard, and she stood back to usher him through it. The way was narrow, and the soldier, turning sideways to pass, misjudged the gap and became jammed in it, held by the rifle slung on his back.

'Here,' said Flora, 'let me help you with that.'

Marvellously, he did not protest when, with shaking hands, she eased the rifle from his shoulder. As he stepped on ahead of her, Flora noticed that he smelled like her Uncle Joseph after one of his nights. What on earth was going on here, she wondered? Then she shook the question from her head: for her purposes, it hardly mattered.

The strange, bedraggled girl sat Moon down at an old kitchen table topped with yellowing formica. He folded his arms and laid his head on them and closed his eyes against the soft light which leaked in from the backyard. He wondered, for a moment, why the kitchen door was broken, and then another wave of pain and sickness broke over him.

The girl disappeared through another door, and when she came back a minute or two later she no longer held the rifle. The weapon was a problem which, Moon was aware, ought to concern him more than it did: but then, he didn't even know whose rifle it was, so it could not formally be his responsibility. If someone like him had been given a weapon, then someone else had clearly blundered.

The girl seemed lost in her long and filthy blue raincoat; the hoodie she wore beneath was stained and darkly smeared. Her black hair was stringy with sweat and there was a large bruise on the right side of her face, which was otherwise pale beneath the dirt. Shadows made saucers of her eyes.

Apart from all that, he thought, she might have looked rather nice, on a good day. She put two white pills and two pink pills on the table in front of him, poured him some water from a jug by the sink, then stood on the other side of the table as he mouthed the pills and took a swig of water. He instantly spat it out again. The pills, already dissolving, flew onto the floor.

'Hey! You gave me dishwater!'

Her eyes remained fixed on him as she shook her head. 'No, that's all we have to drink here. Raw sewage leaks back into the groundwater, because the army won't let in enough parts or fuel for the sewage pumps. Please, pick up those pills and try and swallow them again. They're very valuable. I'll boil some water so we can drink tea. It kills the taste of the water, almost.'

Moon retrieved the pills from the floor and washed them down with a snatched sip of water. The alcohol, he sensed, was clearing from his brain. He was now merely horribly hung-over. He watched the girl fill a kettle and set it on a metal stand by the sink. Then she placed a small white cube under the kettle and lit it with a match; he recognized the cube as a fuel tablet, the kind you get in military field rations.

'Don't you know where you are?' she asked him, without turning around.

He tried to smile, but it hurt his face. 'I barely know *who* I am. I thought I'd take one thing at a time.'

She turned to stare. Why was she so fascinated by him?

'You really don't know, do you?'

'No. I went for a walk last night and I got lost in the tank park. I wandered around for ages before I found a sort of party. I think I remember passing out in the back of a tank, but after that I haven't a clue what happened. All I can think is that those tank guys must have played a really nasty prank on me – I don't recognize this place at all.' A sense of well-being spread through his body, unknotting the pain behind his eyes.

The girl studied his face. 'Are those pills working yet?'

'I rather think they are.'

She leaned back against a cupboard and seemed to reflect for a few moments. 'Good ... I don't want to shock you ... Listen: you're not on your base any more, wherever that is. You're in Hilltown. You're inside the Embargoed Zone.'

He laughed in her face. 'You've got to be kidding me.' The glow was spreading into the tips of his fingers and the balls of his feet. He curled his toes and stretched his back. The pain in his head was a memory now. 'What are those pills you gave me?'

'Codeine and Xanax. Listen, I think you should step over to that door and take a look outside.'

Moon laughed. 'Sure. Why not?'

As he moved around the table the girl sidled away from him, keeping the table between them. Reaching the door, he folded himself comfortably into its broken frame. Outside there was a dirt yard with lines of flapping washing; beyond that was a wall, and the hole they had come through. Then there was a sandy wasteland strewn with rubbish and weeds and bobbing pennants of shredded plastic, and with the rusted abstractions of mangled cars and dumped machinery. And beyond that again was another line of tower blocks, filigreed by shrapnel and bullets. It was still early, but the daylight was full now, and kites were specking the sky beyond the tower blocks. There was no sound of traffic, of any motors at all, apart from a little engine which whined, mosquito-like, high up in the sky.

Moon thought about what he was seeing, and he felt the glow fading within him. He tried to hold it to him, but it too was abandoning him here. At least he couldn't feel any pain now, he tried to console himself. Or any great fear, for the time being, although that would surely come. He turned back to the girl, who was still watching from the other side of the table. The kettle whistled in the corner.

'How did I get here?' He saw how tightly she held herself, her body angled towards the door that led to the rest of the apartment, ready to flee. She looks terrified, he told himself.

'I don't know,' she said, watching him. 'Please come away from that doorway. No one must see you here dressed like that. That's some kind of uniform, right?'

Moon slumped back in his chair. 'It's an air force uniform.'

'You're a pilot?'

Moon stared at the pitted formica. 'You could say that.'

He heard a clatter from the sink, and a cup of strong, red tea appeared on the table in front of him. Her hands, he noticed, were red and swollen, their nails broken and black. A chair creaked as she sat down opposite him.

'Drink your tea,' she told him. 'I've put a lot of sugar in it.'

Moon ignored her. 'Oh, God . . .' He still wasn't sure how

terrified he should be. 'This is for real, isn't it? I'm really in the Embargoed Zone ... That tank I passed out in must have entered last night, and I was so out of it I didn't even notice – I must have drunk a whole bottle of vodka, not to mention all the weed we smoked ...' He looked up at her. 'There must be a way to sneak out of here, right?'

She shook her head, almost too quickly, as if she had been waiting for the question. Who was she?

'Anyone who goes within a few hundred metres of the wall is shot dead,' she said. 'Even little children.'

'But I'm wearing their uniform!'

'So do the resistance, usually, when they try and attack the wall. It doesn't get them very far either.' She took a sip of tea.

'I could call the army, and let them know that I'm coming.'

'I don't have a phone.'

'Couldn't we borrow one?'

She gave a bitter smile. 'The only people in the Embargoed Zone who still have phones that work are the army's secret informers. They don't advertise the fact: if they're caught they get lynched.'

Moon drove his head into his hands again. Then he looked up at her. 'But that means you could be killed for helping me!'

The girl flinched. She really is scared, Moon realized. And of me, too! But her eyes met his evenly. '*Am* I helping you?'

'You're hiding me in your house ...' He sat upright. 'Hey – wait a second: what are you planning to do with me?'

She took another sip of tea. 'Don't bother looking for the

gun,' she said, almost primly. 'I hid it somewhere you'll never find it.'

Moon pushed his chair back. 'I don't want the fucking gun!' he shouted at her. 'I've never fired a gun in my life! But I don't think you could stop me walking out that door, if I wanted to.'

He half expected her to try to flee from him, but she stayed in her chair. 'You're right – I can't stop you,' she said, studying the teacup in front of her. 'But if you do go, I don't think you'll get far before someone sees you. You could also murder me, if you like – there's no one else in the apartment. But then you'd be alone here, with no food and hardly any water, waiting for someone you don't know to start knocking on the door. And when they do . . .'

She reached for her cup again. Despite the calmness of her voice her hand was shaking. Moon flushed. 'I'm not the murdering type.'

He saw her glance down at his uniform, and he exploded again. 'I do my job!' He leaned across the table at her. 'And if unarmed people get hurt it's the fault of the terrorists, for using them as human shields: everyone says so, all of our journalists – it's human rights law!'

The girl looked back at him blankly, then put a hand to her mouth and yawned. 'Sit down and drink your tea,' she said. 'Would you like another Xanax?'

'No!' shouted Moon, who then found himself sinking back into his chair.

She finished the last of her tea, stood up, placed her cup by the sink and turned to face him again.

'I can help you, I think, but you'll have to trust me completely.' She rubbed her eyes, then went on, 'You have no choice but to trust me, because any other course of action will get you killed. Me too, most likely.' She spoke with the tired mumble of a schoolkid rehearsing some phrase or formula half-learned in an all-nighter. 'But right now I don't want any questions from you, and I don't want any arguments.' She leaned her knuckles on the table, swaying a little. 'Because I've got a lot on my mind right now' – and then she was shouting at him – 'and I am *really* fucking tired!'

Moon saw that she was crying. It seemed to him that she was also a little surprised at having heard herself swear.

'Do you agree?' Her voice was muffled.

Moon nodded. He was starting to feel very frightened indeed. His stomach was tight, and his mouth tasted of metal. 'So what do we do next?'

She rubbed her eyes again, and thought. 'I haven't quite worked it out yet,' she said finally. 'I'm too tired to think straight. I'm going to lie down now, just for a couple of hours. There's nothing else for it. You should try and sleep too, I suppose – you can use my little brother's room.'

CHAPTER TWENTY-EIGHT

The terminal which controlled passage to and from the Embargoed Zone had been built, on behalf of the army, by a private consortium. The money for its construction had come from funds allocated by foreign donors for the relief of the Embargoed Zone's civilian population; the army had persuaded the donors that the terminal would serve this very purpose by facilitating visits by UN officials and aid workers, and by giving the inhabitants a means of egress when – as would happen any day now, the army had piously insisted – the embargo began to be eased. So the terminal had been built on a lavish scale, with no expense spared – indeed, with expense encouraged – by the retired generals and colonels who controlled not only the construction consortium but also the private security firm which provided the armed contractors who guarded the regular soldiers who protected the military police who fronted for the spooks who really ran the crossing. The building was made from glass and dull silver metal, a long, tilted span resembling, in cross-section, an aeroplane wing: its architect, himself a reserve colonel in the engineering corps, was hoping some day to graduate to airports, and if the building seemed a little incongruous – not to say mocking – in its geopolitical context, then who really cared? No one was ever allowed to photograph the terminal, and real people never went through it.

Driscoll's footsteps echoed as he crossed the vast tiled floor that morning. High above his head, pigeons cooed and shat on exposed roof girders, flying in and out of windows shattered in previous rocket attacks. Apart from the birds, Driscoll was alone in the hangar-like departure hall.

A dozen passport control booths, screened by bullet-proof glass and plate steel panels, lined the far side of the hall. Only the furthest left booth was occupied. Inside it, a large young woman in a rather small military police uniform was packed into a swivel chair, reading a romantic novel. She did not look up when Driscoll dropped his bag and his armour to the floor beside the booth, nor when he placed his passport and his government press card on the shelf beneath her window. She turned a page, and then, a minute later, she turned another. Driscoll decided to cough.

'Passport,' she grunted, her eyes still fixed on her book.

'It's here,' he said politely, nodding towards it.

She raised her voice angrily, still reading. 'You have to show me your passport.'

'I said, it's here.'

Reluctantly, she turned to scowl at him. 'Press card.'

'That's also here, with the passport.'

The girl made a noise that, if he were honest with himself, Driscoll could only have described as a snarl. She snatched the documents through a hole in the glass and flung them down beside her computer.

'What is the purpose of your journey to the Embargoed Zone?' she demanded, already typing.

'Journalism.'

'Hah . . . What is your profession?'

'Journalist.'

'Hah . . . Will you be meeting any terrorists in the Easy?'

'I suppose so.'

Her scowl darkened, and she picked up a pen and a notebook. 'Then you have to give me their names, addresses and purpose of meeting.'

Driscoll grimaced. 'Erm, it's just that I don't know exactly which terrorists I'll be meeting yet.'

His reply seemed to please her. 'Good. Then you don't have to tell me . . .' She dropped the notebook. 'Do you have any weapons?'

He smiled at her. 'Just one,' he said. 'The truth.'

The girl pressed a red button on her desk. Shoes squeaked behind him, and Driscoll had only a split second to wonder where they had come from before his cheek slammed hard against the booth's glass window. Inside, only inches from his contorted face, the girl was reading her book again.

The interrogation was asinine and repetitive, the search embarrassing and rather painful. And when it was over Driscoll still had to negotiate a maze of steel cages and concrete chutes and cattle bars and turnstiles, observed by swivelling cameras and darkened one-way windows.

Angry loudspeakers barked inaudible instructions, order-
ing him to lift his shirt, drop his pants, place his bags on
the belt, take his bags off the belt and put them back on
the belt facing another way, empty his bags, place their
contents on the belt and stand well back, then watch the
belt go into reverse, dropping his precious camera onto
the hard concrete floor. Each gate or turnstile was locked
when he reached it, and although he was quite alone in
the terminal he had to stand there, appealing to the security cameras, for five or ten minutes before the gate would
click and swing open, and he could pass to the next stage
of his ordeal.

He came to a bank of three full-length turnstiles, installed
in cylindrical steel cages. These too were locked. After waiting
another ten minutes, slumped and sweating under the
weight of his gear, he finally gave up, dumped his stuff on
the ground, and sat on the bare concrete. No sooner was
he seated then he heard a click, and saw a green light winking
over the nearest of the three turnstiles. Scrambling to his
feet, he picked up his gear and rushed towards it, only to
see the light turn red again just as he reached for the bar.

He hurled his kit to the ground again. 'You goddamned
sons of bitches!' he shouted. To his further rage and humil-
iation, it came out as more of a shriek than a bellow.

There was a long pause, and then another green light
winked on, over the turnstile furthest away from him.

This turnstile, he discovered, was so narrow that he could
not pass through it whilst holding the heavy-duty bag
containing his helmet and flak jacket. He tried pushing

the bag through ahead of him, but it got wedged between the cylinder and the teeth of the turnstile, so that he had to lie full length on the ground and stretch his arm through the bars to poke the bag through to the other side. And then he heard a faint click, and saw that the light over the turnstile had gone red again. He closed his eyes and lay there for a while, feeling the concrete rough and cool on his cheek, and then he heard another click. This time it was the middle turnstile that was open. There was a noise from a loudspeaker on the wall, which sounded like people sniggering.

Beyond the turnstiles was a short concrete passage which ended in a wall bare except for a sliding metal hatch, only a little larger than a standard house door. The hatch was painted gunmetal grey, and as he approached it it slid noise-lessly open, flooding the passage with daylight. Driscoll, fearing another last-second reverse, hurried through the door before it could close again. And thus he found himself, with no time to steel his nerves, standing alone in the Embargoed Zone, on the terrorist side of the wall. Dismayed, he spun on his heel, but the door had already slid shut behind him.

Driscoll sunk back against it. The sun was now quite high in the east, and dust and haze had turned the sky the colour of watered milk. He turned his head to squint into the Embargoed Zone. Immediately before him, a long straight road – once tarred, now ripped and scored by tank tracks – led away across the free-fire zone. On either side of it lay heaps of crushed concrete and twisted steel rods, the bull-dozed and bombed remains of houses and factories and border facilities. The nearest intact structures were a group of wood and tin shanties almost a kilometre away. Beyond them, the road stretched on, through ragged fields, towards the broken blocks of Hilltown, perched on their ridge four kilometres off. He heard sparrows in the rubble, and drones wheeling in the sky. A flock of goats was grazing near the road, about halfway to the shanties, but he could see no sign of a goatherd.

Behind him, and stretching off on either side until the land rose or sank to hide it, was the hard grey fact of the wall. A few metres to his right, twin watchtowers guarded a brute metal gate; Driscoll recognized it as the same sally-port which Captain Smith had taken him through in his jeep the day before. He could see no movement behind the tower's tinted windows, but he guessed that there must be soldiers behind them, and that the soldiers must be watching him.

This gave him some heart. He took his flak jacket and helmet out of their bag and put them on, then hid his pass-port and press ID and wallet behind the bullet-proof plate in the front of the jacket. Rallying his nerves, he launched himself out into space.

The way here was flat, the ground hard beneath a thin layer of dust, but as he trudged on, and the wall fell away behind him, Driscoll felt as if he were climbing a steep and narrow path. Before he had walked two hundred metres the sweat was flowing in streams under his helmet and armour. He pressed on. Another hundred metres, and the goats had noticed him now, lifting their heads from the thin green shoots which pushed through the rubble, twitching their ears. A large billy goat took a few steps towards him, head lifted, fixing him with one yellow eye. Do goats attack people? Driscoll asked himself, his steps faltering. Should I make eye contact, to show I'm not scared, or would that just provoke it? The goat bleated loudly, and the other goats became still, all staring at Driscoll. The billy goat took another couple of steps, almost to the edge of the road, as if planning to cut Driscoll's line of advance, and Driscoll came to a halt, frowning past the goat at the towers of Hilltown. I mustn't let it know that I'm scared, he told himself. They can sense that. And before he quite knew what he was doing he had taken the phone from his pocket and was pretending to dial a number.

'Hello?' he told the phone loudly, then closed his eyes in mortification. And then, just as self-loathing was supplying him with the courage to advance, a long burst of automatic fire ripped through the air, seemingly from somewhere behind him. Driscoll spun on his heels, looking frantically about. Dear God, he thought, half-crouching instinctively, has that got something to do with *me*?

There didn't seem to be anyone else around. No obvious target or source for the fire, no one for him to take his cue from. The birds were still singing. The goats were staring at him, unperturbed by the shooting. What was the etiquette for such an occasion? Should he take cover, or would that look silly? Who would know? When he turned to the wall for guidance it stared silently back at him.

Only then did it occur to Driscoll that the grunt soldiers

in the towers might not know who he was. They might well think that he was one of those terrorist-loving journalists and human rights people who caused the army so much trouble. In fact, he realized, they were sure to think so – what other kind of person would want to enter the Embargoed Zone? Perhaps it was the soldiers who had fired the machine gun – as some kind of taunt or warning. He shuddered, despite the heat. Could he decently go back now? Was honour satisfied? He had truthfully been to the Easy that day, so he could justify putting the date-line on his exclusives ... But he had also undertaken to dig out original interviews, to visit the scene of yesterday's terrorist charade, plus there was still the Toploader Project ... The billy goat had lost interest in him, turning its back and wandering off a few paces, and the rest of the herd was grazing again. Driscoll waited another couple of minutes, but there was no more shooting. Steeling himself, he hoisted his kit and trudged on into the Embargoed Zone. There was now a curiously tight sensation between his shoulders.

The shanty huts, which he took to be some kind of border facility, stood at the further end of what must once have been a car park. The door of one hut stood open, with a canvas awning stretched over it. Beneath the awning two men in black polyester trousers and grey polyester shirts sat behind a wooden table. The long walk, the sleepless night, the heat and the sweat and the adrenalin come-down, had all combined to leave Driscoll groggy; he had already handed the pair his passport before he realized what was happening.

He, Flint Driscoll, was face to face with terrorists, on terrorist ground! He watched, fascinated, as the older of the two, a small, very thin man with brown teeth and combed-over hair, opened his mouth. Driscoll heard the terrorist address him.

'Hello and welcome,' said the old man. 'You're the first foreigner to come through this week. Would you like us to fetch you a donkey?'

CHAPTER TWENTY-NINE

Colonel White carefully turned the knob on the door, eased it open two inches and put an eye to the crack. A new shift of drone jockeys had come on duty since his last visit: one of them was hunched blearily over a computer terminal while the other dozed in his chair, unperturbed by the explosions and machine gun fire blaring from the computer speakers, or by the voices screaming 'I surrender!', and 'I'm wounded!' in German. Still with the World War Two games, the colonel thought, feeling a stab of resentment. What was wrong with their own war, the one that they themselves were fighting? Not that it really mattered, he reassured himself: he would have been a fighter ace in World War Two, had he been in it. He was sure of it.

He threw the door open, letting it bang against the wall, and surged into the room. The two drone pilots stumbled to their feet with a pleasing air of fear and confusion.

'Sit down!' shouted the colonel, and came to stand close behind them. 'What is your situation? Lieutenant: report!'

'Um, it's quiet, sir,' said the older one. 'Nothing since we came on duty . . . The artillery are shelling a few places but we're not spotting for them, so I guess they're just shooting blind on a rota or something.'

'Very good,' rapped the colonel. 'Thank you, son. You may consider yourself relieved.'

The two airmen peered up at him, perplexed. 'Relieved, sir? But regulations state . . .'

'Shut up!' roared the colonel. 'Regulations state that lieutenants do whatever colonels tell them! Now get the fuck out of my control room!'

The two kids looked at each other, shrugged, and left. The colonel waited a few seconds and then followed them to the door, opened it and peered into the dark corridor. 'It's clear,' he whispered.

Captain Smith slipped inside. 'You might have been a bit more subtle. People remember being shouted at.'

'Don't tell me how to deal with my non-flight personnel, Captain. I've been doing this for years.'

Smith sat at the console and took a cell phone and a laptop from his bag. 'Well, remember, Colonel, they didn't see me: unlike you, I was never here this morning. Now, if you could kindly take command of the drone systems, Daddy Jesus is on stand-by at the wall, ready to go back into the Easy as soon as we hunt up a lead for him.'

'Right . . . So where do we begin?'

'I suppose I might as well start with Cobra. You never know, he might be stupid enough to have switched his phone back on.'

He punched a number into his cell phone, listened for a few moments and then his face lit up. 'It's ringing! Good old Cobra! . . . Hello, Cobra? I hope I find you well . . . No, the line's pretty bad at this end, too. Perhaps you're having trouble with your aerial . . . Yes, yes, I know it's too early for you to have anything new for me, I just wanted to make sure you were okay. I heard there was some kind of explosion in your neighbourhood last night . . . You didn't know? The locals are blaming the air force, as usual, but the army press office says it was a terrorist bomb that went off prematurely. The important thing is that you're okay . . .'

Colonel White leaned over and snatched the phone from Smith's hand. Glaring at his subordinate, he switched the phone to loudspeaker then handed it back.

Cobra's voice crackled loudly in the darkened control room. 'Hang on a minute, Captain. I'll just go upstairs and see if I can get a better signal outside. I'm unplugging now . . .' Smith and White heard several seconds of static, and muffled steps and clangs, and then Cobra's voice burst forth again, clear and loud.

'Okay, I'm outside now – Holy God! What the . . . ? Where the hell . . . ? My God, Captain, half the street is missing!'

Smith rolled his eyes at the colonel. 'Oh, dear. That does sound serious.'

'There are rescuers digging in the rubble . . . They're still pulling bodies out . . . How the hell did this happen?'

'Like I said, Cobra, we're still not sure.'

'Nobody in Hilltown could have built a bomb that big without me knowing about it. God . . . Could you call me back in five minutes? I need to find out if anyone survived. My cousins lived in that building.'

The phone went dead. The two officers exchanged glances, then simultaneously reached into their breast pockets and pulled out their cigarettes. Smith deployed his lighter, and they hunched, smoking in silence until it was time to call again.

'Cobra,' said Smith urgently, 'please, before we go any further, tell me: are your relatives okay? Is there anything I can do to help? Medicine? Cash? I might be able to swing permission for children to be treated in our hospitals, if their parents agree to work for us. Just say the word: I'm here for you.'

There was a long pause before Cobra spoke. 'That's all right, Captain. They're all dead.'

'I'm most dreadfully sorry.'

'They're all dead,' Cobra repeated, sounding baffled now. 'The whole building imploded on them. God . . .'

'There there, Cobra,' soothed Smith. 'There there. I'm sorry for your loss.'

Cobra said nothing for a while, and then he spoke again. 'I heard something else, too, from the rescuers. At the same time that my cousins were killed, your drones attacked 24/7's jeep in Hilltown. They killed that guy Tony I told you about last night, and a whole lot of other people who came into the street.'

'Yes, I heard that too. Very sad business. I'm still trying to find out why that happened. Probably a mistake, I should think. Wrong place, wrong time, sort of thing.'

Smith and White took synchronized pulls on their cigarettes and hunched in on themselves, waiting.

'It seems a bit odd,' mused Cobra. 'Do you think it might have something to do with that washing machine business? Tony was involved in that . . . And so am I, come to think of it . . .' His voice rose suddenly. 'Good God, Captain! Are you trying to kill me? Was that bomb last night meant for *me*?'

Colonel White winced. Smith opened his eyes wide and then closed them again, for maximum concentration. His fingers drummed a temple. 'Dear God, no, Cobra! After all we've achieved together? I would never allow you to come to any harm . . . But you know – hang on – there is one possibility: it could be that new commanding officer I told you about. The one who's a bit of a cunt' – White gave him a foul look, but Smith waved him off – 'He keeps me in the dark about a lot of things, and I'm not sure that he even knows what he's doing himself, half the time. He's the one who wants that washing machine so badly. I don't know why – he's quite mad. Maybe – just maybe – he's got something to do with these regrettable incidents.'

'Oh, my God!' shrieked Cobra. 'Your commanding officer wants me dead? What on earth can I do?'

'Let me think about that for a moment . . . Cobra? It occurs to me . . . There's just one way that maybe we can solve this thing . . . Here's a thought: if you find that washing machine, and hand it over to me, I can intercede for you with the colonel – that would probably work. But without the washing machine I've got nothing to work with; the colonel hates my guts. I'm hanging on by my fingernails as it is.'

White grunted his agreement.

There was another wait before Cobra spoke again. 'Okay – I'll find your goddamn washing machine. But the price has gone up, Captain: I want twenty grand now, not what we agreed last night. And when this is done you're going to take me out of the Embargoed Zone. I can't go on like this any more: I want to go into your relocation programme.'

'But Cobra, what would I do without you in the Easy? You're my best operator!'

'Not for much longer, Captain – I'm living on borrowed time here. The few men I still have are beginning to suspect me. And that mad American bitch from People for the Ethical Treatment of Animals has started putting up posters of me all around the Easy, saying I'm wanted for donkey murder – I'm the laughing stock of the militant community. And now your boss is out to kill me as well! You have to get me out of here – let me go abroad and join my family.'

'Oh, very well. Twenty grand it is, and when it's over I'll put you in the programme. Just get us that washing machine. Go and see that girl again – there's no time to waste. I still think she might know something. And don't try making any side-deals with the Iranians, Cobra. We know all about them. They'll be no use to you.'

'Iranians? What Iranians?'

'Don't play games with me. Go find the girl.'

Smith hung up the line.

'He can't be all that stupid,' commented the colonel. 'He's smart enough to demand twenty grand and a place in the programme.'

216

Smith lit another cigarette and puffed meditatively. 'Oh, he's stupid, all right . . . There is no relocation programme – we don't have a budget for one. It's just something I made up to keep my agents happy.'

'Really? So what happens when an agent is blown?'

'Well, obviously, we can't leave them in the Easy – they'd tell the other terrorists all they knew, under torture. Worse, they might even start talking to journalists about some of our more . . . *proactive* programmes.'

'So you give them a new identity on this side of the wall?'

'Yes, you could say that . . .' Smith took another expansive drag on his cigarette. 'What normally happens is that Daddy Jesus picks up the blown agent at an agreed rendezvous inside the Embargoed Zone. He takes them out through the wall, and then he drives them on a way, alone, out into the national park. And that's where he puts them in the programme.'

The colonel shook his head. 'That's pretty cold-blooded,' he marvelled.

Smith gave a little bow. 'I'll take that as a compliment, coming from someone who used to fly attack helicopters.'

'But you've worked with these people. Surely some kind of bond forms with them . . . like a reverse Stockholm syndrome?'

Smith looked pained. 'I'm doing them a kindness, sir! It wouldn't do to leave them in the Easy, to be tortured to death. Daddy Jesus is very quick and business-like, when he wants to be.'

'I have to admit, Smith, that I may have underestimated you. So what shall we do now? Sit and wait?'

'No, we'll keep working my contacts. We can't put all our eggs in one basket.'

The colonel sat back and drummed his fingers on the arm of his chair. A frown spread slowly across his face. 'There's something else that's bothering me,' he said finally. 'Why is Cobra *upping* his price to twenty thousand euros? I thought you'd agreed twenty grand with him already?'

Smith's phone, which he'd placed on the console, beeped twice.

'Oh good!' he said brightly. 'This could be a break! One of my leads has just sent me a text message!'

CHAPTER THIRTY

The driver of Driscoll's cart was a toothless young man with dull eyes and a massive goitre. He wore what was left of a double-breasted pinstripe suit, now buttonless, with two loops of twine to hold it closed against the chill. It seemed to Driscoll that his driver was also slow or deranged in some way; asked to drive to the scene of the big air strike that had killed lots of people – Driscoll was in a sense working under cover now, and trimmed his sails accordingly – the driver had slowly scratched his bottom, and asked, 'Which one?' He seemed to have trouble swallowing, and spat after each stumbling phrase.

Driscoll had never travelled by donkey-cart before, and the trip from the border was one he would already like to forget. The last time he had been in Hilltown, years before, he had been a guest of the army, then still in formal occupation. In those days, before blockade and bombardment had become acceptable tools of indirect administration, the streets had still been paved, more or less, and the municipality had enough diesel and spare parts to collect the rubbish and pump the sewage. Now, heaps of rubble and rotting food scraps stood on every corner, each with its shifting corona of flies. The wind, gusting from behind the cart, carried the stink of the sewage lake, a mile to the north. What must it be like, Driscoll wondered in horrid fascination, to actually stand on the banks of that square-mile sump of shit? How would it feel to fall into it? Rivulets of raw sewage trickled down the gutters on either side of the road, past bombed-out stores and workshops. He felt himself starting to gag, and lifted his eyes from the ground. Here and there, rubble had been shovelled back to clear the thoroughfare, and militant flags fluttered from each mountain of debris, as if claiming responsibility. From the pavements, where pavements existed, pedestrians glanced sideways at the well-dressed foreigner, showing flashes of quickly stifled curiosity, almost of hope, clownish in their charity-shop coats and their shuffling, plastic-soled shoes, before letting their eyes drop again. Only the children – who did not yet know that they were less than alive, and ought to behave accordingly – intruded frankly on Driscoll's existence. Filthy, taunting boys swarmed after his cart from every muddy junction.

'Hey, mister!' shouted a skinny, bug-eyed little brute, trotting effortlessly by his side. 'Hey, mister! That's a fine big black helmet you have on you there! Any chance of a go of your big black helmet?'

The other urchins laughed and whooped, nudging each other and pointing at Driscoll's flushing face. He fixed his gaze between the donkey's twitching ears. The bug-eyed kid scampered out in front of the cart, back-pedalling, and addressed him again.

'Hey, mister! Are you a reporter? Do you want to see some dead bodies? If you give me ten euros I can show you some. Just give me the money now, and I'll go and arrange it, eh?'

The others giggled knowingly. One reached up and tapped Driscoll's knee. 'Please, mister,' he whispered. 'Just give me one euro, eh? I won't tell anyone. Just one euro, please?'

His eyes still fixed to the front, Driscoll leaned sideways to murmur to his driver: 'Can't you make this cart go any faster?'

The driver shrugged and flicked his whip. The donkey shivered once at its touch and then, without changing its gait or troubling to lift its tail, released a stream of yellow, liquid dung down its withered haunches. The sweet stench flooded Driscoll's nostrils. He closed his eyes and cringed. What was wrong with these people? Was their hatred and ignorance really so all-consuming that they would choose to endure such a fetid, hopeless existence rather than abjure their wrong-minded, criminal delusions? Perhaps blood and shit really *were* their natural humours; perhaps those who had walled them up here were right when they hinted at that.

The children were making chicken noises at him. Driscoll considered the sky. The sun was higher: the day must surely be warmer by now. Stiffly, he took off his helmet and flak jacket and returned them to their bag, which he clamped firmly between his feet on the floor of the cart. Beneath the jacket, his blue shirt had turned white with the sweat from his journey.

They turned a corner into a quiet side street and the boys

lost interest and turned back whence they'd come. Swishing the diarrhoea from its tail, the donkey came to the edge of a trash-strewn field overlooked by skeletal apartment blocks. The winter sun shone through glassless windows and shattered walls.

Driscoll recognized this landscape: it had been burnt into his memory the night before, by repeated viewings on Captain Smith's computer. There was the treeless wasteland, there were the uneven goalposts, there the mangled cars and pitted buildings. And there, in the foreground, only fifty metres away, was the infamous bank of dirt and gravel, scene of the dumbshow he had come to unmask.

'Wait here,' Driscoll told the driver. The donkey made a half-hearted effort to kick him as he passed its heels, then tore at some weeds in the gutter.

Driscoll scrabbled up the dirt bank and peered into the crater at the top. It was lined with stinking, slimy soot, and surrounded by a penumbra of carbonized dirt and gravel. Here and there lay scorched pieces of green plastic circuit board, marked with fragments of code. Driscoll picked up a piece and looked more closely. The letters on it read: 'J2 FINS & PS UMBILICAL'. He smiled grimly to himself as he tossed it away into a clump of weeds. You had to hand it to the terrorists: they were nothing if not thorough.

Looking around, he noticed a kite flying high above the football pitch, its string slanting down behind a wrecked truck. Scrambling down the bank, Driscoll threaded his way through heaps of ordure, rounded the truck and came to the end of the string; it was clutched in the hand of a twelve-year-old boy, who frowned up at his kite with total concentration. He barely glanced around as Driscoll stepped up to him.

'Flying a kite, eh?' said Driscoll, smiling down at the boy. The kid glanced at him again, but said nothing. He was a wizened homunculus, with dark, darting eyes. His green cotton jacket had faded with age, and the kite string cut pink and white tracks in the skin of his hand. Driscoll tried again.

'So, uh, son . . . Do you come here often?'

A look of faint alarm appeared on the child's face. 'What do you mean?' he squeaked. He began to wind in the kite, wrapping the string around a square wooden frame that served as a spool.

'Well, I mean, were you here yesterday, for instance, when the explosions happened?'

'No.' The boy scowled. 'My mother wouldn't let me out yesterday, because of the tanks. That's why I missed it. It would have been cool.'

'Cool?' Driscoll took the notebook from his pocket. 'Surely that's a funny way to describe what supposedly happened here yesterday?'

The kid gave Driscoll a 'how stupid are you?' look. 'It was totally cool!' he insisted. 'The guys were making explosions with cleaning fluid and aluminium foil. It's a trick, but I don't know how they did it – I was trying at home last night, until my mother caught me, but I couldn't get it to work. There must be a knack to it.'

Driscoll felt his pulse quicken. 'You're saying that they *faked* explosions here yesterday?'

223

The kid rolled his eyes. 'Of course! They were playing a game, and some TV guy was filming them.'

'Wow!' Driscoll licked his dry lips. 'Listen, son, what's your name?'

'Cole Harrah.'

'How would I spell that, Cole?'

'Anyway you like, mister.' The boy backed away from him, still reeling in the string, then grabbed his kite and prepared to flee. Driscoll put a hand on his shoulder to detain him.

'Listen, Cole,' he wheedled, 'I really must have you on camera. Nobody has to know about it – we could go behind that bank of dirt over there, just the two of us. I'll pay you well if you'll do it with me.'

The child blanched and ripped his shoulder free. 'Get your hands off me, you filthy bastard!' he squealed, and dodged away through the wreckage.

Driscoll watched him go, aghast. What had gone wrong? Was there something amiss with his interview technique? He was, he had to admit to himself, unused to dealing directly with such plebeian elements . . . Dear God: had he blown his exclusive by failing to nail the boy's story on camera? Perhaps not entirely – he still had his notes of the conversation. And he had the child's name, too, and could use it if he wanted; the boy had foolishly omitted to specify in advance that they were talking off the record. But did that give him enough material to stand up his story, enough so he could leave? This place was giving him the creeps – all these distracted, shambling people in dirty ragged clothes, deficient in morals and vitamins, with their swarming feral children and their stinking open drains ... It was time he got out, while the going was good, before he was rumbled ... But no, goddamn it, he didn't have enough yet, not quite. There was still the Toploader story. And he did have one more lead to follow ...

Driscoll dodged another kick from the donkey.

'Could you take me to this address?' he demanded, showing his notebook to the driver. 'It should be very close.'

CHAPTER THIRTY-ONE

Flora's alarm clock nagged her back to wakefulness. Evil memories jostled for place on the pillow before her, against the cracked white plaster of the wall. She heaved herself into a sitting position, wincing at the pain in her face and her ribs, her feet already reaching for the cold concrete floor.

Ten o'clock, she told herself viciously. She had already given her enemies – Cobra, the little soldier, whoever else might be lurking out there – hours in which to turn up at the apartment and ruin her game. Her feet found her slippers in their usual place, neatly set at the side of the bed, yet they could not slide into them. Looking down, she saw that she was still fully dressed, sneakers and all, in the clothes – now filthy and bloodstained – that she had put on the previous morning.

The door of Gabriel's bedroom was open. Moving as quietly as she could, Flora stepped into the room and opened the wardrobe opposite the bed. She had been saving Jake's clothes for when Gabriel would be big enough for them; the pilot, she judged, was a little taller and somewhat heavier than her dead brother, but at a squeeze his clothes would do.

She took a pair of jeans from a shelf, and a T-shirt and an old woollen sweater, and laid them softly on the foot of the bed. The pilot would need socks and – she reluctantly supposed – underwear too. These were kept in a drawer at the foot of the wardrobe, and despite her efforts to remain silent the drawer squeaked loudly as she pulled it. A head emerged from under a pillow.

'Hello,' said the pilot groggily. His voice sounded loud in the bare concrete room, its walls softened only by a picture of a football team. Pale squares, higher up the walls, showed where Jake's militant posters had once been tacked.

'Hello,' said Flora, not looking at him. 'Did you put your clothes in that laundry bag I gave you?'

The pilot rubbed his eyes and sat up in the bed. He seemed to be naked. 'I did what you told me. The bag's in that basket, hidden under the other clothes.'

'Good.' She wrapped some underpants and a clean T-shirt into a towel and tossed them onto the bed. 'What size shoe do you wear?'

'Forty-five . . .' The pilot, she saw from the corner of her eye, was looking at the ancient PC that sat on a wheeled desk at the foot of the bed. Tony's manual lay on the keyboard, where she had left it the night before.

'Megaware Flight Simulator 2001,' he marvelled. 'That's a real classic, that game. I used to play that all the time.'

She ignored him, picking through Jake's shoes.

'That game's impossible to get now, legally,' he went on. 'It was the last flight simulator game to include the World Trade Center in its 3D model of Manhattan. They had to take it off the market after the attacks, so as not to upset people.'

Flora picked up a pair of shoes and shook them, frowning. The pilot tried again. 'We used to play it a lot when I was in training.'

Flora dropped the jeans on the bed and began looking for a jacket. When she spoke she didn't look at him. 'Why were you playing an old game like that? Surely you'd have had access to professional simulators?'

'Oh, sure,' said the pilot, and looked away from her. 'It was just a kind of retro thing we were into . . .'

. . . Sweat trickled into Moon's eyes, and his hand felt slick on the joystick. Blinking, he hurled his lumbering 767 into the prescribed sequence of high-speed manoeuvres: first an Immelmann turn, then a split S and finally a victory roll, pulling straight and level again just as the nose of his aircraft hit the South Tower, impacting at exactly the right speed and angle for its flaming debris to pepper and ignite the North Tower as well.

There was a silence, and then voices behind him began to whoop and call:- 'Sssstttrike!' Moon shot-gunned another can of beer, as tradition demanded, and then the chief instructor slapped him on the back and pinned his new drone wings to his collar, and eager hands pulled him away from the old PC so that another cadet could take his turn . . .

The girl was picking through another drawer. 'You'd better wash before you get dressed,' she said.

'Why do *you* play that old game?' he asked her. 'Is it the only one you can get in here?'

'No . . .' She turned to look at him. 'That also happens

to be the only flight simulator game in which the Embargoed Zone has its own airport – the game went on sale just before your engineers finished the wall and blew up our runways. When I play it, I can take off from my own home and fly to Paris or New York or Beijing, just like a normal person. And then if I feel like it I can fly back home again.'

She jerked her finger at a pair of sneakers in the bottom of the wardrobe. 'These are only forty-threes, so you should probably wear your own sneakers. They're covered in sick, but they're civilian. And you can have that green jacket, the one on the back of the door.' She prepared to leave the room. 'The bathroom is the next door along. There's a plastic bucket beside the shower stall, about half full of water. You pour the water over yourself with the scoop you'll find floating in the bucket. But leave some water for me - it's expensive. There's soap in there too, and some towels. When you're dressed again meet me in the hall. We have to go outside and take your picture.'

'*What? . . .* Why?'

'I need to take a picture that proves that you're okay, and shows where you are. Then I can try and find a way to send the picture to your bosses, so we can get you out of here.'

'I thought you didn't have any contact with the other side.'

'I know someone who does. A journalist. We'll have to find him, though, which means going to the city on foot. We should be okay, so long as you don't talk to anybody.' A thought occurred to her. 'So if we do get stopped you're going to have to pretend to be simple.'

'*What?*'

'You're my retarded big brother. And please don't argue – it's the best idea I can think of right now.'

Moon had never washed himself with cold water before. When the ordeal was over he felt wide awake, and cold, and very small. The girl was waiting in the hall with an ancient digital camera, almost as big as her hand.

'Come on,' she said, and led him outside. 'We have to be quick, before someone tries to talk to us.' Moon stepped gingerly out of the vestibule and into the baleful light of day. The sun was bright overhead but had yet to warm the street. He had forgotten the jacket, and the wind blew fresh through his clothes. A few people straggled up and down the street, paying no attention to Moon and the girl. A drone bumbled high overhead, and Moon jerked his head back to search for it.

'Wow,' he said. 'Where is it? I've never seen one from this perspective. I wonder who's flying—'

'Shut up and look at the ground!' the girl hissed at him. 'Nobody looks up at the sky here! People think the drones can recognize them.'

'They can. But I want them to see me – then they can come and get me.'

'That's not the point! You'll stand out like a sore thumb, gawping there like that. People will think there's something wrong with you!'

'There is. I'm simple, remember?'

'Shut up and stand over there, in front of that Land Rover.'

She pointed towards a patch of street blackened by a recent fire. The mangled remains of a jeep had been pushed to one side of the road, and a few little boys were picking through clumps of charred debris.

'What happened to that Land Rover?'

'It doesn't matter.' She raised the camera. 'Look at me, please.' She clicked her camera, frowned at the viewing screen and lowered it again. 'Now back inside. I have to wash and change, and then we can get out of here.'

Flora left the pilot in the kitchen while she collected some clean clothes and went into the bathroom. With the door locked, she sat on the lid of the disused toilet, sealed with yards of duct tape to keep in the rats, and took the captain's cell phone and battery from her pocket. The phone had a camera of its own, but she couldn't have used it in front of the pilot; if he had found out that she had her own means of communication he would simply have taken it from her, and made his own arrangements.

She slipped the memory card out of her camera and paused for a moment, steeling herself: this would have to be done as quickly as possible. Once ready, she reconnected the battery to the cell phone and switched on its power. Humming with frustration, she watched the phone slowly boot itself up and connect to a civilian network on the other side of the wall. Then she inserted the camera's memory card into the phone's slot. It was years since she'd held a working cell phone, and this one had an unfamiliar operating system, so it took her three eternal minutes to work out how to attach the photograph to a text message. That done, she assigned the message to the captain's speed dial number and pressed send. As soon as it was gone she released the breath she had been holding and dismantled the phone again.

The weight of the previous twenty-four hours bore down on her now. When she stood up again she staggered, caught herself, then stripped her clothes off and stepped into the shower stall. She would treat herself to a proper wash this time, no scrimping on water. As she poured scoop after scoop over herself the cold cleanness revived her, her hair wet down her back. Then she looked at the floor, and saw the mingled blood of Adam and Gabriel and Tony, running thinly down her legs. It pooled on the tiles and seeped sadly away down the drain.

The pilot was loitering in the corridor when she came out, her hair still damp. 'Come on,' she said. 'We have to move.'

'Let me get that jacket and I'll follow you out.'

Flora took a clean raincoat and a fresh scarf from the hallway, opened the door and stepped out into the vestibule. There was a movement in the shadows behind her, and a hand reached out and grabbed her arm. Flora screamed.

CHAPTER THIRTY-TWO

Captain Smith sat back in his chair and read the text message aloud. 'I have something you are looking for. I will exchange it in return for safe passage overseas for myself and my brother. I want foreign media to witness the exchange to guarantee that all promises are kept. I will contact you again when I am ready.'

'I don't get it,' said Colonel White. 'What the hell is it supposed to mean?'

Captain Smith tapped his fingers on the edge of the drone console, frowning. 'The text itself is clear enough – the girl either has the washing machine or knows where it is, and wants to trade. It's the picture she's attached to the message that's confusing me. I have no idea who this chap is . . .' He puzzled over the picture displayed on his phone. It showed a stooped and slightly stocky young man in jeans and an old sweater, hugging himself against a background of burnt wreckage. Smith zoomed in on the image, peered closer, then turned to the colonel. 'That mess in the background would seem to be the press Land Rover that you took out last night. So even if we don't know who this man is, we know where he was when this picture was taken. Do you know him, Colonel?'

White studied the face for several seconds. 'I've never seen him before in my life.'

'Okay, then, let's run his picture through the biometric database.' He forwarded the text message to his own email account, opened the biometric application on his laptop and fed the photograph into it.

'Ah,' he said after a few seconds. 'Now this really is interesting . . . The face in this picture is not registered in our database of Easy residents. Nor does it belong to any of the journalists and aid workers who we've previously admitted to any of our terrorist enclaves – we take their DNA and full biometrics on their way back out, when we do the full body scan and cavity checks. Which means that whoever this man is, he's not from the Embargoed Zone, and nor has he gone there with our permission.'

'But that can only mean? . . .'

'That's right, Colonel: this man is a foreign infiltrator. And in light of what we've learnt elsewhere in the past day or two, there can only be one conclusion: this is the face of an Iranian agent!'

'Dear God!' The colonel leaned forward to stare at the screen. 'After all these years talking about it, we've actually found one! . . . How do you think he got into the Embargoed Zone, past all our layers of security? Frogman suit? HALO jump? Miniature submarine? I know for a fact that the smugglers would never let him in: they're under strict instructions about what they can and can't bring into the Embargoed Zone – no proper anti-tank weapons, no anti-aircraft missiles, no outside activists and above all, no foreign agents.'

'I don't know how he got there,' pondered Smith. 'He's a clever one, your Johnny Farsee. But all we need to know right now is that he did get in there, and that having done so, he can probably get out again. And he's clearly on the trail of that washing machine.'

'Oh, God!' The colonel covered his face with his hands.

'Now now, sir. There's no need for panic. The girl is offering to sell him to us. All we have to do is agree to whatever terms she asks and then go and fetch him. After Daddy Jesus has had a chat with him, I'm sure he'll be happy to give up the washing machine if he has it already.'

The colonel looked aghast. 'But we can't give her what she wants! Safe passage, yes; asylum, just maybe: but media witnesses to guarantee the handover? That would blow the whole thing wide open! Even if we got the washing machine back, we'd still be court-martialled for running a rogue operation! And for cocking it up, which is even worse!'

Smith glanced heavenwards. 'You really aren't cut out for this sort of work, are you, Colonel? Listen: we can agree any terms we like with the girl, because we don't have to honour them. All we have to do is string her along until she shows her full hand, and then we'll know how to cheat her.'

An idea blundered across the colonel's face, unfamiliar terrain. 'Perhaps you could offer to put them in the programme?'

'Exactly, sir – now you're getting it! I could put them in the programme ... Though not unless I really have to: I prefer to throw back the little ones, whenever I can. Perhaps I'm a little too sentimental ... Now let's get a bite to eat. There's nothing for us to do now but wait for her next move.'

CHAPTER THIRTY-THREE

Flora screamed and jumped away from her assailant, but his grasping arm dragged both of them off balance. She fell, sliding on the wet floor. There was a dull thud against the wall of the vestibule, and Flora saw her attacker stagger, clutching his head in both hands.

'Oww!' the man grunted through clenched teeth. He took one hand away from his head, to steady himself against the wall, and Flora, scrambling to her feet, saw that he was quite bald. He was also positioned between her and the apartment door. Flattening herself against the wall, she inched away from him, working to improve her angle for a dash across the vestibule, to the safety of the street.

'Who are you?' she demanded, hearing her voice waver. 'What are you doing here?'

The intruder swore again, rubbing his head, then turned to squint at her. 'I was just about to knock! And then you frightened me by opening the door all of a sudden, and I tripped over my armour' – he pointed to a heavy bag that sat on the floor.

He took a step towards her. The angles had changed again.

Flora slid back along the wall the way she had come, towards the door of her apartment. It was, she saw, still slightly ajar. 'Who are you?' she demanded again. 'What do you want from me?'

A funny look came over the stranger's face, an ugly combination of nervousness and excitement; he recognizes me, thought Flora. She slid closer to the door, and the stranger took another step towards her. He was very big.

'I've come to have a little talk with you,' he said, showing her his teeth. 'Let's go inside, shall we, for some privacy?'

'Get out!' she screamed, and darted back through her door. Turning fast, she tried to slam it, but a huge foot, clad in some kind of nylon and leather hiking boot, shot between the door and the frame. The stranger swore and the door heaved, hurling Flora back into the hallway. She fled towards the kitchen; if she could only make it into the backyard she might find some neighbours there to rescue her.

She reached the angle of the corridor, skidding into the wall, and tried to accelerate away again. But her old sneakers, worn smooth, slipped on the tiles, and pain seared the sore half of her body as she crashed to the floor again. There was the clump of boots, and she screamed again as she felt the stranger's hands on her.

'Now you hold it right there!' he shouted, pulling her back towards him. 'I know what you've been up to!'

'Let me go!' She struggled, feeling his grip tighten, his breath hot on the back of her neck, his feet shuffling behind her, gaining leverage, and then there was another flurry of movement and the stranger screamed and jerked away from her. She tore free of his grasp and escaped down the hallway.

'You hit me!' she heard him shout as she skidded into the kitchen. There was a thud. 'Ow! You hit me again! ... Ow! Stop doing that, please! For the love of God, that thing might go off!'

Flora's feet faltered. She came to a stop in the yard, just outside the back door. 'Oh,' she said, and she turned and went slowly back through the kitchen.

Her attacker was on his knees in the dimly lit hallway, cringing sideways against the wall, his arms raised to protect his head. The pilot was standing over him, grunting strangely and jabbing the stranger's ribs with the muzzle of his rifle. The stranger saw Flora and raised a hand imploringly. There was blood trickling from his shaved scalp.

'For God's sake, tell him to stop!' he pleaded. 'Ow! Please, tell me what you want me to do, anything at all, but don't kill me! Ow!'

Flora closed her eyes wearily. 'Oh . . . Yeah, right . . . Look: my brother doesn't say much – he's simple. But he does everything I tell him. And if you don't go away right now, I'm going to tell him to shoot you . . . In fact, I'm now giving you thirty seconds to start running, and after that we're coming after you.'

The stranger scrambled to his feet and fled down the corridor. The pilot stood back and whooped in triumph. The front door slammed behind the fleeing man, and Flora hurled herself at the pilot and ripped the rifle from his hands.

'What the hell do you think you're doing?' she shrieked, punching him in the chest. 'You could have ruined everything if he'd worked out who you are! And where did you find that gun? There's a good reason why I hid it, you know. Or are you really retarded?' Her rage was shaking her.

'Hey! I saved your life, or something. And it's your fault that I found the gun. Or did you really think that the last place anyone would look for it was under the bed? I dropped my jacket on the floor and when I went to pick it up there was the gun, looking back at me. And lucky for you, too!'

'I'd have talked my way out of this!'

'Bullshit! Did you see that guy? He had evil and stupid written all over him. I think your wit would have been wasted on him.'

They stood there, glaring at each other. Flora was suddenly aware that she was still holding the little carbine by its muzzle. With a jerk of her arm, she tossed it into her father's workshop. It clattered against the wall and slid down behind a refrigerator.

'We have to go right now. Out the back. That thug might have some friends with him.'

The pilot followed her down the hallway. 'Who was he?'

'He must have been one of Cobra's goons. Cobra threatened to get me.'

'Who's Cobra?' They passed through the kitchen and into the yard.

Flora felt the cold returning to her. 'You don't need to know.'

CHAPTER THIRTY-FOUR

The donkey was tired and fractious from its escapade the night before, and no amount of beating could persuade it to cross the carpet of wet acid soot around the dead Land Rover. Cobra was forced to dismount and lead it through a gap in the rampart of mangled cars. Once off the road, the donkey dug its heels in and refused to move any further. Cobra gripped its bridle close, in case it tried to bite him again, and pulled its eyes down level with his own.

'Listen, you big-eared cunt, I've had enough of your arse-dragging. So guess what – you've just volunteered for my next little mission!'

The donkey twitched its ears contemptuously.

Cobra's whip had just completed its backswing when there was a scuffle of running boots. A man came hurtling out of Flora's apartment building and made blindly for the gap where Cobra's cart was stranded. His flying knees caught the rim of its frame and he tumbled face-down onto its wooden bed, screaming with pain, then spun off to lie in the road. Cobra watched as the stranger rolled from one side to the other, clutching both knees and moaning in agony. He was, Cobra noted with interest, expensively dressed. He was also bleeding from a small cut on his bald head.

Cobra touched the stranger on the shoulder. 'Hey, mister,' he said, putting on a smile, 'are you all right?'

The stranger squinted up at him. 'Please,' he begged, 'get me out of here! I'll pay whatever you like!'

'Pay? . . . What do you mean? What's wrong?'

The stranger tried to struggle upright, but his feet slipped in the dirt. 'Please, help me get away from here. They're going to kill me! They have a gun!'

Cobra backed away from the stranger, looking worriedly about him. 'A gun? Who?'

The stranger grabbed Cobra's hand. 'That terrorist bitch back there, and her retarded brother! They assaulted me! I've got to get out of here before they come after me! Help me escape and I'll make it worth your while.'

Cobra knew of no one on that street who matched the stranger's description, and he knew all of the operators in Hilltown. He also knew an opportunity when he saw it. 'How much worth my while?'

'Two hundred euros.'

'Five hundred.'

'Fine. But for the love of God, let's go!'

Cobra studied the stranger's boots. They looked rather like army boots, only much more up-market. 'Okay . . .' he said slowly. 'Tell you what, if you don't want them to see you, why don't you hide under that tarpaulin on the back of my cart?'

The stranger hurled himself onto the cart and pulled the blue plastic tarpaulin over himself. Cobra tugged and kicked his donkey around until it was facing back down the hill. There was no hurry; he needed time to think. Should he merely rob this idiot and let him go, or would it be better to shoot him first? He took up his whip and climbed back onto the driver's seat. All things considered, he decided, a bullet would be best: the stranger was very much bigger than him, and dangerously mad.

Axles squealing, the cart started back down the hill, the donkey propelled, despite itself, by the weight of the cart behind it. Cobra heard the tarpaulin rustle.

'Are they coming after us?' whispered the stranger. 'Can you see them yet?'

Cobra, who was lighting a cigarette, glanced back up the street. It was quite clear. 'Erm, yeah. They're back there, all right, looking around the place … They have a gun, like you said. You'd best stay hidden under there until I say it's okay for you to come out. Don't worry: I'll take care of you.'

He heard a shuddering sigh under the tarpaulin. 'Thank you,' whispered the stranger.

'Believe me, you're welcome.'

They turned a corner and drove on northward for a spell, until they reached the disused repair shop where Cobra had his place of business. It was deserted, the metal doors open on the black space within. Cobra wheeled the cart smartly inside and reined in the donkey. 'Just make sure you stay hidden,' he told the tarpaulin urgently. 'They're not far behind us!'

'Oh, God!' There was a crackle of agitated plastic. They had stopped in a dark corner of the loading bay, beside the heap of old fertilizer bags. The donkey snuffled and stamped its hooves, the echoes dancing on the concrete.

'Hey,' whispered the stranger. 'It sounds like we're inside now. What's going on?'

'It's a ruse – I'm trying to shake them off,' whispered Cobra, dismounting. He took the pistol from the waistband of his trousers and glanced around. A couple of metal pipes, future mortar tubes, leaned against a nearby wall. Cobra reached with his right foot and kicked the lower ends of the pipes away from the wall so that they fell, clattering and clanging, onto the bare concrete floor. As they did so, he worked the noisy slide on his pistol, coughing loudly for good measure, then gently slipped the hammer forward with his thumb.

The tarpaulin twitched and yelped when the pipes fell, but the stranger said nothing. Cobra took a step closer. 'Hey,' he whispered, 'they're almost here. You need to roll yourself up tight in that tarpaulin, like a carpet, so that none of you sticks out.'

He waited while the stranger rearranged himself into an easily disposable, drip-free package, then raised his pistol to take aim. And then it occurred to him that he didn't know at which end of the package the stranger's head was to be found.

'Hey,' Cobra whispered again. 'Just lie totally still . . . So, uh – I didn't catch your name – why do you think these terrorists are after you?'

The tarpaulin trembled. 'Oh, God . . . I can't tell you my name . . .' Cobra shrugged, raised his pistol and took aim at the talking end of the tarpaulin. There was a gentle click as he thumbed back the hammer. The voice continued: 'The terrorists must know who I am, and that's why they turned on me. It's because of the Toploader, and the Iranian connection. And now they're going to murder me, to cover it all up. Oh God . . .'

Cobra pulled the trigger. His thumb gently eased the hammer back to the safe position.

'What did you just say?' he asked politely.

CHAPTER THIRTY-FIVE

Moon was unused to walking long distances, and his feet were already blistered from his odyssey the night before. The road's remaining patches of tarmac burnt his soles, while the soft sand between them made his heels work back and forth against his sneakers, bursting the blisters and chafing the sores. There was no way to shut out the pain: each step required his conscious attention, as they scrambled over heaps of rubble, threaded their way through piles of rubbish, skipped across rivulets of sewage.

Hilltown was busy with carts and pedestrians passing to and from the UN food depot. People brushed past him, showing him the hems of their cheap skirts and trousers, their filthy plastic shoes. Sometimes a child would look up into his face and Moon, playing the part assigned to him, would stare dully back: perhaps he ought to add some tics to his performance; perhaps every adult here behaved like this. The girl ignored him, unless he lagged too far behind.

'You have to keep up,' she whispered. 'What if somebody tries to talk to you?'

'You could always slow down a bit.'

'Time's not on our side.'

'Then why can't we hire a donkey cart? I'll pay, if you like. I still have some euros.'

'No! I don't need your money. Look: if we get on a cart the driver is bound to try and talk to us. I should have thought that was obvious.'

Moon understood that although she was still plainly terrified, she was no longer frightened of him. Back to that, he told himself, a little regretfully.

After another kilometre they passed from the broken-backed ruins into the more open terrain between Hilltown and the city. The few buildings here were two- or three-storey farmhouses, set in a checkerboard of scorched fields and splintered groves, the fields separated one from the next by sagging strands of wire. Only a few other people straggled on the road, and the girl allowed Moon to fall back a little way, until all he could see of her was the frayed hem of her jeans, bobbing along in front of him. Then her feet slowed, and Moon lifted his head and saw a crowd of people milling around two Red Cross ambulances. The ambulances were idling in the middle of the road, facing away from him, the drivers leaning out of the windows and staring ahead. Three hundred metres beyond them the road was choked between two small but steep hillocks, which rose on either side of it. A bank of dirt and rubble had been bulldozed across the choke-point. Smoke was rising beyond the small hills.

The girl weighed up the situation. 'You stay back here,'

she decided. 'I need to ask those people what's going on.'

Moon tried to object, but she was already walking ahead with hesitant steps. And then he saw that several of the men in the crowd were wearing masks, and carried rifles and RPG launchers.

He cast about for an escape route: there was nothing on either side of him but ragged, wintery groves. Behind him was the nightmare of Hilltown, along a road that his imagination already saw as swept by humming bullets. In a moment of inspiration, he decided to go into the trees and pretend to take a piss: if the girl betrayed him to the terrorists he would be able to see them coming, and could run for it into the grove. He was too frightened to go for real. As he peered through the leafless twigs he saw the girl talk briefly to one of the gunmen, then turn and start back towards him.

Something slammed into the earth somewhere just beyond the hillocks, a dull lurch in the soles of his feet. Then there was another louder, brighter concussion, followed by three jack-hammer bursts of heavy machine gun fire. Moon sank to his knees behind the tree. The crowd in the road split and contracted, balling up in the lee of the ambulances like shoals of frightened fish. The gunmen vanished into the weeds by the road. The girl faltered, glanced over her shoulder, and stepped on again. She reached the point where she had left him and stood, frowning, her hands on her hips, as he skulked back onto the road. Ahead, the people were drifting back into the open, out from the illusory shelter of the ambulances.

253

'The army has blocked the road to the city,' the girl told him. 'We'll have to go another way.' She set off down a path that led through the trees towards the coast.

Moon caught up with her again. 'What were those explosions and that shooting?'

'Just some tanks. They weren't shooting at us. They're invading the next village.'

A standard up-tit operation, Moon realized: uprooting the infrastructure of terror. There would be tanks protecting the armoured infantry and the bulldozers. Sniper teams hidden on the taller buildings – and doubtless, on the two hillocks in front of him – would be watching over the tanks. There would be artillery on standby, and attack helicopters. And above it all, tying the whole thing together, would be the drones. Making an effort, Moon could hear at least two of them, loitering smugly overhead: it was amazing how easily you forgot that they were there, like the cameras in a reality show. He took stock of the nearby farmhouses that rose above the groves. The closest, on the girl's line of march, was a hundred metres away. It stared back at him through glassless windows, its walls a mosaic of discoloured concrete and flaking plaster. There was, he noticed, a small round hole in the wall near the roof: a sniper's loophole, or merely a drain?

Moon felt naked. 'Wait a minute,' he called after the girl. 'There could be more tanks or snipers hidden this way. Or what if a drone sees us? They might think we're terrorists, sneaking off through the trees.'

The girl shrugged. 'There's no other way,' she said. 'Unless you want to go back to Hilltown.'

He had to think about each step again, although the way was level and unobstructed, and the pain in his feet no longer concerned him. The path led them under the walls of the farmhouse. Moon felt a curious tightness in his throat and chest, and an urge to sigh, and to curl his toes and fingers as he walked towards it. The right side of his body, the one facing the house, seemed to swell in size. He dared not look at the house itself, as if it were a dangerous animal, and it was better not to challenge it. An old bicycle lay in the weeds along its wall. Only feet away now, the windows yawned at him, exhaling a musty breath of mildew spores and ancient cooking. They were past the house, crossing the edge of a weedy dirt yard, scattered with faded plastic toys, then entering the groves again. Moon felt the house watching him through the spot between his shoulders, still trying to make up its mind.

The girl tramped onwards. He felt as if he were tethered to her. They left the groves and entered a stretch of fields and scrubby pasture, where smoke rose from kitchen fires, and sheep grazed, and dogs barked from higgledy-piggledy shacks. Cresting a dune, they saw the sea before them, blue and wrinkled and wind-blown, its horizon broken by the grey scaffolds of offshore gas platforms. Closer in, the conning tower of a patrol boat bobbed on the waves, its hull intermittently hidden in the troughs. Moon stared at the boat, then turned to the north, towards the distant grey smudge of the wall and – just beyond it, he knew – the lost Eden of his base.

'It's so close,' he said, but the girl had already started down the dune, slipping and stumbling in the loose sand. Behind them, just over the crest, there was another brace of explosions, dulled now by distance, and the rattle of automatic fire. Invisible jets moaned in from the sea.

They slid down the last few feet of the dune and turned southwards onto the road which skirted the coast. Beyond the road, straggling along the beach, were the houses and huts of what once had been a fishing village, before the army banned boats from taking to sea. A knot of children was hunkered down in the shelter of a beach shack, clutching twigs, while an old woman walked back and forth in front of them, her face veiled against the stinging sand, pointing with a stick of her own.

'What are they doing?' he asked the girl's back.

'Learning the alphabet.'

'What? In the sand?'

The towers of the city reared over the dunes. 'Paper and ink are very precious here. The army doesn't let them in. We can't get chalk either, or textbooks.'

Moon understood now that he had, for some time, been looking for something to fight about. 'That's absurd!' he retorted. 'We would never ban schoolbooks, not even for terrorists' children!'

She answered without looking. 'I didn't say you banned them. You never ban anything, openly – that might look bad overseas. You just stop letting it in, for months at a time, saying it's for security reasons, then let a little bit in, then block it again. It has the same effect as a ban, but without having to admit that you're doing it.'

'Why would we want to stop your children learning? That would just make them even more savage when they grow up.'

The girl stopped and turned. 'Did you see those boys back there at the barricade, the ones with the guns?'

He glared at her. 'I saw the terrorists, yes.'

'Do you know what they were doing there?'

'Planning some terrorism, I expect.'

'Sure, if you like. They were hanging about there, trying to work up enough courage to make a terrorist attack on the tanks you sent in to their village. And if they do attack they'll almost certainly be killed, most likely without even seeing your soldiers, let alone harming them.'

'Serves them right for being terrorists. And what has that got to do with schoolbooks?'

The girl closed her eyes. 'Do you know anything about bullfighting?' she asked finally.

'God. Can't you get to the point?'

'I *am* getting to the point. Apparently, the bulls they use for bullfighting are selectively bred, down the generations, to be fast and strong and aggressive. But they're also bred to be stupid, otherwise they'd be too dangerous to get in a ring with. They'd ignore the red rag and go straight for the man, and kill him every time.'

'Sounds like bullshit to me.'

'There's a lot of money in bullfighting, apparently. Both for the people who fight the bulls and for the people who breed them. And there's power, too. That's why the Roman emperors spent all their money on circuses – the Romans had bullfights in their circuses, along with the lions and gladiators.'

'That is the most cynical thing I've ever heard.'

'Thanks,' she said, setting off down the road. 'I heard my father say it once, in a row with my big brother. My brother didn't listen, but I did. And there was something else my father said: he said that this isn't a real war, it's a war in a bottle. Whenever it suits them, the politicians and generals just give it a shake.'

'So where are your father and brother now?' demanded Moon. 'There was no one else in your apartment.'

'You don't want to know.'

They were rounding a shallow curve of the seashore, and Moon saw the scree of rubble and twisted metal heaped about the feet of the tower blocks ahead. The sun, dipping to the west, shone in the few intact panes still facing the sea. Howitzer shells were stalking the land again, off to the south-east. Smoke rose from several points above the dunes.

CHAPTER THIRTY-SIX

Captain Smith felt indecisive, an unfamiliar sensation for him. On the one hand – the hand which was about to close the door on a fridge full of beer – it really was too soon yet to celebrate: the bird was in this hand, so to speak, but not yet in its cage. On the other hand – the hand which had reached in to gather two bottles – he had never yet failed to win after drawing such excellent cards.

A delicious smell rose from the two steaming plates of goulash and chips set on the tray in front of him. The smell urged yes. But the captain's professional caution, the glare of a blank, random day through the mess-room skylight, told him no. He slid the beerless tray along the rails, bypassing the cakes and the fancy, cellophane-wrapped granola bars, until he reached the till, operated by a pert blonde sergeant who had rather less than the regulation number of buttons done up. Having signed for both meals himself, Smith pushed the tray to its penultimate halt at the condiment and cutlery counter. Then the phone in his pocket rang. Answering, he listened for a few seconds, then abruptly walked out of the mess-room and into the corridor, the phone clamped to his ear. Colonel White reached a hand out to stop him as he whisked past their table, but Smith side-stepped, dipping his hips and shoulders like a good wing three-quarter.

When he returned to the mess a few minutes later he saw that Colonel White had retrieved their tray from the counter and was stealing some of his chips; the colonel's own plate was already wiped clean. White froze, guilty, but Smith ignored him, tripping back to the counter to collect two bottles of beer. He signed for them both with a flourish and returned to the table, beaming at the colonel.

'Wouldn't you like another one of my chips, sir? Please, help yourself.' He opened both bottles and set one down in front of each of them. 'We've just had some very good news.'

Colonel White eyed his beer suspiciously, but scooped up another handful of chips. 'What's that?' he grunted, filling his mouth.

Smith leaned towards him, still smiling, his eyes flicking around the room to make sure that none of the other early diners was close enough to eavesdrop. 'Cobra just called,' he confided. 'Guess what: he's got the Iranian!'

'What? But that's brilliant! How did it happen? I thought the girl had him.'

'That's just it – Cobra picked him up outside the girl's house in Hilltown, about an hour ago. He'd been roughed up a bit, and he was babbling about how the girl was trying to kill him because of the washing machine. I guess he must have worked out that she was going to double-cross him and sell the machine to us, and he made a run for it, while he still could. It looks like I underestimated that girl – she has some serious muscle working with her.'

'No matter. And it's definitely our man?'

'It has to be. He was babbling hysterically about Iran and the toploader – Cobra had to gag him to shut him up. Also, Cobra texted a picture of this guy to Daddy Jesus, which is normal procedure when we take an interest in someone. When Daddy Jesus fed it into the computer it didn't match anyone on our terrorist database.'

'Fantastic! It must be the same guy as the one in the girl's picture! Are you going to compare the pictures to make sure?'

'As soon as I get back to my office. It's a formality, though.'

'So where is this Persian prick now?'

'That's where it gets even better. He's all trussed up and ready for collection. And there's a routine up-tit operation south of Hilltown right now, which Daddy Jesus can use as cover to scoot in and pick up the Iranian. With your permission, of course, sir.'

The colonel raised his beer to Smith. The two men clinked bottles. Smith picked up his phone again, glanced at White, and switched it to speaker.

'Hello, Daddy Jesus?'

'Boss.'

'The colonel says go get him. Just wait until it's getting dark.'

'After I pick him up, do you want me to put him in the programme?'

'Good Lord, no! He's a bona-fide Iranian spook! If we bring him in alive I'll retire on a general's pension . . . No, take

261

him to the lock-up and loosen him up a bit, so he'll be ready to chat when the colonel and I come to see him.'

'Right, boss. Loosen him up. And what about Cobra? Is *he* still going into the programme?'

'No . . . No, I don't think so, Daddy Jesus, not yet. We may still need him to help retrieve the washing machine. We'll just give him some more money, to buy him off for now.'

White took a long pull on his beer and groaned. 'Oh man, how I've earned that . . . Tell me, Captain, where do you propose to get the extra money you need to keep Cobra happy?'

'I was just getting to that.'

The colonel smiled archly. 'How much do you need?'

CHAPTER THIRTY-SEVEN

The attack on 24/7's jeep, coming so soon after Joseph and Tony's big scoop, had driven the rest of the Embargoed Zone's press corps underground. When Flora and the pilot reached the media centre that evening – sore, hungry, no longer pretending to be on speaking terms – the Land Rovers were all parked outside the building, abandoned by their crews. Locked doors greeted the pair on each darkened landing. The frosted glass in 24/7's door was unlit, but Flora knocked and tried the handle a few times, hoping that her uncle might yet be lurking inside. The pilot stood close behind her, trying to recover his breath.

'Let's try the roof,' she said, looking away from him. 'My uncle often goes up there.'

'Your *uncle*?'

The stairs brought them up into the last of the daylight. Flora saw at once that Joseph's couch was empty. But she cast about anyway, amongst the ventilation ducts and service huts and satellite dishes. The pilot leaned back against the parapet, still breathing heavily, and she felt his eyes on her.

'Your uncle isn't here, is he?'

She turned. 'No, he's not. I'm sorry.'

'Couldn't we try his home?'

'He doesn't have one. He lives in his office. He must have gone into hiding, after what happened to Tony.'

The pilot yawned, raising one hand to cover his mouth. 'Okay,' he said, drawing the syllables out. 'Okay,' he said again, 'so there's a Tony in the story now? What do I need to know about this Tony?' When his hand dropped away he was smiling, but not in a nice way.

Flora felt her temper stir. She welcomed it: it was a familiar thing. She leaned against the further parapet, with the sunset behind her, and smiled back at the pilot, equally unpleasantly. 'Okay,' she said, mimicking his cadence. 'I'll tell you about Tony: Tony worked for 24/7 Television, and so does my uncle. Tony was murdered last night, by one of your drones, while he was driving down my street in a press jeep. That's the same jeep I took your picture with earlier, as it happens.'

The pilot bounced away from his wall and stalked across the roof towards her. 'Don't be ridiculous!' he spat at her. 'We respect the freedom of the press!'

He loomed over her, stiff with rage and resentment, and Flora noticed again how much taller he was than her, and stronger, and she remembered for a moment the fear she had felt for him. And then she found herself laughing. At what, exactly, she could not be sure. The pilot had started it, no doubt, but there was much more to it than that: a cartoon image of Gabriel and Tony and herself, hunted merrily through day-glo canyons by fizzing Acme rockets; a glimpse of her father in a heaven of useless appliances;

Cobra, falling off his donkey cart, and his bald bony henchman, begging *her* for his life! And there was Adam, and the surprised, slightly peeved look which had remained on his face after he was dead. Flora closed her eyes and bent forward and laughed until sobs were tearing themselves from her, and tears burned down her face. When she opened her eyes again, still whimpering, she saw that the pilot had retreated several steps from her. The look on his face sobered her. She ought, she heard her mother whisper from somewhere, to remember her manners.

'Please excuse me – it's not you,' she lied, raising a hand to detain him. She saw the bitterness drawing down the corners of his mouth. He backed another step away and half-turned, as if to go.

'Listen,' she called after him. 'You may as well hear what I have to say; you don't have to believe it. My friend Tony really *was* killed last night, by one of your drones. Why exactly I don't know, but it ties in somehow with the washing machine, and with the dead children, and—'

'*Washing machine?*' he interrupted.

Flora saw that she was losing him. 'Okay,' she conceded, 'forget the washing machine – that really is too weird to worry about for now. But everything that's going on is definitely linked somehow to a story that Tony and my uncle shot yesterday morning. I think the army wanted to kill them to cover it up, or something.'

'What story?'

'They filmed a drone strike yesterday morning. It killed some boys who were playing some stupid game near my house.

I was there myself, with my little brother. The story became important in the real world, because 24/7 got really graphic close-up footage. So then the army killed Tony, and my uncle too, for all I know.' She recalled the phone in her pocket, and piously continued, 'and I think the army might be after me and my brother, too. And then, which I don't get at all, there's the whole bizarre business with the washing machine . . .'

She trailed off. The pilot had crossed to the far corner of the roof and was staring to the west. Naval gun boats broke the horizon, patrolling in line a few kilometres apart. The sun had sunk into the sea, dying the water a wintry red. She gave up on him, and crossed the roof. The wall was hidden from here by other buildings, and by the rising ground to the east. To the north, plumes of smoke from the invaded village had merged into one thick cloud, low and flat in the evening inversion layer. She listened for gunfire, but could near nothing except the wind in the wires, the buzz of the drones, and the murmur of tired voices below in the street. The rooftop was a blessed island of indecision, but soon she would have to descend from it, and think of somewhere to go. She went to stand beside the pilot. He spoke without looking at her.

'There's no way I can phone for help without your uncle, is there?' His tone was conversational. 'And the terrorists will kill you if they find me with you . . . I guess I should go it alone now. Try and find my own way back.'

Flora had never hated him more. She made an impatient gesture with her hands. 'Don't be silly. You'd be killed for sure.'

What do you care? his face asked her, without expecting an answer. And to her surprise and further anger, she felt herself stung.

'Oh, stop feeling sorry for yourself! I'm the one who has to live here! All *you* have to do is find a way out.' She put her hand in her pocket, pulled out the cell phone and battery and waved them in his face. 'Look: here's your ticket out of here! Nobody's going to let you die!'

The pilot stared at the objects in her hand. 'What? ...' He started to frown. 'But you told me you didn't have a cell phone.'

Flora gave him her pertest smile. 'I lied!' Then, as the pilot took two quick steps towards her, she began to wonder why she was feeling so smug. He grabbed her upper arms, his fingers biting into them. His face, inches from hers, was white.

'You mean to say' – he ground the words out – 'that you made me walk all the way here, through terrorist patrols and up-tit operations, when we could have just made a phone call from your apartment, and waited for them to come and pick me up? I could have been killed, you stupid bint! So could you! What the fuck were you playing at?'

She shook herself free. 'I had my reasons! I'm risking my life to save yours, and I don't trust your bosses not to cheat me. The way I'd planned it, they'd have to give me what I wanted in exchange for your safety.'

'Oh, yeah? And what's that? Money? Or guns for your terrorist friends?'

'I want to live!' She hurled the words in his face. 'And I

want my little brother to live too! I want them to stop trying to kill us, and to let us both out of this place for ever, so we can look for a real life, in some place that's real!'

'What, just you and your brother?' he sneered. 'Don't you want to save the rest of your family too? Don't you care about them? What about your mum and dad, and that big brother you keep going on about?'

Her anger folded its arms and stepped smartly away from her, watching, intent, to see what she'd do next. It was the pilot who had brought it to this, not her. He had handed her the game, the one she hadn't thought that she was playing. For an exquisite moment, Flora felt she might not be able to keep a straight face. The moment passed.

'They're all dead,' she told him coldly. 'They were killed by your drones. My older brother and mother died two years ago. My father was killed in the jeep with Tony last night – I didn't bother telling you that before. My little brother is in hospital – he was injured in the air strike yesterday morning. He's all I have left now.' She offered the phone to him. 'Here. Make your call. Just press and hold the 1 key and it will speed-dial a creepy little soldier whose friend wanted to rape me last night.'

The pilot was staring at the phone in her hand, or perhaps not quite at the phone, but just past it, as if his attention had been diverted inward, to some other problem. Then, still not looking her in the eye, he reached out his hand and – absentmindedly it might have seemed – collected the phone and the battery.

'You can still set your price,' he told her gruffly, turning

268

away to examine the phone. 'I'll make sure they honour it. They're bound to be grateful to you.'

She snorted. 'I'm not so sure, and I've met them. I think they'll want more than ever to kill me. I know too much about what's going on.'

'And what *is* going on?'

She thought about that. 'I have no idea.'

Rage and energy ebbed from her, and she felt almost unable to stand. She leaned over the parapet, looking down into the street. Only a handful of people were still about, picking their way homewards. Raising her head, she studied the sky until she saw the sun flash red on a tiny, cruciform shape that seemed to hang motionless over the city. Other drones, invisible, whirred in the dusk. They could be looking for me, she thought dully. She laid her arms on the parapet and rested her forehead on her laced fingers, closing her eyes and giving in to the darkness.

She felt a tap on her shoulder, and heard something click on the concrete in front of her. When she opened her eyes the phone and battery were inches from her face.

'Take it,' the pilot said. 'It's not over yet. We can still look for your uncle, and try and handle things your way.'

I ought at least to look at him, she thought. If he were anyone else, I would owe him a smile. Instead, she watched her hand pick up the phone. Guiltily, she stuffed it into her pocket.

'My uncle could be anywhere,' she told the parapet. 'We can't look for him now – it's not safe on the streets after dark.'

'Right ... Well, is there somewhere we can hide for the night? Only we can't stay here: a drone might spot us.'

Don't you want them to spot you? she almost demanded. But she stopped herself in time. It did not seem a fair question right then, to ask or to answer. She applied herself instead to the practical problem: 24/7's office was locked, and if they broke into it others – Cobra, the soldiers – might come there searching for them, or for Joseph ... Then she remembered her uncle's special place, and saw the surprise on the pilot's face. She was, she realized, smiling.

CHAPTER THIRTY-EIGHT

Cobra unhitched his donkey and led it back outside the workshop, tethering it to graze on the weeds by the road. He stationed himself in the shadows inside the door, sitting on the cart with pistol in hand, smoking cigarette after cigarette. Nobody came to trouble him. Beside him lay a seven-foot sausage of blue heavy-duty polythene, tied up with nylon cord. Every now and then the sausage would wriggle and moan, and Cobra would reach back, without looking, and tap it sharply with the butt of his pistol.

'Now then,' he'd say. 'Now then.'

Day drained from the workshop and off down the street to the sea. Still Cobra sat smoking. Finally, as the grass outside the door turned grey, he heard the rumble of a diesel engine. A Toyota twin-cab with UN markings turned in through the door. Cobra blinked as the lights clicked off, then stretched himself and rose. The jeep's door opened.

'Just yourself, Daddy Jesus?' Cobra called, trying to sound hearty. 'Where's the captain tonight?'

Daddy Jesus's bulk billowed from the cab like a slow-motion air-bag. 'Busy,' he grunted. 'Where's the package?'

'All wrapped up for you. Actually, he did the job himself,

which was nice of him. I had to gag him, though. He wouldn't stop bawling and whingeing.'

Daddy Jesus brushed past Cobra and went to examine the sausage. It started to thrash about as Daddy Jesus picked it up and flung it on the floor in the back seat of the jeep. Leaning in, he quietly addressed it.

'You. Make one more move, make any trouble at all, and I will fucking cripple you.' Cobra could not but shudder at the loving menace in Daddy Jesus's tone; he had heard it before, in even less pleasant circumstances. The parcel whimpered once more, then lay still. Daddy Jesus waited a few moments, hoping for an infraction, then grunted again and shut the back door. He was opening the driver's door when Cobra, alarmed, jumped to his feet.

'Hey! Aren't I coming with you? The captain said he told you to take me out!'

With one hand, Daddy Jesus took a car battery from the floor in the front of the cab, turned and walked back towards Cobra. In the gloom of the workshop, Cobra could just make out that he was smirking. A smile was never a good thing, he knew. Daddy Jesus raised his free hand and pushed him gently backwards until he was sitting on the cart again.

'Change of plan. I'll take you out later. The boss needs you to stay live for the next few days. Here – he's sent you that new battery you've been asking for.' He dropped it contemptuously on the cart.

Cobra's face was quivering. 'But he promised to put me in the programme! I've packed a bag!'

'Hey, don't blame me,' protested Daddy Jesus. 'If it was

up to me, I'd put you in the programme right now. I wanted to. But the boss said no. He said he might still have a use for you.'

Cobra stared at him suspiciously. 'You know, the captain never actually told me what this programme involves. What have you got planned for me?'

Daddy Jesus's smile changed, until it almost looked pleasant. 'The plan is that I'll fill you in when the time comes,' he said, and patted Cobra on the cheek.

Cobra felt himself shudder again. 'Well, what about the money you owe me, then? If I'm staying a bit longer there's stuff I'd like to settle. My cousins need burying.'

'How much money did you get from the Iranian?'

Cobra looked innocent. 'What are you talking about?'

'Our friend in the parcel here must have had quite a bit of money on him, unless the girl and her goons already took it. I'll be asking him about that myself, very shortly, when I get him back to our lock-up. And as you know yourself, he won't lie to me.'

Cobra's lips were dry. 'He had three and a half thousand euros in a money-belt, since you ask. I reckon it's mine. I earned it – finder's fee.'

'It's not yours. That money is forfeit to military intelligence. The Iranian belongs to us – him and everything he had on him. But I'll tell you what: you can keep the cash from the money-belt. Let's call it a down-payment on your back pay. You'll get the rest of what's coming to you when I put you in the programme.' He chuckled to himself.

'You bastards!'

'What else did he have on him?'

'A notebook,' said Cobra, reluctantly. 'A very fancy smart phone, and a video camera. Several pens and highlighters, all different colours – blue, red, yellow and green. Mostly green.'

Daddy Jesus stretched out an oar-sized hand. 'Give it all here. Did you find any chips on him?'

'He had some breath mints, but I already ate them.'

'Computer chips.'

Cobra looked puzzled. 'No. Nothing like that. No passport or wallet or any other kind of ID, either. But I only gave him a quick frisk. You'll probably want to search him more intimately when you have him on the other side of the wall.'

'Yes. I probably will.'

CHAPTER THIRTY-NINE

Joseph finished his last cigarette, tossed it out of the car window and put both hands on the steering wheel. The grain of the wood reassured his fingers. He sighted with one eye down the centre of the bonnet, watching it stretch away from him, beige and gleaming, towards the green roller door at the end of the garage. His feet found the pedals, and he allowed one hand to slip from the wheel, falling, as if from long habit, onto the gear stick.

'Vroom,' he ventured aloud, rolling the 'R'. 'Vroom *vroom* . . .'

He was working the clutch and the gear stick – just a little heel and toe drill, he told himself – when he heard a scraping noise from the front of the garage. He became very still. Had he imagined it? Could it have been the wind? And then he heard it again, louder this time. It was definitely coming from the door. And he was sure that he saw the roller door move a fraction. Someone was trying to get in.

With exquisite care, he lifted the spring-loaded latch on the car door. Meanwhile, his other hand reached across his body to hold the door closed, so it would not pop audibly open. There was the faintest of clicks as the latch gave and then, slowly exhaling, Joseph allowed the door to glide open six inches. He was about to bring his knees across, to slip quietly out of the car, when the garage door thundered.

Joseph shot, as if propelled by an ejector mechanism, out of the driver's door, and pressed himself against the wall. Someone was pounding on the door. He caught his breath: if he could only keep quite still, and wait, they might give up, whoever they were, and go away . . . And then he saw that his discarded cigarette had fallen into a heap of oily litter, which was smoking alarmingly. He stretched out a foot to tramp the fire out, but his toe caught an old oil can that lay hidden in the rubbish, and it skittered rowdily off into a pile of clinking cans and bottles. There was a moment's silence, and then the pounding redoubled. The door shuddered and jerked as someone tried to wrench it upward. Joseph crouched down, his back against the wall, and cringed, despising himself.

'Hey!' called a female voice. 'Uncle Joseph? Are you in there? Please open up: it's me!'

'Flora?' Joseph felt his knees stiffen, as fear turned to fury. 'What the fuck are you doing out there? You frightened the shit out of me!'

'Sorry,' she answered, calling through the strips of the door. 'We looked for you at the media centre, and then I thought we'd come here, to hide for the night. Please, open the door before somebody sees us.'

Joseph squeezed along the gap between car and wall to

unlatch the door and heave it upwards. His niece ducked in from the alley, followed by a tall, scared-looking kid he'd never seen before. Joseph pulled the door down again and tripped the latch with his foot. There was still a little daylight in the garage, from a window set high in one wall; Joseph could just see his visitors' faces, but their bodies were lost in the shadows. Joining them at the dark end of the garage, he peered at the stranger again, trying to make him out, then kissed his niece on both cheeks. 'You know about Tony, I guess,' he said.

'My dad was in the car with him, Uncle Joseph. He's dead too.'

He could only stare at her. 'Oh God, Flora . . .' he said, finally. 'I didn't know.'

I should embrace her, he thought. But she's always been so formal . . . He reached both hands out to her and she held them for a moment, firm in her own, then pushed them away.

'You don't have to say anything,' she said. 'There isn't the time. Listen: do you have your camera with you?'

'I've always got my camera with me: I'm a professional. For the time being, at least – my bosses think I faked yesterday's footage and they'll fire me, if they can find me . . .' The youth, he noticed, had moved to the front of the car and was fiddling with the bonnet. 'Hey, son!' he called. 'Don't touch that!'

'Listen,' said Flora. 'We need to video this guy, and then we need to send the clip to a mobile phone on the other side of the wall. Can you do all that?'

Joseph rammed his hands in his pockets. 'Flora. What the hell is going on here? Who is this kid?'

'He's an air force pilot. He's lost in the Embargoed Zone.' Joseph sat back on the tail fin of his car. He felt the rivets on his jeans grind against the paintwork.

Flora went on: 'I found him, and I'm going to try and get him out in return for a way out of here, for Gabriel and me. Would an exclusive like that help you to make things right with your bosses?'

Joseph jumped to his feet. 'Better than that! A story like that could get me out here, with you and Gabriel . . .' Joseph looked across at the pale blur of the stranger's face. 'Hey kid, is this true? Are you really a *pilot*?'

The blob nodded. 'Uh, yeah.'

'Fuck me! . . . Come on, let's step outside.'

Joseph took his camera from a metal shelf in the corner, opened the roller door and then stooped and peered outside. 'It's clear,' he said, and scrambled out under the door. Flora passed him the camera, then followed. The pilot came out last of all.

'What do you want me to do?' he asked, looking warily around him. They were standing in an unpaved alley lined on both sides with lock-up garages and workshops and fenced-off junk-filled yards. They were alone. The media centre was visible above the eastern end of the alley, recognizable from the dishes and aerials sprouting from its roof.

Flora thought for a moment. 'Just look at the camera and say your name and the date, and that you're trapped inside the Easy and that you want to go home. Tell your family that you love them, or something. I'm sure they'd appreciate that.'

'I don't have any family. They all died years ago.' Joseph, setting up his tripod, glanced over: the kid sounded pleased with himself, for some reason. Flora did not seem to hear him. The kid waited a few moments and then tried again.

'Do you want me to say that you're treating me well?' he asked, sarcastically.

'That's up to you.'

'I suppose it would be polite.'

When they had finished they retreated into the garage and rolled down the door again. Flora lit some candles and set them on shelves and crates, their light dancing on the car's polished skin. Joseph installed himself, along with his laptop and camera, in the back seat, pushing to one side a tangle of blankets and pillows, and Flora pulled an old bar stool over and sat by the open car door, so she could brief her uncle on her scheme. Meanwhile, the pilot made his way slowly around the car, furtively dragging his hand along its curves.

'That's a nice old car,' he ventured.

'Yeah?' said Joseph, distracted by his keyboard. 'It's a Triumph 2000. My dad bought it a long time ago, back in the good old days, before they walled us up in here. He was a real car-lover. Come to think of it, the guy he bought it from was a pilot, like you. He made us promise that it was going to a good home.'

The pilot finished his orbit of the car and halted by Flora. 'Does it still go?'

'Oh, sure. It helps to keep me sane – polishing it, fixing it up, turning the engine over sometimes. It makes a wonderful noise.'

'Where do you get the petrol?'

Joseph was frowning at the screen. 'It's not a question of *where*, son. It's a question of *when* – I still had half a tank in it when the army stopped letting the smugglers bring fuel in. There must be four or five litres left in it still . . . Not that it matters, since your drones started attacking all private cars on sight . . . I'm ready to compress this file now, Flora, and then we can send it.'

'I've got an army cell phone.'

Joseph looked up at her. 'Really? . . . Is it his?'

'No.' She wouldn't meet his eye. 'Look: I'll explain about that later. The number we want is on speed dial – when you've set up the message just press and hold the 1 key. Here.'

Joseph did not take the phone. 'You said you wanted to stay hidden until the exchange is about to happen, which means we can't use that thing. They'd be able to trace its signal instantly. We should send your message over the internet.'

'You have internet? In *this* place?'

'No. But we have a wireless network back in the office, and this garage is just within range of it. If we route the text message through a Skype account, then your pals in the army' – he scowled – 'won't be able to fix our position so easily.'

CHAPTER FORTY

Captain Smith lay on his back, eyes closed, trying to ignore the pressure of his bladder. He wasn't getting any younger, and he should not have had that second beer, still less the fourth or fifth one. But the colonel had been insistent, and they were spending the colonel's money . . . It was warm beneath the doubled-up army blanket, and the folding camp-bed was adequate for a man of his size. The wind nestled agreeably in the eaves of his office, and the roof creaked like an old wooden ship riding a gentle sea. He was going to be rich, he reminded himself: perhaps his wife would let him go with them to Paris? . . . If only he could get back to sleep again. He had had so little rest the night before, and something else was nagging him, something other than the insistent call of nature, something he'd forgotten . . . Then his cell phone rang, and he opened his eyes, cursing himself: he had left it recharging on his desk, on the other side of the room.

Emerging fully dressed from the blanket, Captain Smith tap-danced across the darkened office and flicked his desk light on, fumbling for the phone.

'Daddy Jesus?' he yawned. 'Are you back? . . . Well, I'm at

the office. When you get here, put the Iranian in the lock-up and I'll stroll over as soon as the colonel arrives. He's very keen to see the prisoner for himself . . . Yes, soften him up a little – I'll leave the details to you, if you don't mind.'

Smith left the phone on his desk and skipped over to the door which led to the anteroom and, beyond it, the toilet. His hand was reaching for the doorknob when his phone beeped twice, loudly. Swearing, he darted back to the desk, snatched up the phone and took it with him through the door.

Silence returned to the office, apart from the sound of the wind, and a faint hum from the photocopier/scanner. And then, echoing from the toilet, reverberating through the anteroom, came a terrible bellowed oath, and an instant later the captain shot back into the office, his flies still disordered, and hurled himself across the desk. Grabbing the land phone, he punched in a number.

'Colonel? We have a massive problem. I can't explain on this phone – I'll meet you outside the drone room in ten minutes . . . Yes, I'm deadly serious – we are one hour away from being utterly fucked!'

The colonel was lurking in the shadow of the doorway, and Smith collided with him as he came panting down the ill-lit corridor. He shoved his cell phone in the colonel's face.

'Take a look at this!' he said, and pressed play. The colonel watched, puzzled.

'Now read the text!' urged Smith. The colonel pressed the menu key and read. 'They're going to tell the press about the Iranian, within the hour!' he said, aghast. 'How the hell are we going to keep a lid on this now?'

He threw open the door to the drone room. It exploded inwards, smashing into the wall. The two duty drone jockeys jumped in their chairs.

'Fuck off!' Colonel White screamed at their astonished faces. 'Get the fuck out of here now!' They fled wordlessly into the night. Smith logged on to the tactical computer as the colonel hurled himself at the drone controls.

'What kind of a name is Moon, anyway?' he demanded. 'Is it Farsee, or Turkic, or whatever the hell kind of language they speak in Iran? It sounds oddly familiar. And why is he only a poxy lieutenant?'

'Don't be stupid,' muttered Smith, checking his screen. 'That's not his real name or rank. He's still trying to maintain some kind of cover, like the top agent he is – the girl obviously hasn't broken him yet ... Damn: this message wasn't sent over the mobile phone network.'

'What does that mean?'

'It means they sent it using an internet account. Which means we don't know where they are – if they'd used a cell phone we could've traced its signal.' The captain plunged his face into his hands and became very still apart from one index finger, which slowly tapped his temple. The colonel jumped to his feet.

'Oh, no! If the girl still has the Iranian – which she clearly does, judging from this video clip – then who is Daddy Jesus interrogating?'

The captain's index finger stopped tapping for a few

moments, then started again. 'It doesn't matter . . . Not important right now,' he muttered. 'What's important right now
is that they say they're going to send this clip to 24/7's
London bureau within the hour . . . Sure, 24/7 won't broadcast the clip straight away: they'll sit on the story until
closer to the supposed handover, so they can have exclusive
coverage for themselves. But let's face it: once 24/7 has any
footage at all we'll never be able to make this story go away
again; it's bound to come out sooner or later . . . And if that
happens, we'd be lucky to end up in prison: if I were in
charge, I'd give us both to Daddy Jesus . . .' Smith raised his
face from his hands and looked grimly at the colonel, who
was staring back in open-mouthed terror. 'I hate myself for
saying this, Colonel, but there's only one thing for it – we're
going to have to do this your way.'

'Right . . . What way is that?'

'We're going to have to kill them before they can send
that footage. We need to throw everything we have at them!'

White slumped, despairing. 'But we don't even know where
they are!'

The captain took out his phone and played the clip through
again, holding the screen close to his face. Then he looked
at the colonel. 'Actually, we do know where they are – sort
of. They're somewhere within a few hundred metres of the
Easy's media centre – that's the building where all the
foreign-owned press bureaux are based. You can just see a
couple of the broadcast dishes in this shot, on that rooftop
in the top left-hand corner . . .' He smacked the console. 'Yes,
that's it! They must be using one of the centre's wireless

networks to communicate with us. It's one of the few places in the Easy that we're still forced to allow to have the internet.'

'But that means they could be anywhere within a few hundred metres of that building. We need to be much more specific than that; we can't just carpet-bomb that big a radius in the middle of a crowded city – someone might start asking questions.'

Captain Smith lowered his face into his hands again. The finger tapped his temple some more. When he raised his face again, White saw that he was smiling.

'Then we'll just have to do it the old-fashioned way!' Smith said, and took a land phone from the console. 'Hello? Switchboard? Put me through to the artillery, please.'

CHAPTER FORTY-ONE

To conserve its battery, Joseph had set his computer to run at minimum processor speed. With each instruction the screen froze for several seconds, then shook itself awake again. Flora and the pilot drew close, watching, as he edited the clip to a usable length. Then a new window popped up on the screen, uninvited, and the computer began to chime at them.

'They're calling us back!' said Joseph. 'Here, Flora.'

He tried to pass her the computer, but Flora shook her head. 'You do the talking, Uncle Joseph. I want them to know they're dealing with someone with connections in the real world.'

'Me? You're sure?' She nodded. 'Well, I hope you're right, only you've been the brains so far . . .'

He clicked on the computer. Flora and the pilot leaned in through the window, their heads almost touching.

'Hello again, Flora,' said a voice from the computer, distorted by the long-range wi-fi connection. 'You say you have what we're looking for.' Joseph and the pilot looked at Flora. 'It's him,' she mouthed silently.

Joseph addressed the computer. 'You're not talking to Flora.

This is Joseph West – Easy bureau chief for 24/7 Television News. Flora has asked me to talk on her behalf. What's your name?'

'Me? . . . Well, Brown, I suppose. And you must be Uncle Joe. Tell me: is the girl listening to us?'

Joseph looked at Flora. She nodded. 'Yes,' he said.

'Good . . . Then we can get down to business. We agree to your terms. We only ask that you delay sending the advance footage to your London bureau for the time being. If the news leaks out from there before the exchange takes place you'll have every terrorist in the Embargoed Zone combing the streets for you. Even if they didn't find you, which they probably would, it would make it very difficult for us to extract you.'

Joseph looked at Flora again. She shook her head. 'I can't do that,' he said. 'That footage is our guarantee that nothing funny will happen.'

'Really? . . .' There was a click and a long pause, and then the voice resumed. 'So, if you can just tell us where you are, I'll start making preparations for your extraction.'

Flora shook her head so violently this time that she accidentally butted the pilot.

'No,' said Joseph. 'We're not telling you where we are until our footage is sitting in 24/7's in-tray. But I'll tell my bosses to embargo the story until we're ready to show the pilot being handed over live, via the internet.'

'One moment, please.'

Captain Smith pressed the hold button on his cell phone.

'*Pilot?*' Colonel White demanded. 'What the hell does he mean by *pilot?*'

'The Iranian must be a pilot,' said Smith impatiently. 'They would naturally use someone with an aviation background for a mission like this.'

He picked up the land phone from the console. 'Hello, Fifth Battery CP? Could you put one ranging round – high explosive, if you please – on the coordinates I already gave you? Then wait for further instructions. Thanks so much.' He put the receiver down and activated his cell phone again.

'That will be fine, Mr West,' he continued. 'Would you like to tell us where you and your niece wish to go after we extract you, or shall we wait until we can talk face to face? By then we should have established some trust, eh?'

'Once you have the pilot, and 24/7 has the exclusive, trust won't be an issue for . . . Holy God! What was that?'

Smith gave Colonel White a silent thumbs up. 'What?' he asked the phone anxiously. 'Is there something wrong, Mr West? Did I just hear some kind of explosion or something?'

Bruised and breathing heavily, Joseph picked himself up from the ground. Moon, hurled to the front of the garage when Joseph flung his door open, had banged his head against the roller door. Flora sprawled against a half-toppled rack of tools and old car parts. The computer lay on the floor in the car's rear foot-well. Joseph picked it up and sat in his seat again.

'We're still here . . . There was a big explosion, pretty close by. I heard a whoosh just before the bang – some kind of artillery shell. What the hell is going on, Brown?'

'I don't know, Mr West, I really don't. I just thank God you're okay. Let me check something on my tactical computer

289

here . . . Oh dear . . . Oh dear . . . Look, Mr West, there may be a bit of a situation developing . . . The tactical computer tells me that several artillery-fire missions are starting right now – just routine interdiction barrages, fired at random map references to send a message to the terrorists. Unfortunately, you must be very close to where one of the ranging shots fell, which means you could accidentally be caught up in one of those bombardments.' Smith winked at the colonel. 'Now, I'm not asking you to tell me where you are, or anything like that, but if you could just tell me where and how far away that particular shell fell *in relation* to where you are now, compass-wise, I can instruct all of the artillery batteries to shift their fire in the opposite direction. That way you'll be safe, no matter where you are.'

'I'm not sure I follow you, but anyway: that shell must have fallen due south of us. I can't say how far exactly. Maybe a hundred and fifty metres or so.'

'Excellent . . .' Captain Smith pressed the hold button and picked up the landline. 'Hello, Fifth Battery? Adjust fire one hundred and fifty metres due north . . .' He nudged the colonel. 'Old-school but effective, eh? Who needs lasers and GPS and anti-radiation homing systems?' The colonel scowled at him.

'Okay, everything's taken care of now,' Smith told his cell phone. 'Now tell me, Mr West, what are your preferences for the post-extraction period? Will you be wanting publicity for your own role in this rescue? You could be a hero on the lecture circuit.'

'Are you kidding me? I want you to say that you abducted

the kids and me when you picked up the pilot. We don't want to look like traitors. Who knows, maybe someday we'll be able to go home again, if the walls come down.'

'Who knows indeed? – Dear Lord! What was that?'

This time the explosion was so close that its shock wave threw Flora and Moon to the ground. The walls of the garage heaved, and dust poured from the roof and rose from the floor, acrid and choking. Motor parts and tools clattered off the shelves. Flora and Moon could barely see each other as they dragged themselves to their feet again, trembling from shock. Moon's head throbbed, as if it had been kicked. Joseph coughed and spluttered, gagging on the dust.

'Brown!' he screamed. 'They've gone the wrong way! That last shell was almost on top of us!'

'Oh dear! What a dreadful mistake! . . . Did it fall just east of you, or west?'

'You treacherous bastard!' Joseph, tears of dirt streaming down his cheeks, cut the connection. He looked at Flora. 'He's trying to kill us! Don't you see what he's doing? He's getting you to tell them where to shoot!'

Moon slid in behind the steering wheel, settling his hands on it. 'I get it now,' he said. 'They want me dead, not alive! I know too much: they're afraid that now I'm in touch with the media I'll go public about all the terrible stuff I've done.'

Flora stared at him. 'You? Terrible stuff? You seem pretty geeky to me . . .'

'I *am* a geek – I'm a drone pilot, not a real pilot!' He looked at her imploringly. 'It was *me* who fired that missile yesterday morning, the one that hurt your brother and killed all those other kids! God knows what else I've done over the past couple of years. They give me a target and I engage it, that's all I do … And the targets are always terrorists …'

Joseph reached between the seats and punched him on the shoulder. 'You self-important little prick! The army doesn't give a shit about stuff like that. What happened yesterday happens all the time here; all they have to do is cook up some half-arsed denial and they're back in the clear. They couldn't care less about you, so long as you don't get killed or captured, and get your picture in the news. But if people know that you're here they'll have to do a deal to rescue you.'

'That's just it! I don't think anybody else *does* know that I'm here. Which means it could be easier for them to cut their losses!'

'And to keep it secret,' concluded Flora, 'they'll need to kill us as well.'

Another shell slammed to earth, right outside the garage, and then another, and another. Flecks of twilight appeared in the dust and the cordite smoke, as shrapnel tore holes in the roller door and skittered along the walls. As one, they ducked inside the car, seeking the frail protection of its metal skin. The windscreen was speckled with stars.

'Well, that's that,' commented Captain Smith. 'Now that the Fifth Battery is firing for effect, the rest of the Sixth

Regiment will join in and lay a standard concentration on that area. It might flush our friends out into the open, in which case you can get them' – he indicated the drone console. 'And if they stay put, well' – he gestured at the screen which was relaying footage of the scene. Shells were falling every few seconds, flashing white for an instant then blossoming into filthy clouds of smoke and debris. A whole city block, a post-industrial jumble of two-storey warehouses and one-storey lock-ups, was crumbling into rubble and flame.

Colonel White looked sad. 'I can't help thinking about that washing machine, Smith. Do you think it's down there, somewhere, in all of that?'

'Most likely. This West fellow must have been working an angle all along – him, his niece, and his mate Tony, the one you killed yesterday. The Iranian must have hired them to help him, perhaps because of their access to motor transport. But then they decided to double-cross him, and sell the washing machine to us instead. So they brought it here in their jeep yesterday, and stashed it close by their office. Probably in one of those lock-ups down there. We can send Cobra to look for what's left of it later. Enough of the chip might survive . . .' He shook his head. 'It was a pretty smart play, from their point of view: if only they hadn't decided to drag 24/7 into it, and forced us to do this.'

'But we'd have had to kill them anyway, to shut them up.'

'Yes, but we'd have done it neatly. Professionally. Not

like this ...' Smith gestured sadly at the shell-bursts on the screen.

With each impact it felt as if all the air were being sucked from the room, then allowed to smack home again. The concussions slammed into Moon's skull, pounding his chest and abdomen. Jagged holes appeared in the walls of the garage, and smoke flashed mauve with each new shell burst. The car rocked and danced on its ancient suspension, and shrapnel scuttled around the walls of the garage like rats frantically seeking escape. The girl was lying on top of Moon, her weight jamming his face against the pedals. He put an arm around her, as if to protect her, and she turned her face to him. They were inches apart, but he had to shout at the top of his voice to overcome the thunder of the shell fire, and the ringing in his ears.

'We need to get out!' he bawled. 'I know how this works: they'll keep firing until they've flattened the whole area!'

'That would be suicide! Our only hope is to lie here.'

Moon wriggled out from underneath her. 'We can't stay here! Even if we survive the shellfire, as soon as it stops they'll send people to look for us! What about the car? Can't we use that to escape?'

Joseph had shoved his head forward between the seats. 'Don't be stupid: the drones would destroy the car in seconds! Besides, it doesn't work.'

'But you said that it did!'

'That was just something cool to say. In real life it was

always rubbish. We had to tow it in here after my dad bought it.'

The Triumph bucked as if stung by the revelation, and shrapnel ticked through a body panel.

'We can't just stay here and wait to die!' shouted Moon. He opened the driver's door, then wormed out from under the girl. She tried to stop him but he pulled himself free and staggered to the roller door.

'Come back!' she shouted, 'You can't go out there!'

Moon turned at the door and showed her the phone which he had stolen from her pocket. 'I can try and draw their fire!' he shouted. Then he pulled up the door, and vanished from her sight.

The alley was full of smoke and dust, so thick that Moon could barely see his hands. A shock wave hurled him to the ground and he cowered there gratefully, face pressed into the rubble, head covered by his arms. His lungs were seared by brick dust and the hot reeking fumes of explosives. He had hoped that he might find some pattern to the shellfire, something he could work with, to move in leaps and bounds, like they did in the movies, but the explosions, every four or five seconds now, hammered their point home to him: there was no way of cheating this game, he'd just have to play it. Blindly – his eyes burnt, or clogged, or simply shut; he didn't know which any more – he crept and crawled. Rubble bruised and snagged him, and shell fragments seared his hands and knees. He vomited. Blast waves battered him, and he knew that at some point he must, having had no say in the matter, have fouled himself.

He was crawling again. A shell blasted him sideways, and his shoulder struck metal, which swung away from him: he had somehow found a door. He wriggled his body around it. Another shell sucked the door shut, just as he pulled his foot clear of it. He was inside.

Moon lay still for a while, waiting for his eyes to clear. There was a heavy, almost stinging smell of must and ammonia. Beneath him was a concrete floor, scattered with a fragrant substance that scratched his cheek. Another salvo of shells crumped into the alley outside, and Moon, surfeited with terror, was merely puzzled to hear screams and bellows erupt all around him, with a frenzied drumming sound and the splintering of wood.

He crawled a couple more feet into the room, pushing his face along the prickly mass on the floor. He could recognize the smells now: urine, animal shit and straw; opening his eyes, he saw that he was in a stable, warmly lit by two overhead light bulbs and lined on either side with wooden stalls. Four of the stalls were occupied by panicking beasts of some kind, blurs of bloodstained, drumming hooves and foam-flecked teeth, frantic to escape this hideous storm. A fifth animal had already kicked its way free of its stall, and Moon saw it cowering against another door in the further wall, a thick steel door, mounted on heavy-duty sliding rails and painted an oddly-familiar shade of gunmetal grey. The beast was a donkey. Another shell fell, and the donkey reared on its hind legs and clawed with its front hooves at the unyielding metal door, lips curled back from teeth bloodied and broken. The donkey saw him and wheeled around to face him, braying hysterically. Moon, still sitting, scooted slowly back against the door he had come through. You don't want to get killed by a donkey, he told himself. That would be taking the joke too far. He fished the phone and battery out of his pocket, fumbled them together, switched on the phone and pressed 1. And as he did so something occurred to him: from where, he idly wondered, did those light bulbs get their current?

Colonel White was lighting another cigarette when Captain Smith's cell phone, face up on the console, started to buzz. The two men looked at it, and then an alarm beeped in the drone console, and a flickering pink disk appeared on the lower left-hand corner of the video screen, on the edge of the bombarded zone. The phone rang again, once, then twice more, and as it did so the circle on the screen slowly contracted and adjusted its centre, until it formed a hard, red dot, overlaying what looked like a two-storey warehouse.

'It's them, on the phone, in that building!' White crowed. 'They're trying to cut another deal with us! And now we know exactly where they are!' The phone rang again. 'Aren't you going to answer it?'

Captain Smith picked it up. 'Hello? Yes? . . . Moon, you say? How nice to hear from you – one moment please.' He pressed the hold button. 'It's the Iranian.'

'Great! What shall we say to him?'

'Nothing. Let's just get this over with. Can you please direct an anti-radiation missile onto that signal?'

'With pleasure!' The colonel made some adjustments to his controls, flicked a couple of switch-covers to the 'on' position and then thumbed a large red button on the end of his joystick. The two men watched the screen until a white blur streaked across it and the warehouse vanished in a burst of white light and a ball of swirling darkness. A single pale pressure wave pinged across the screen.

'That ought to give them something to think about!' exulted the colonel. He glanced at Smith, his face flushed. 'I have to admit, in some ways this is actually more fun than flying a real aircraft! You can really see what's going on!' He checked the screen again. 'The cell phone signal has disappeared! We got them! Now, what shall I try next, to confirm the kill? Maybe I'll bring up a second drone, one that's packing a little white phosphorus – cook them nice and slow, eh?'

Captain Smith stared blankly back at him until the colonel, unabashed, returned to his video game. Then Smith picked up the desk phone. 'Hello, Sixth Regiment CP? Please have all guns adjust fire onto these new co-ordinates' – he mouse-clicked on the warehouse. 'Target is a two-storey building, terrorist base. Ten rounds HE per gun, delayed fuse, fire for effect. Then you can stand down your detachments.'

The first shells fell a few seconds later, pulverizing what was left of the building. Colonel White swore, then flung down his joystick.

CHAPTER FORTY-TWO

Flora and Joseph lay in the old car, curled up like sleeping runaways. The barrage swelled to a ground-heaving drum-roll, spattering the car with falling masonry, and then it seemed to shift away from them, even more intense now, and then the shells stopped falling. The only sound was the whine of tinnitus. Painfully, Flora extricated herself from the pedals and gear stick and climbed back onto the passenger seat. It was covered in little chunks of wind-screen glass, too small and blunt to cut her. Joseph shifted on the back seat. It was too dark for them to see each other, and they were too deafened yet to talk. They sat there together for a few minutes, resuming their identi-ties, and then they each pushed open their door, straining against the debris piled outside. Joseph peeled back the remains of the roller door and peered out into the alley.

'We should go,' he said, shouting against the hum in his ears. 'Before they send someone.'

The alley was filled with broken blocks and splintered wood and torn plastic. Flames licked the tumbled buildings, their smoke sheltering the two fugitives from the sky. They had to pick their way over heaps of rubble barbed with twisted steel and torn roofing, pulling their shirts over their faces to gasp the poisoned air. An unexploded howitzer shell ticked as it cooled, half-buried in the rubble; they tiptoed around it, and found their way blocked by the remains of a much larger building, ploughed and harrowed and sifted by the shells. The rubble flooded the mouth of the alley, spilling into the street beyond. A bright metal sign lay on top of the ruins.

'"Donkey Sanctuary", Joseph read, disbelieving. '"Wanted: war-donkeys. Rewards paid."'

Flora ignored him. 'I don't suppose he survived all that,' she said.

They walked on a few more yards, and then Joseph spoke again.

'He's underneath all of this, somewhere . . . You do understand, Flora, that we can't ever mention him again? If anybody here finds out we tried to help him we'll be killed as collaborators. So forget you ever heard his name.'

'I never did hear his name. I never told him mine, either.'

'Really? . . . Well, I suppose he's not worth mourning – he did run out on us in the end.'

'I wonder.'

They came to the edge of the beaten zone, where the last flames guttered on the wreckage. Before them, a street gaped black and perilous beneath the open sky, a river to be crossed.

Joseph stopped, considering. 'So we're back where we started. You and Gabriel are stuck here in the Easy, on somebody's hit list for God knows what reason. And I'm still going to lose my job, and whatever privileges I have left: my bosses will fire me if I don't hand over all the footage that I shot yesterday. And they'll do worse than fire me if I do give them the disk and they see all the stuff that I didn't send.'

Flora shook her head, impatiently. 'Honestly, Uncle Joseph . . . Do you have the disk on you now?'

'Sure.'

'Can I see it, please?'

Doubtfully, he took a plastic cartridge from his pocket and handed it to her. With a flick of her wrist she tossed it into the heart of the fire. Joseph leaped after it. 'For God's sake, Flora, what are you doing?' He tried to reach for it, but the flames were too hot, and already the plastic was blackened and melting.

'That disk was in your Land Rover, Uncle Joseph,' Flora explained, slowly and carefully, as if speaking to a child. 'It was destroyed yesterday, when the drones killed Tony and Dad. Do you understand what I'm saying?' She glanced at the humming sky, steeled herself, then sprinted off across the road. Joseph stared after her, then roused himself and followed.

'That's pretty clever,' he admitted, joining her in the shadows on the other side of the street. They were almost at the media centre now. 'But what will you do now?'

She made an effort to smile. 'I'll just have to hope that they leave us alone.'

Captain Smith watched the two glowing figures as they stood conversing in the shadow of a wall. He clicked a menu option, slid his finger along a scale, and the camera zoomed in, the image brightening and sharpening as the camera switched from infrared to intensified starlight. One of the figures looked up for a moment, as if suddenly aware of him. Smith saw her face and smiled. Colonel White looked up suspiciously from his controls.

'Look! Those terrorists down there are breaching the curfew! Let's kill them! They're breaking the law!'

Smith yawned and rubbed his eyes, then pushed his chair back and stood. 'It's not worth it, Colonel. They're just some wretched survivors from the bombardment, I expect.'

Smith switched the camera back to infrared. The girl darted off across the road, a shining aurora in the heat-sensing image, and a moment later her companion followed her. Together again, they vanished down an alleyway.

Smith stretched, flung both his arms back, then reached for his cell phone. 'We have more serious business to worry about,' he told White, and dialled. The phone rang for a long time before it was answered.

'Hello, Daddy Jesus? . . . Yes, sorry: we were delayed – something came up. Tell me, this prisoner of yours – what does he look like? . . . I see . . . And has he told you who he is yet? . . . Right . . . Right . . . Oh, dear . . . I see . . . The thing is, Daddy Jesus, he may not be lying about that . . . No, you weren't to know, not having met him. It could make our situation a bit ticklish, all right. But tell me, has he seen your face at all? . . . Really? So he's been blindfolded all the time, except for when you had your special mask on? And he has no idea who you are, or which side of the wall he's on? . . . Well, good. That does give us something to work with. Let me think for a minute . . .'

Smith lowered the phone, frowning. He tapped his left temple for a few seconds, and then he put the phone to his ear again.

'Right: take a shower, put some civilian clothes on, then go over to the armoury and draw two sub-machine guns, a hundred rounds of blank nine-millimetre and half a dozen stun grenades. I'll pop around to the office and pick up some balaclavas, then I'll meet you back outside the lock-up.'

He put the phone down and turned to the puzzled colonel. 'Sorry, sir, but it seems that Flint Driscoll went into the Easy by himself today, was abducted by terrorists and treated rather horridly. We're going to have to stage a rescue.'

CHAPTER FORTY-THREE

The winter dawn climbed a clear eastern sky, over the flat, monotonous fields of the farming co-ops, the moaning highway, the sleeping army base. It did not stop at the wall, but extended its blessing over the Embargoed Zone, which sent pillars of smoke up to greet it. The dawn shone in the fighter-bombers' con-trails, blazed on the hulls of patrol boats, glinted on the ever-wheeling drones.

Only one of our friends saw that dawn: not Captain Smith nor Colonel White nor Daddy Jesus, who slept deeply in their quarters; not Flora and Joseph, who were sprawled, oblivious, on couches in the office of the Xinhua news agency; not Cobra, who was digging angrily in a smoking pile of bricks and donkey shit; not Flint Driscoll, who lay, heavily sedated, in his bomb-proof little room; not our soldier boys, David and Johnny, and Lenny and Harry, who were on a weekend pass, at home with their loving families. But little Gabriel, wide awake, impatient, gazed out the window of his ward, watching the day take form around the hospital, the first kites swaying up from the earth, and wondering why his sister hadn't come for

him yet, and what the hospital might give him for breakfast.

Captain Smith came into his office rather late that morning,
with a take-away coffee and an Egg McMuffin. He placed the
coffee and the McMuffin in the centre of his desk, stared at
them for a while, and then he yawned and used his knee to
nudge a drawer open. The forged receipts which he had swept
into it two days before, when the colonel had burst in on him,
demanded his attention. He extracted a fistful, took a sip of
coffee and a bite of his McMuffin, and looked at the receipts
glassily for a while. Giving up, he took a key from his pocket
and opened a locked drawer on the other side of his desk. This
was empty apart from a green nylon zip bag. He picked up the
bag and tested its weight: it was heavy. Unzipping it, he extracted
a large bundle of high-denomination euro notes, then tested
the weight of the bag again: it felt hardly any lighter. Captain
Smith grinned broadly, replaced the money in the bag, put
the bag in the drawer and relocked it. He swept the blank
receipts back into the other drawer, slammed it shut and sat
back in his chair, whistled a few notes, then took another sip
of coffee.

There was a knock at the door and Colonel White shuffled in. He was wearing his number one uniform, gorgeous
with ribbons and braid.

'Good morning, sir!' said Smith, not rising from his
chair. 'I trust you got some sleep in the end. I'd offer you
a coffee' – his face became apologetic – 'but I'm afraid
I've only got this one here.'

The colonel dropped into the chair across the desk, picked up Smith's coffee and took a gulp. His eyes were bruised. He took a form from his pocket and flung it on the desk.

'I need another officer from the Slob to countersign that,' he said. 'You'll do.'

'What is it?'

'A discharge for some little shit who's gone AWOL. If I send the military police after him it'll create more paperwork than he's worth – he's due to be discharged in a month anyway. He's a nonentity. No one will miss him.'

Smith signed the form, then smiled at the colonel.

'If you don't mind me saying, sir, you *are* dressed smartly today.'

The colonel looked miserable. 'I've been summoned back to headquarters,' he confessed, and fumbled a cigarette from his jacket. 'They called me this morning. 24/7 is alleging that we attacked their jeep in order to cover up the truth about that air strike a couple of days ago. They say their footage was destroyed with the jeep, to prevent them refuting Flint Driscoll's allegations. It's making him look pretty bad, too.'

Smith lit his own cigarette. 'Driscoll will be fine. Nothing can stop him. All he needs to stay in business is a fixed opinion and a broadband connection.'

'If only we'd left that story alone, it would have been forgotten already.'

'That's what I tried to tell you at the time, but you were most insistent, Colonel. It was your decision.' Smith leaned forward. 'In fact, everything we did over the last two days

307

was your decision. And that's what you're going to tell them back at HQ.'

'But you were running the show yesterday! That's what we agreed!'

Smith cocked his head, smiling. 'But Colonel, *I* am just a humble captain, a lowly gunner eking out the last few years to his pension. Do you mean to say that you abdicated your command to such a one as me? *That* won't wash back at HQ.' Smith smiled. 'Besides, Colonel, *you* are the one who privately stole secret technology from our allies to sell on his own account, and then lost it inside the Embargoed Zone. If I thought I was going to take the drop, I'd have no choice but to mention that.'

'You bastard! You wouldn't!'

Smith stopped smiling. The two men stared at each other grimly, until Smith smiled again. 'Am I bluffing?' he asked.

'No,' White said. He sank lower in his chair and gestured vaguely around him. 'It doesn't look like I'll be coming back here, Smith – I suppose you'll have to be acting CO until they appoint a replacement. Oh, well. All I can do now is polish my boots, front up, and try and talk my way out of it.'

Smith nodded approvingly. 'That's the spirit, sir. And may I say again how smart you look in your nice air force uniform.'

'Bollocks,' said the colonel, rising slowly to his feet. 'Look' – he pointed to his chest. 'The shirt's ruined – all grey and streaked and mottled-looking! It's supposed to be regulation white!' He shuffled towards the door. 'I gave it to one of those slags who run the VIP compound, so she could launder it, and this is how it came back to me! And it's the only regulation shirt I have on the base! So now I have to go to the most important interview of my career looking like a tramp . . .' He trailed off in disgust.

As his hand curled around the doorknob his rage spilled over. 'And when I took it back to the girl and told her to sort it out, she actually refused – the little bitch of a sergeant refused a direct order from me! She said it wasn't her fault, that it was because of some dodgy new washing machine the general made them install yesterday morning. She said it's ruining everything they put in it!'

'Ah, yes,' said Smith. 'Our general is very fond of that old dodge: you indent for a new piece of kit from the Supply Corps, and then when it comes through you sell it, pocket the money and replace it with something cheaper from the local black market. The general is very friendly with the local gypsies, as it happens.'

The colonel left the room. Smith waited until the door clicked shut and then he smiled to himself and sucked in a mouthful of McMuffin. He was still chewing when the phone rang. He picked it up.

'Captain Smith?' It was a woman's voice, cold, knowing. 'This is the bureau of the Chief of Military Intelligence. I have some people from Washington on the line who want to talk to you, on a matter of the gravest importance. They're going to ask you some questions, and I strongly advise you to cooperate.' The phone clicked.

'Oh, dear God,' whispered Smith.

'Captain Smith?' It was a grim baritone voice. 'This is

Special Agent Winton from the Federal Bureau of Investigation.' Smith shut his eyes and rocked back and forth in his chair. 'I'm joined by Special Agent McCabe from the Bureau of Alcohol, Tobacco and Firearms, and by Chief Officer Birnbaum from US Customs and Border Protection.' Smith clutched his head in silent despair. 'Oh,' Winton added, 'there's also Special Agent Zanetti from the Drug Enforcement Administration.'

Smith stopped rocking. 'Drug enforcement?' he whispered.

Agent Winton went on: 'Tell me, Captain, what do you know about the Aryan Brotherhood?'

Smith blinked, sat upright. 'Only what I saw on the Discovery channel.'

'Good. Then you'll know that they are a brutal white supremacist prison gang involved in the traffic of drugs and weapons into and across the United States. Captain, we have recently obtained compelling evidence that the Aryans have linked up with terrorist groups active in your Embargoed Zone. We view this alliance as a major new threat to homeland security, and we're going to need your help to fight it – your cooperation has already been cleared with your own people, all the way to the top. It's not going to be easy, Captain, but with enough firepower, men and money, I'm sure we will prevail.'

'You can count me in,' said the captain stoutly. 'I'm your man.'

Smith placed the telephone reverently back on his desk, stood, and walked slowly around his office. He glanced at the papers protruding from his fax machine, then dumped them in the bin. Stretching, he smiled sadly at the dead, yellowing terrorists whose pictures lined his walls, then tripped back to his desk and reached for the phone again.

'Daddy Jesus? . . . Yes, good morning to you, too. And what a lovely morning it is. Look, something has come up – can you get Cobra on the phone for me? . . . No, he's not going into the programme yet. Tell him I have some new work for him. But try and be nice to him this time: we might have to ask him to get some tattoos.'

EPILOGUE

The blast from the first missile sent Moon flying across the room. His back thudded dully against the gunmetal door, and his eyes misted over. 'So this is what it's like . . .' somebody murmured. As he slid to the floor, he was dimly aware of sharp hooves trampling him, and the screaming of terrified beasts. The building itself began to heave and dance. The air was full of stinging fragments of brick and concrete, and as Moon closed his eyes for what he hoped would be the last time he saw rubble and dust flood the room from all sides. He could no longer hear very much, but he felt hot animal breath on his face and then sharp, peg-like teeth fastened into his shoulder, and he guessed that he was screaming. But his back was no longer supported, and he was toppling backwards, and the donkey had released his shoulder and disappeared from the equation. Something else was biting his legs now, a growing, vice-like pressure, and Moon opened his eyes and saw that he was lying in the glare of two bright, golden eyes, and that his legs were being crushed together by a metal door, which was grinding slowly shut on them. Desperately he twisted himself onto his side, freeing his legs enough to pull them through the door after him. On his stomach, he crawled a few feet more into the light and collapsed there, gasping. A damp concrete floor heaved beneath him, yet the sound of the shells was muted now by more than his own broken eardrums. What is this place? he wondered, and then the two golden eyes blinked – first one, then the other – and he realized that they were headlights, and that someone or something had just crossed in front of them. A moment later his ribs were jabbed painfully, and Moon understood that someone was kicking him.

'You there!' shouted a querulous voice. 'What are you doing in this tunnel? Go back at once – you're not allowed to be here!'

Twisting onto his side again, Moon squinted into the glare and beheld his new adversary. Above him stood a small, dumpy woman of about sixty, who was glaring down at him with an expression pitched neatly between anger and exasperation. She had grey hair and wore thick-framed owl glasses, a beige sleeveless safari vest, pressed blue jeans and a pair of clean white sneakers, one of which now kicked him in the belly.

'Get out!' she shouted, blinking crossly. 'I'm only allowed to take donkeys through the tunnels – those are the rules. I'll open the door again, so you can go back where you came from.'

Moon felt the ground heave as another salvo of shells fell outside. The old lady was, he reflected, by quite a long way the least scary thing he had encountered in what felt like a very long time. He heaved himself to his feet: he towered above her.

'I'll be killed if I go back out there,' he told her. 'You can't make me.'

She took a step back from him. 'I could always shoot you,' she said, doubtfully. 'That's what the general told me to do, if a terrorist ever tried to escape this way. Oh, dear . . . Oh, dear . . .'

And Moon now saw what he had not noticed before, that in her left hand, down by her side, the old lady was holding an automatic pistol. He watched its barrel lift towards him. 'Oh, for fuck's sake,' he said aloud, and closed his eyes.

And then he heard a click, and then another, and another, and Moon opened his eyes to see the old lady, her gun still pointing at his face, tugging vexedly at its double-action trigger, the hammer swinging forward and back on an empty chamber.

Gently, he relieved her of the pistol. 'I think you're supposed to pull back this slide thing here at the back before you can shoot someone,' he told her. 'Otherwise it's not really cocked, or something like that.'

'Oh, dear,' she said again, and blinked at him through her large spectacles. 'I knew I shouldn't have come here without my gypsies. I'm not supposed to. But I just so wanted to feed the poor things, and the gypsies were all rather drunk today – they came into some extra cash this morning, I don't know how . . . Are you going to kill me now?'

Moon stretched his aching shoulders, looked at the pistol in his hand, then shoved it into his waistband, like he'd seen in the movies. 'Not if you get me out of here.'

She shook her head quickly. 'I can't do that. The tunnels

are so secret that hardly anyone knows about them – apart from the top generals and the gypsies, of course. If they found out that the tunnels had been compromised they'd stop letting me use them for my rescues.'

Now that Moon's eyes had grown used to the tunnel he could see that the headlights belonged to a quad bike, which was attached to a trailer loaded with hay bales. The quad bike almost filled the tunnel, and he smelled rather than heard that its engine was still running. He looked at the old lady again. 'Who are you?' he demanded.

She drew herself up a little straighter, and stuck her chin out. 'People for the Ethical Treatment of Animals.'

Moon shrugged. 'Fine,' he said. 'That makes sense, I suppose. Listen: we have the same problem; you don't want me to be in this tunnel, and I don't want to be in it either. And neither one of us wants anyone else to ever know that I was here. So I'll tell you what: if you can get me to the other side of the wall safely, I promise that I will utterly disappear, and you'll never hear of me again.' He was handling this quite well, he realized. He thought of the girl. She would have been quite pleased with him.

The old lady looked at him suspiciously. 'You won't do any terror?'

'I won't do any terror.'

'And you'll let me have my gun back? It's only that the general gave it to me himself. He's very fond of animals.'

'I'll give you your gun back when we're on the other side. But I'll keep the bullets, if you don't mind. I expect you can always get some more.'

She pondered his proposal. 'But how do I know you won't tell people about all this?'

Moon wormed his way in between the bales on the trailer. 'Because no one would want to believe me.'

Somewhere in the darkness, far off down the damp, echoing tunnel, a donkey brayed.